A STUDY IN

Charlotte

A Charlotte Holmes novel

A STUDY IN
Charlotte

A Charlotte Holmes novel

BRITTANY CAVALLARO

KATHERINE TEGEN BOOKS
An Imprint of HarperCollins Publishers

Katherine Tegen Books is an imprint of HarperCollins Publishers.

A Study in Charlotte

Library of Congress Cataloging-in-Publication Data
Cavallaro, Brittany.
  A study in Charlotte / Brittany Cavallaro. — First edition.
    pages cm
  Summary: Sherlock Holmes and Dr. Watson descendants, Charlotte and Jamie, stu-
dents at a Connecticut boarding school, team up to solve a murder mystery.
  ISBN 978-0-06-239890-1 (hardback)
  [1. Mystery and detective stories. 2. Murder—Fiction. 3. Love—Fiction. 4. Boarding
schools—Fiction. 5. Schools—Fiction.] I. Title.
PZ7.1.C42St 2016   2015015669
[Fic]—dc23   CIP
                                                                               AC

16 17 18 19 20   CG/RRDH   10 9 8 7 6 5 4 3 2 1
❖
First Edition

For Kit and me, at sixteen

I had no idea that such individuals
existed outside of stories.
A Study in Scarlet, Sir Arthur Conan Doyle

one

THE FIRST TIME I MET HER WAS AT THE TAIL END OF ONE OF those endless weekday nights you could only have at a school like Sherringford. It was midnight, or just after, maybe, and I'd spent the last few hours icing my sprained shoulder in my room, the result of a rugby scrimmage gone horribly wrong just minutes after it'd started. Practices tended to do that here, something I'd learned in the first week of school when the team captain shook my hand so voraciously I thought he was about to pull me in and eat me. Sherringford's rugby team had landed at the bottom of its division at the end of every season for years. But not this year, no; Kline had made a point of reminding me of that, smiling with every one of his strange little teeth. I was their white whale. Their rugger messiah. The reason why the school shelled out not just a tuition scholarship for my junior year but my transportation costs, too—no mean feat when you visit your mother in London every holiday.

The only real problem, then, was how much I hated rugby. I'd made the fatal mistake of surviving a maul on the rugby field last year at my school in London before accidentally sort of bringing our team to victory. I had only tried because, for once, Rose Milton was in the stands, and I had loved her for two passionate, secret, awful years, but as I learned later, the Sherringford athletic director had been in the stands as well. Front row, scouting. You see, we had quite a good rugby team at Highcombe School.

Damn them all.

Especially my cow-eyed, bull-necked new teammates. Honestly, I even hated Sherringford itself, with its rolling green lawns and clear skies and a city center that felt smaller than even the cinder-block room they gave me in Michener Hall. A city center that had no fewer than four cupcake shops and not one decent place to get a curry. A city center just an hour away from where my father lived. He kept threatening to visit. "Threatening" was the only word for it. My mother had wanted us to get to know each other better; they had divorced when I was ten.

But I missed London like an arm, or a leg, even if I had only lived there for a handful of years, because as much as my mother insisted that my coming to Connecticut would be like coming home, it was more like coming to a manicured jail.

All this is just to give you an understanding of how, that

September, I could have struck a match and happily watched Sherringford burn. And even so, before I had ever met Charlotte Holmes, I was sure she was the only friend I would make in that miserable place.

"YOU'RE TELLING ME THAT YOU'RE *THAT* WATSON." TOM WAS delighted. He smashed his round Midwestern accent into the flattest Cockney I'd ever heard. "My dear chap! My dear fellow! Watson, come here, I want you!"

The cell of a room that we shared was so small that when I flipped him off, I almost poked out his eye. "You're a genius, Bradford. Seriously. Where do you get your material?"

"Oh, but dude, this is perfect." My roommate tucked his hands in the pockets of the argyle sweater-vest he always wore under his blazer. Through a moth hole, I watched his right thumb wriggle in excitement. "Because the party tonight is at Lawrence Hall. And Lena is throwing it because her sister always ships her vodka. And you *know* who Lena rooms with." He waggled his eyebrows.

At that, I finally had to close my book. "Don't tell me you're trying to set me up with my—"

"Your soul mate?" I must've looked violent, because Tom put two very serious hands on my shoulders. "I'm not trying," he said, enunciating each word, "to set you up with Charlotte. I'm trying to get you *drunk.*"

Charlotte and Lena had set up camp down in the Lawrence Hall basement. As Tom had promised, it wasn't hard to get past the hall mother. Each dorm had one (in addition to our army of RAs), an older woman from town who oversaw her students from the front desk. They sorted mail, arranged for birthday cakes, lent an ear when you were homesick—but they also enforced the hall rules. Lawrence's was famous for sleeping on the job.

The party was in the basement kitchen. Though it was stocked with plates and pots and even a spindly four-burner stove, the pans were all so dented they looked like they'd been worn to war. Tom squeezed against the stove while I shut the door behind us; within seconds, one of the knobs rubbed a half-moon of grease onto his sweater-vest. The girl next to him smiled thinly and turned back to her friends, a tumbler of something dangling from her hand. There had to be at least thirty people in there, packed in shoulder to shoulder.

Grabbing my arm, Tom began shouldering us to the back of the tiny kitchen. I felt like I was being pulled through a dark, dank wardrobe into some boozy Narnia.

"That's the weird townie dealer," he whispered to me. "He's selling drugs. That's Governor Schumer's son. He's *buying* drugs."

"Great," I said, only half-listening.

"And those two girls? They summer in Italy. Like, they use 'summer' as a verb. Their dads run an offshore drilling operation."

I raised an eyebrow.

"What, I'm poor, I notice these things."

"Right." If it was a joke, it was a lame one. Tom might've had a hole in his sweater-vest, but back in our room, he also had the smallest, thinnest laptop I'd ever seen. "You're poor."

"Comparatively speaking." Tom dragged me along behind him. "You and me, we're upper-middle class. We're peasants."

The party was loud and crowded, but Tom was determined to drag me all the way to the far wall. I didn't know why, until a strange voice curled up through the cigarette smoke.

"The game is Texas Hold'em," it said, hoarse, but with a bizarre, wild precision, like a drunk Greek philosopher orating at a bacchanal. "And the buy-in tonight is fifty dollars."

"Or your soul," chirped another voice, a normal one, and the girls in front of us laughed.

Tom turned to grin at me. "That one's Lena. And that one's Charlotte Holmes."

The first I saw of her was her hair, black and glossy and straight down to her shoulders. She was leaning forward over a card table to pull in a handful of chips, and I couldn't see her face. This wasn't important, I told myself. It wasn't a big deal if she didn't like me. So what if somewhere, back a hundred years and change and across the Atlantic Ocean, some other Watson made best friends with some other Holmes. People became best friends all the time. There were, surely, best friends at this school. Dozens. Hundreds.

Even if I didn't have one.

She sat up, all at once, with a wicked smile. Her brows were startling dark lines on her pale face, and they framed her gray eyes, her straight nose. She was altogether colorless and severe, and still she managed to be beautiful. Not the way that girls are generally beautiful, but more like the way a knife catches the light, makes you want to take it in your hands.

"Dealer goes to Lena," she said, turning away from me, and it was only then that I placed her accent. I was forcibly reminded that she was from London, like me. For a moment, I felt so homesick I thought that I'd make an even worse show of myself and throw myself at her feet, beg her to read me the phone book in that extravagant voice that had no business coming out of such a thin, angular girl.

Tom sat down, flung five chips on the table (on closer inspection, they were the brass buttons from his blazer), and rubbed his hands together theatrically.

I should have had something witty to say. Something strange and funny and just a little bit morbid, something I could say under my breath as I dropped down on the seat beside her. Something to make her look up sharply and think, *I want to know him.*

I had nothing.

I turned tail and fled.

TOM ARRIVED HOME HOURS LATER, CHEERFULLY EMPTY-handed. "She cleaned me out," he laughed. "I'll win it back next time." That's when I learned that Holmes's poker game had been running weekly since she showed up the year before. They'd just gotten more popular since Lena started bringing vodka. "And probably more lucrative for Charlotte too," Tom added.

For the next weeks, I hit snooze over and over in some wild hope that the morning would just pack up and leave me alone. The worst of it was first-period French, taught by the autocratic, red-suspendered Monsieur Cann, whose waxed mustache looked like it belonged on a taxidermist's wall. Almost every other Sherringford student had been there since freshman year, and that early in the morning all anyone wanted to do was sit by their oldest friends and catch up on the night before. I was no one's oldest friend. So I took an empty double desk for myself and tried not to fall asleep before the bell rang.

"I heard she made, like, five hundred dollars last night," the girl in front of me said, pulling her red hair into a ponytail. "She probably practices online. It's not fair. It's not like she *needs* money. Her family has to be loaded."

"Close your eyes," her seatmate said, and blew lightly on her friend's face. "Eyelash. Yeah, I've heard that too. Her mom is like, a duchess. But whatever. It's probably just going up her nose."

The redhead perked up at that. "I heard it was going into her arm."

"I wonder if she'd introduce me to her dealer."

The bell rang, and Monsieur Cann shouted, *"Bonjour, mes petites,"* and I realized that, for the first time in weeks, I was completely awake.

I spent the rest of the morning thinking about that conversation and what it meant for her. Charlotte Holmes. Because they couldn't have been talking about anyone else. I was still mulling it all over as I walked across the quad at lunch, dodging people left and right. The green was choked with students, and so in a way, it wasn't a surprise when the girl I was thinking about stepped out from what seemed to be an invisible door and directly into my path.

I didn't run into her; I'm not that clumsy. But we both froze, and began doing that awful left-right-you-go-first shuffle. Finally, I gave up. *Screw all of this,* I thought mulishly, *it's a small campus and I can't hide forever, I might as well go ahead and—*

I stuck out my hand. "Sorry, I don't think we've met. I'm James. I'm new here."

She looked down at it, eyebrows knitted, like I was offering her a fish, or a grenade. It was sunny and hot that day, early October's last gasp of summer, and most everyone had slung their uniform blazer over one shoulder or was carrying it under their arm. Mine was in my bag, and I'd loosened my tie, walking down the path, but Charlotte Holmes was as fastidiously put together as if she were about to give a speech on etiquette. She had on slim navy pants instead of the pleated skirt most of the girls wore. Her white oxford shirt was buttoned up to her neck and her ribbon tie looked as if it'd been steamed. I was close enough to tell that she smelled like soap, not perfume, and that her face was as bare as if she'd just washed it.

I might've just stared at her for hours—this girl that I'd wondered about off and on my whole life—had her colorless eyes not narrowed at me suspiciously. I started, as if I'd done something wrong.

"I'm Holmes," she said finally, in that marvelous, ragged voice. "But you knew that already, didn't you."

She wasn't going to shake my hand, then. I slid both of them into my pockets.

"I did," I admitted. "So you know who I am. Which is awkward, but I figured—"

"Who put you up to this?" There was a flat kind of acceptance in her face. "Was it Dobson?"

"Lee Dobson?" I shook my head, bewildered. "No. Put me up to what? I mean, I knew you'd be here. At Sherringford. My mum told me that the Holmeses had sent you; she keeps in touch with your aunt Araminta. They met at some charity thing. Right? They signed the *His Last Bow* manuscript? It went for leukemia patients or something, and now they write emails back and forth. Are you in my year? I was never clear on that. But you've got a biology textbook there, so you must be a sophomore. A deduction, ha. Maybe best avoid those."

I was babbling like an idiot, I knew I was, but she had been holding herself so straight and still that she looked like a wax figurine. It was so at odds with the commanding, freewheeling girl I'd seen at the party that I couldn't make heads or tails of it, what had happened to her since then. But my talking seemed to calm her down, and though it wasn't funny, or morbid, or witty, I kept on going until her shoulders relaxed and her eyes finally lost some of their sharp sadness.

"I know who you are, of course," she said when I finally stopped to draw breath. "My aunt Araminta did tell me about you, and Lena, though it would have been obvious anyway. Hello, Jamie." She extended a small white hand, and we shook.

"I hate it when people call me Jamie, though," I said, pained, "so you might as well call me Watson instead."

Holmes smiled at me in a closed-mouth kind of way. "All right, then, Watson," she said. "I have to go to lunch."

It was a dismissal if I'd ever heard one.

"Right," I said, tamping down my disappointment. "I was going to meet Tom anyway; I should go."

"Right, see you." She stepped neatly around me.

I couldn't leave it at that, and so I called after her, "What did I do?"

Holmes flung me an unreadable look over her shoulder. "Homecoming's next weekend," she said drily, and went on her way.

By every account—and by that, honestly, I meant my mother's—Charlotte was the epitome of a Holmes. Coming from my mother, that wasn't a compliment. You'd think that after all this time, our families would have drifted apart, and in most ways I suppose we had. But my mother would run into the odd Holmes at Scotland Yard fund-raisers or the Edgar Awards dinners or, as in the case of Holmes's aunt Araminta, an auction of my great-great-great-grandfather's literary agent's—Arthur Conan Doyle's—things. I had always been enthralled with the idea of this girl, the only Holmes who was my age (as a kid, I thought we'd meet and the two of us would go on wild adventures), but my mother always discouraged me without saying why.

I knew nothing about her but that the police had let her assist on her first case when she was ten years old. The diamonds she helped recover were worth three million pounds. My father had told me about it during our weekly phone call, in an attempt to get me to open up to him. It hadn't worked. At least, not in the way that he'd planned.

I dreamed about that diamond theft for months. How I could've been there by her side, her trusted companion. One night, I lowered her down into the Swiss bank from a skylight, my rope the only thing holding her above the booby-trapped floor. The next, we raced through the cars of a runaway train, chased by black-masked bandits shouting in Russian. When I saw a story about a stolen painting on the front page of the newspaper, I told my mother that Charlotte Holmes and I were going to solve the case. My mother cut me off, saying, "Jamie, if you try to do anything like that before you turn eighteen, I will sell every last one of your books in the night, starting with your autographed Neil Gaiman."

(Before they'd divorced, my father was prone to saying, "You know, your mother's only a Watson by marriage," with a pointedly lofted eyebrow.)

The only real conversation my mother and I'd had about the Holmeses happened right before I left. We'd been discussing Sherringford— Well. *She* had been monologuing about how much I'd like it there while I packed up my closet in silence, wondering if I flung myself out the window, would it properly kill me or just break both my legs. Finally, she made me tell her something I was looking forward to, and to spite her (and because it was true), I told her I was excited, and nervous, to finally meet my counterpart in the Holmes family.

Which didn't go over well.

"Lord knows how your great-great-great-grandfather put

up with that man," she said with a roll of her eyes.

"Sherlock?" I asked. At least now we weren't talking about Sherringford.

My mother harrumphed. "I always imagined he'd just been bored. Victorian gentlemen, you know. Didn't have too much going on. But it never seemed to me that their friendship ran both ways. Those Holmeses, they're *strange*. They still drill their children from birth in deductive skills. Discourage them making friends, or so I've heard. I can't say it's healthy to keep a child away like that. Araminta is nice enough, I suppose, but then again I don't live with her. I can't imagine what it was like for the good Dr. Watson. The last thing you need is to take up with someone like her."

"It's not like I'm going to marry this girl," I said, digging in the back of my closet for my rugby kit. "I was just interested to meet her, that's all."

"I've heard that she's one of the stranger ones," she insisted. "It's not as if they've sent her away to America on a lark."

I looked pointedly down at my suitcase. "No, that's usually not a reward."

"Well, I hope for your sake she's lovely," my mum said quickly. "Just do be careful there, love."

It's stupid to admit to it, but my mother isn't usually wrong. I mean, the whole sending me to Sherringford thing was a terrible idea, but I understood it at its core. She had been paying quite a bit—money we didn't really have—for me to attend Highcombe School, and all because I'd insisted that I wanted to be a writer. There were a few famous novelists who taught there . . . not that any of them had really taken to me. Sherringford, despite its obvious drawbacks (Connecticut, my father) had as strong an English program, or better. And they offered to take me for free, as long as I did my best impression of an excited rugger for them now and again.

But at Sherringford, I kept the writer thing to myself. A constant, low-level drone of fear kept me from showing my work to anyone; with someone like Dr. Watson in your family, you didn't want to invite any comparison. I did my best to hide my work away, so I was surprised when it almost came up that day over lunch.

Tom and I had grabbed sandwiches and sat down under an ash tree off the quad with some other guys from Michener Hall. Tom was digging around in my bag for some paper to spit his gum into. Normally it would've annoyed me, having someone shuffle carelessly through my things, but he was acting like any of my old Highcombe friends would, and so I let him.

"Can I tear a sheet out of this?" he asked, holding up my notebook.

It was only through sheer force of will that I kept from grabbing it out of his hands. "Yeah," I said indifferently, fishing chips out of a bag.

He flipped through it, quickly at first but slowing as he went. "Huh," he said, and I shot him a warning look that he didn't see.

"What is it?" someone asked. "Love poems? Erotic stories?"

"Dirty limericks," Dobson, my hallmate, said.

Tom cleared his throat, like he was about to perform a page from what was, to be honest, my journal.

"No, drawings of your mom." I snagged it and tore a page from the back, making sure to tuck it under my knee afterward. "It's just a journal. Notes to myself, that kind of thing."

"I saw you talking to Charlotte Holmes on the quad," Dobson said. "You writing about her?"

"Right." There was a nasty note in his voice I didn't like, and I didn't want to encourage it with a real response.

Randall, his ruddy-faced roommate—he was on the rugby team with me—shot him a look, and leaned in like he was about to tell me a secret.

"We've been trying to crack that nut for a year," he said. "She's hot. Wears those tight little pants. But she doesn't go out, except for that weird poker game, and she doesn't drink. Only likes the hard stuff, and does it alone."

"They're trying PUA," Tom said to me mournfully, and at my blank look, he elaborated. "Pick-up artistry. You neg the girl—like, an insult hidden in a compliment. Dobson keeps telling her he's the only guy who likes her, that everyone else thinks she's ugly and strung out but that he *likes* the junkie look on girls."

Randall laughed. "Doesn't fucking work, at least not for me," he said. "I'm moving on. Have you *seen* those new freshmen? A lot less work for a lot more payoff."

"Not me. I cracked the nut." Dobson smirked at Randall. "And, you know, she might do me some favors again. Since I can be such a charming date."

Liar.

"Stop talking," I said quietly.

"What?"

When I get angry, my English accent thickens until it's clotted and snotty, a full-on cartoon. And I was furious. I probably sounded like the bloody Queen.

"Say it again, and I'll fucking kill you."

There it was, that weightless rush, that floor-bottoming-out exhilaration that comes from saying something you can't take back. Something that would lead to me smashing in some deserving asshole's face.

This was the reason I played rugby in the first place. It was supposed to be a "reasonable outlet" for what the school counselor called my "acts of sudden and unreasonable aggression." Or, as my father put it, snickering like it was some joke, "the way you get a little punchy sometimes." Unlike him, I never looked back on them with anything like pride, the fights I got into at Highcombe and, before that, in my public school in Connecticut. I always felt disgusted with myself afterward, ashamed. Classmates I liked just fine the rest of the time would say something that would set me off, and immediately, my arm would cock back, ready to swing.

But I wasn't going to be ashamed this time, I thought, as Dobson jumped to his feet, swinging wildly. Randall grabbed his shirt to hold him back, his face a mask of shock. *Good, hold him,* I thought, *that way he can't run,* and I applied my fist to Dobson's jaw. His head snapped back, and when he looked at me again, he was smirking.

"You her boyfriend?" he said, panting. "'Cause Charlotte didn't tell me that last night."

In the background, shouting—the voice sounded like Holmes's. A hand pulled at my arm. In the second I was distracted, Dobson broke free of Randall's grip and tackled me to the grass. He was the size of a steam liner, and with his knee on my chest, I couldn't move, couldn't breathe. Leaning into my face, he said, "Who do you think you are, you little prick?" and spat, long and slow, into my eye. Then he hit me in the face, and hit me again.

A voice cut through the blood-roar. "Watson," Holmes shouted, at what sounded like an enormous distance, "what the fuck do you think you're doing?"

I was maybe the only person to ever have his imaginary friend made real. Not entirely real, not yet—she was still dream-blurred to me. But we'd run through London's sewers together, hand in muddy hand. We'd hidden in a cave in Alsace-Lorraine for weeks because the Stasi were after us for stealing government secrets. In my fevered imagination, she hid them in a microchip in one small red barrette. It held back her blond hair; that's what I'd pictured her with, back then.

Truth be told, I liked that blurriness. That line where reality and fiction jutted up against each other. And when Dobson had said those ugly things, I'd lunged at him because he'd dragged Holmes kicking and screaming into *this* world, one where people left litter on the quad and had to leave a conversation to use the toilet, where assholes tormented a girl because she wouldn't sleep with them.

It took four people—including a visibly shaken Tom—to haul him off me. I lay there for a moment, wiping the spit out of my eyes, until something leaned in to darken my view.

"Get up," Holmes said. She didn't offer me a hand.

There was a crowd around us. Of course there was. I swayed a little on my feet, flushed with adrenaline, feeling nothing. "Hi," I said stupidly, wiping at my bleeding nose.

She looked at me for a measured moment, then turned to face Dobson. "Oh baby, I can't believe you fought for me," she drawled at him. There was a smattering of laughter. He was still restrained by his friends, and I could hear him panting from where I stood. "Now that you've *won* me, I guess I'll lay down and spread for you right here. Or do you only like your girls drugged and unconscious?"

Shouts, jeers. Dobson looked more shocked than angry; he went limp against his restrainers. I snickered; I couldn't help it. Holmes spun, and stared me down.

"And you. You are not my boyfriend," she said evenly, the drawl completely vanished. "Though your wall-eyed stare, your ridiculous rambling, and the way your index finger twitches when I talk says you so very much want to be. You think you're defending my 'honor,' but you're just as bad as he is." She jerked a thumb at Dobson. "I don't need someone to fight for me. I can fight for myself."

Someone whistled; someone else began a slow clap. Holmes's expression didn't change. Some teachers showed up, and after that the dean; I was questioned, given a compress, questioned again. The whole time I couldn't stop replaying it.

As I bled onto my shirt in the infirmary, waiting to see if I'd be expelled and shipped back home, it was still the only thing I had banging around in my head. *You're just as bad as he is,* she'd said, and she'd been absolutely right.

But I had never wanted to be her boyfriend. I wanted something smaller than that, and far, far bigger, something I couldn't yet put into words.

The next time I sought out Charlotte Holmes, it was because Lee Dobson had been murdered.

two

IT WAS CLOSE TO DAWN WHEN THE SHOUTING STARTED.

At first, it only registered as part of my dream. The shouts were those of an angry mob; someone had armed them with torches and pitchforks, and they chased me into a barn under a sky full of stars. The only hiding place I could find was behind a nonplussed cow, chewing her cud.

You didn't need to be a psychologist to understand what it meant. After my fight with Dobson, I'd gone from being unknown to notorious. People who didn't even know me suddenly had *opinions* about me. Dobson wasn't very popular; he was a meathead, and nasty to girls, but he had a number of thick-necked friends who made their presence known when I walked into the dining hall. Tom, for his part, was secretly thrilled. Gossip was Sherringford's favorite currency, and by his reckoning, he'd found a key to the Royal Treasury.

But for me, not much had really changed. I was still uncomfortable at Sherringford, only more so. My French class began falling silent when I walked in. A freshman girl stammered out an invitation to homecoming one morning outside the sciences building while her friends smothered giggles behind her. She was cute, in a blond, wispy kind of way, but I told her that I wasn't allowed to go. It was almost true. I'd been suspended from all school functions for a month—clubs, days in town, and thank God, the rugby team, though I'd been assured I would keep my scholarship—but they'd forgotten to ban me from the dance. It was a light punishment, I was told by the nurse who examined my broken nose. To me, it didn't seem like a punishment at all.

After the fight, I'd kept an eye out for Holmes, though I didn't know what I could possibly say if I did see her. That week, she canceled her poker game, though I wouldn't have gone anyway—showing up would've made me look like the awful stalker she already thought me to be. It was hard to avoid someone at Sherringford, with its five hundred students and postage-stamp campus, and yet somehow she had managed it. She wasn't in the dining hall; she wasn't on the quad between lessons.

I don't think I would have spent so much time thinking about it—about her—if I wasn't also coming to grips with how poorly I fit in at Sherringford. By the time all the trouble with Dobson started, I'd made friends—mostly through Tom, who seemed to know everyone from the cute girls in my classes to the upperclassmen playing ultimate Frisbee in the quad. Soon, I knew them too. But there was a flimsiness to all of those friendships, like a strong wind might blow them away.

For one thing, people were always talking about money.

Not upfront, not *How much do your parents make?* More like, *What do your parents do?* Was your mom a senator? Did your dad manage a hedge fund? *Oh my God, I'll be in the Hamptons for Christmas, too,* I heard one girl tell another in a voice that carried across the room. More than once, I saw students buying drugs from the creepy blond townie who lurked in the corners of our parties and around our quad at night. When they weren't using their parents' money to fund their coke habits, my classmates were globe-trotting. I overheard the girls in my French class trading notes on who was building orphanages in Africa last summer (never a specific African country, just "Africa"), who was backpacking through Spain.

Sherringford wasn't one of those schools like Andover or St. Paul's, filled with future presidents and baseball stars and astronauts. Sure, we had electives like screenwriting and Swahili, teachers with PhDs and tweed jackets, students sent off to the lesser Ivy League schools—but we were a rank or two below extraordinary, and maybe that was the problem. If we weren't in the fight to be the best, we'd fight instead to be the most privileged.

Or *they* would, anyway. I'd just landed myself a front-row seat to their match. And somewhere out there, in the dark, Charlotte Holmes prowled, playing entirely by her own rules.

The night of Dobson's murder, I'd been up late mulling over how to fix things between us. Holmes and I. I was fairly sure that I'd blown any chance of our ever being friends, and that thought kept me up until half past three. I'd been asleep for what felt like a moment when I was woken by the panic spreading down our hall. Tom had already thrown on clothes and gone to investigate before I'd even dragged myself from my bed. I thought, hazily, that it must be a fire drill and that I had somehow missed the alarm.

But there was a crowd gathered at the end of the hallway: guys from our floor, mostly, but our gray-haired hall mother was there as well, and beyond her was the school nurse and a knot of policemen in caps and uniforms. I pushed through them until I found Tom, staring blank-faced at a door wrapped in police tape. It stood open about an inch, and beyond it, the room was dark.

"What is it?" I asked him.

"Dobson," Tom said. When he finally turned to face me, I saw the frightened look in his eyes. "He's dead."

I was shocked to realize he was frightened of *me*.

The guy behind me said, "That's James Watson, he's the one who punched him," and the buzz around me ratcheted up to a roar.

Mrs. Dunham, our hall mother, put a protective hand on my shoulder. "It's all right, James," she said, "I'll stay here with you." Her glasses were askew, and she'd thrown a ridiculous silk robe over her pajamas; I hadn't known that she stayed nights in the dorm, or that she even knew my name. Still, I was fiercely glad she was there, because a man in a button-down shirt broke away from the policemen and crossed straight over to me. "James, is it?" he asked, flashing a badge. "We'd like to ask you some questions about tonight."

"Oh no, you don't," Mrs. Dunham said. "He's a minor, and you need his parents' permission to question him without a guardian present."

"He's not under arrest," the man insisted.

"All the same," she said. "Sherringford policy."

"Fine." The detective sighed. "Do they live close by, son?" He produced a notepad and pen from his trouser pocket, like this was *Law & Order*.

Well. It kind of was.

"My mother lives in London," I said, and my voice sounded strained even to my ears. Tom's stare was hardening into something like a glare. Behind him, a boy who lived next door to me was quietly crying. "My father lives here in Connecticut, but I haven't seen him in years."

"Can you give me his number?" the detective asked, and I did, pulling out my phone to read out the digits I'd never once called myself. He said some other things about staying put, and getting some sleep, and them coming by to see me in the early afternoon, all of which I agreed to. Did I have a choice? He gave me his card: it read *Detective Ben Shepard* in a businesslike font. He didn't look much like the other policemen I'd seen, on-screen or otherwise. On first glance, he gave an impression of grocery-store averageness, but as I stared at him, holding his card, I saw that his face had an unusually eager cast to it, like a dog eyeing a lofted ball. He didn't look like he had a tragic past, some murdered mother or brother that drove him to become a detective. He looked like someone who played video games with their kids. Who did the dishes without being asked.

That impression of goodness unsettled me more than if he'd been a mustache-twirling villain. Because it was clear that Detective Shepard thought *I* was the bad guy.

He gave me what was meant to be a reassuring smile. Then he left, him and the other policemen, and everyone else milled around for another few minutes until Mrs. Dunham sent them back to their rooms. They shoved past me. All of them did, Harry and Peter and Mason and even Tom, wrapped in his ubiquitous sweater-vest. The looks they gave me were uniform. *Outsider,* their faces said. *Killer, you deserve what's coming to you.*

Mrs. Dunham offered to make me some cocoa, but I had no idea what I'd say to her, or to anyone, so I said thanks but no thanks, I'd just go to sleep. As if sleep was even a remote possibility.

Tom wasn't in our room. He'd probably decided to sleep on someone's floor, I thought. He was afraid of me now. In a flash of rage, I picked up my pillow to chuck it across the room—and stopped cold. If someone heard me on a rampage, it wasn't going to help my case in the slightest. It was this anger that had gotten me into this mess in the first place, I reminded myself, and squashed the pillow against the bed instead.

Anger, and Charlotte Holmes.

When I snuck back down the hallway, the yellow tape over Dobson's door caught the light like a mirror, one I refused to look too closely into. I kept moving.

I made it all the way to Lawrence Hall before I realized I didn't have her number. Her phone number, or her room number—in fact, I was only vaguely sure she lived in this dorm. The rows of darkened windows stared down at me as I struggled to make a decision. Any moment now, the sky would start to brighten. Lights would begin to go on. The girls who lived here would shower and dress and gather their textbooks on the way out the door. How far would they get before they heard that one of their classmates had been murdered? How long would it take for them to start believing I'd done it?

I didn't even know what I'd say when I found her. What possible reason did she have to believe I was innocent? The last time she saw me, I was beating the daylights out of the victim.

My sense of purpose dissipated like a sputtering balloon, and I sat down on Lawrence's front steps to get my head on straight. Campus was silent and dark, except for the lights of the emergency vehicles that crowded around Michener.

"Watson," the voice hissed. "Jamie Watson."

Holmes stepped neatly out of a small stand of trees; I hadn't seen her there at all. In fact, I didn't think that I was meant to, as she was dressed in head-to-toe blacks: trousers, gloves, a pair of dark sneakers, a jacket zipped all the way to her chin, even the backpack slung over her shoulders. Her face was a pale moon against all that darkness, her lips compressed in anger until she opened her mouth to say something that, from her expression, I didn't want to hear.

So I spoke before she did. "Hi," I said, in my usual stupid way. "I was looking for you."

Her eyes widened, then narrowed, and I watched her rapidly recalculate something in her head. "This is about Dobson."

I didn't bother to ask how she knew. She was a Holmes. But I must've looked surprised enough for her to fill in the gaps. "Look, Tom texted Lena, and Lena texted me. Relatively straightforward. Unfortunately, I was wearing this when I heard"—she indicated her outfit with a frustrated hand—"and so I decided to stay away from the dorm so that nobody would see me. It's bad form to be dressed as a burglar on the night of anyone's murder, much less that of someone you hate."

"Oh," I said. "What were you actually burgling?"

A quicksilver smile flitted across her face. "Pipettes," she said. "I went to go work in my lab after night check."

"You absolute *nerd*," I said, laughing, and her smile came back, and stayed. Incredible. "You have a lab? Wait, no. Later. Because Dobson's dead, and we're easily the prime suspects, and we're *laughing*."

"I know." She scrubbed at her eyes with her hands. "Do you know, at first I thought you came here to accuse me of it."

My eyebrows must've shot up into my hair. "Absolutely not—"

"I know," she said, cutting me off with a searching look. I felt as if she were X-raying me. Her eyes flickered from my face, to my fingers, to my beaten-up Chucks. "But I told him I would kill him. I should have been your primary suspect. And I'm not."

There were a lot of answers to that not-question: *I'm a Watson, it's genetically impossible for me to suspect you* or, *In my imagination, you weren't ever a villain, you were always the hero*, but everything I came up with sounded flip or cute or melodramatic. "Like you said, you can take care of yourself," I told her, finally. "If you'd murdered him, I bet there would be twenty witnesses who saw him put the gun to his own head."

Holmes shrugged but she was clearly pleased. We sat there for a minute; in the distance, birds started calling to each other.

"You know," she said, "that bastard has hit on me in every disgusting way since the day I arrived. Shouted at me, left notes under my door. He slapped my ass in the breakfast line the weekend my brother was visiting." She shook her head. "It took some persuasion on my part, but Dobson wasn't immediately napalmed. Or made the target of a drone hit. Actually, Milo quite wanted to play the long game, wait a few years and then just disappear him from his bed, make it look like aliens. Or so he said. He was trying to cheer me up. . . ." She trailed off; it was clear she'd said more than she meant to. "I should still be mad at you."

"But you aren't."

"And we shouldn't be talking about Dobson like this." She got to her feet, and after a second's hesitation, offered me a hand up.

"I didn't think you'd be so respectful of the dead," I told her. "Just a few hours ago, he was alive and kicking, and practically begging to be napalmed."

The sun was rising in the distance, pulled up by its lazy, invisible string, and the sky was shot through with color. Her hair was washed in gold, her cheeks, in gold, and her eyes were as knowing as a psychic's.

In that moment, I would've followed her anywhere.

"We shouldn't be *talking* about Dobson," she said, starting off across the quad, "because we should be examining his room."

I stopped short. "I'm sorry, what?"

IT WAS ALREADY TEN PAST SEVEN, AND OUR HALLWAY IN Michener was on the second floor. I had no idea how we'd sneak by Mrs. Dunham at the front desk, not to mention the hordes of junior boys emerging from their rooms to shower before breakfast. I watched Holmes consider it for a moment, frowning, before she slid around to the side of the ivy-covered building.

She told me to stand back, then flung herself down on the ground, examining it inch by inch. For footprints, I realized. If we'd thought of accessing Dobson's room this way, someone else probably had too. Nervously, I looked around to see if we were being watched, but we were shrouded by a cluster of ash trees. Thank God Sherringford was so damn picturesque.

"Four girls went by here last night in a group," she said finally, getting to her feet. "You can tell by the stampede of Ugg boots. But no solo travelers, not even to smoke. Strange, this seems like a good spot for it." She methodically brushed the dirt and grass from her clothes. "They must have entered through the front doors. Michener isn't connected to the access tunnels, the way Stevenson and Harris are."

"Access tunnels?" I said.

"You really should explore more. We'll remedy that, but not now." Holmes glanced at the first floor's thick stone windowsills, at the windowsills above those, and bent down to untie her shoes. "Stuff these in my bag, will you," she said, putting a socked foot up on the sill. "Yours too. And put your gloves on. We can't leave prints of any kind. Come on, quickly, they might open their blinds at any moment. At least his roommate is away on that rugby tourney."

"Don't you need to find out which room is theirs?" I asked.

She tossed me a look, like I had asked her if the earth went around the sun. "Watson, just give me a lift."

I cradled my hands for her to step into, and in seconds she had climbed up the ivy to Dobson's second-floor window. Clinging to the sill with one hand, she used the other to pull a length of wire from her pocket, and bent one end into a hook with her teeth. I couldn't see what she did next, but I could hear her humming. It sounded like a Sousa march.

"Right," I whispered. "When I found you, you were just going to your *lab.*"

"Shut up, Watson." With a slight hiss and crack, the window opened. Holmes eased herself inside, as delicate as a dancer.

Her head reappeared. "Aren't you coming?"

I swore. Loudly.

Thankfully, all that rugby I'd been playing meant I was in passable shape. I had a good six inches on her too, so I didn't need a leg up to reach the hanging ivy. When I scrambled into Dobson's room, she patted me on the shoulder absently; she was already surveying her surroundings.

Dobson's was the sort of room I'd seen all over Michener: he had that black-and-white poster of two girls kissing, and the floor was thick with crumpled clothing. Randall's side wasn't any cleaner, but at least his bed was made. Dobson's sheets were a mess, kicked down to the end of his mattress. The coroner must've already removed the body.

There was a framed photo of him and what looked like his sister on the bedside table. The two of them were squinting into the lens, big smiles on. I felt an unexpected pang of guilt.

Holmes had no such hesitation. "Hold my bag," she said, and immediately fell to her hands and knees. I jumped back about a foot. From what seemed like thin air, she produced a penlight in one hand, a pair of tweezers in the other.

"Did you order some sort of spy kit online?" I asked, irritated. I'd had barely an hour of sleep, and, to be honest, I was trying hard not to give in to a lurking sort of terror. Anyone could come in at any moment and catch us tampering with the crime scene for a murder I'd sort of wanted to commit.

And then there was Holmes. While I stood there, shaking with fear, she was efficient, cool-headed, working swiftly to get us absolved. I thought once more about the two of us racing through a runaway train and smothered a laugh. In reality, she'd make a clean escape while I'd trip over my own feet and get hauled away for waterboarding.

"Be quiet," she whispered back. "And pull one of those specimen jars from my bag, I've found something."

I took a small glass bottle from her backpack and undid the stopper, then crouched so she could tip the tweezers in. Through the glass, the sample looked like a sliver of onion skin; as I examined it, she added another piece, and a third. She pulled up a bit of the carpet and tucked that into another jar, and used her piece of wire to poke around under the bed, dislodging a number of pens, an old toothbrush, some odds and ends. She inspected a glass of milk by his bed and the old-fashioned slide whistle beside it. With one gloved finger, she traced an invisible line from a high vent down the wall to Dobson's pillow. Then she looked up, sharply, at the ceiling, and I heard her counting—why, I wasn't sure. Every small noise sounded to me like our inevitable imprisonment, and my heart hammered in my ears.

She bent to examine Dobson's pillow and gestured me over. The indentation that his head had made was still visible. "Is that spit?" I whispered, pointing.

"Excellent." She scraped at it with the edge of her tweezers. I'd said it just to make her laugh, but I warmed at the compliment anyway. "Jar," she said, and I handed her one.

"I don't see any blood," I said, and she shook her head. There wasn't any to see, not anywhere.

Outside the door, I heard footsteps—more than one

set—and people talking. To my horror, I heard the edges of my name, of Dobson's. Above the din, a grizzled voice said, "Is this the boy's room?"

"We need to go," I told Holmes, and for a second she looked like she was about to protest. "*Now*," I said, pulling her to the window—I swear I saw the doorknob begin to turn. Without waiting, I lowered myself down the outside of the building, then jumped the rest of the way.

The second my feet hit the ground, my fear broke open into exhilaration.

I heard the window shut with a snap. Holmes landed behind me, and I spun her around by the arm.

"Were you seen?" I asked breathlessly.

"Of course not."

"Holmes," I said, "that was *brilliant*."

That flicker of a smile again. "It was, wasn't it. Especially for a first effort."

"A first—you hadn't done that before."

She shrugged, but her eyes were gleaming.

"You had us break into a crime scene to steal evidence— something that could make us look even more guilty than we do already—and you've *never done that before?*" If I sounded a bit shrill, it was because I felt a bit shrill.

Holmes had already moved on. "We need to get to my lab," she said, pulling her shoes from her bag, "without arous- ing any suspicion for why we're together. Do you want to split up and meet there in twenty? Sciences, room 442." She tossed my sneakers to me in an elegant, underhand lob. "And take the long way, will you? I want to get there first."

SCIENCES 442 WAS A SUPPLY CLOSET.

A big one, but still.

When I walked in, Holmes was already bent over her chemistry set. It was the real deal, the kind I'd only seen in movies—tall beakers, and big fat ones, smoke coming off of the strange green substances inside. Bunsen burners all lit like a row of stage lights. This setup had pride of place in the middle of the room, and she'd lashed a pair of desk lamps to a neighboring bookshelf for light. That bookshelf was filled with a collection of battered-looking textbooks, everything from Darwin's *The Origin of Species* and *Gray's Anatomy* to huge tomes with names like *The History of Dirt* and *Baritsu and You*. There was an entire shelf just on poisons. At the bottom, I spied the famous biography of Dr. Watson, the one my mother had told me was too scandalous to read. (Which meant I had read it immediately. Apparently, he was really, really . . . popular with girls.)

Next to it was the only fiction in the entire bookcase: a handsome leather-bound set of Dr. Watson's Sherlock Holmes tales. The whole series, from *A Study in Scarlet* to *His Last Bow*. Their spines were all broken like they'd been read a million times.

If I was harboring any doubts about my part in this investigation—and to be honest, I'd had some *Titanic*-sized ones ever since we broke into Dobson's room—seeing those well-thumbed books made me feel better. I belonged here, I thought, with her, as surely as anyone belonged anywhere.

As weird as *here* was.

Because there was just so much else crammed in that space, and any one part of it would have made her Prime Suspect #1 in Every Murder Ever. One wall was plastered with diagrams of handguns, obscured by a hanging set of giant bird skeletons. (A vulture peered knowingly at me, its eyehole bullet-black.) The tatty love seat against one wall was spattered in what had to be blood, dripped, most likely, from the riding crops hung above it. There were sagging shelves filled with soil samples, blood samples, what looked like a jar of teeth. Beside the jar was a violin case, a lone bastion of sanity.

I fervently hoped that I was the only visitor she'd ever had to this lab. Or else she was most definitely going to jail.

"Watson," she said, gesturing to the love seat with a set of tongs, "sit." I grimaced. "The blood's all dried," she added, as if that helped.

It was a measure of how tired I was that I obeyed her. "How goes—whatever you're doing? What did you find, anyway?"

"Twelve minutes," she said, and busied herself with her chemistry table.

I waited. Impatiently.

"I don't like to hypothesize in advance of the facts," she said finally. "But what I *have* found suggests that our killer wasn't leaving anything to chance. He used at least two methods of poison, maybe three."

"Poison?" I asked, unable to hide the relief in my voice. I knew nothing about poison; there was no way I could be accused of killing Dobson.

But Holmes could.

I swallowed. "I thought you were a sophomore. You haven't had chemistry yet."

"Not here," she said, holding a pipette to the light. "But I was privately tutored when I was younger."

Of course she was. I thought again of what my mother had said, that the Holmeses drilled their children from birth in the deductive arts. I wondered what else Holmes had learned up there in their vast, lonely Sussex manor.

She cleared her throat. "How to defend myself. How to move silently through a room, how to locate every possible exit within seconds of entering a space. Entire city plans, beginning with London, including the names of every business on every street, and the fastest way to get to any of them. How, in short, to be always aware of what everyone is doing and thinking. From there, you can reason to why they do the things they do." For a moment, her eyes went dark, but her face cleared so quickly I decided I had imagined it. "And I was taught all the other subjects one learns in school, of course. Is that enough of an answer?"

I had no idea how to handle these conversations, where the questions were picked right out of my head. "It sounds incredible," I said honestly, "but I don't know if I'd want to always know what other people are thinking. Where they come from, what they want. Where's the mystery in that?"

She shrugged her shoulders with a nonchalance I didn't quite believe. "I suppose few people hold up to the scrutiny. But my family's business was never in maintaining mysteries. It's in unraveling them."

I wanted to ask her more questions, but I was exhausted. I caught myself smothering a yawn. "What time is it?"

"Eight," she said, and eye-dropped a clear substance onto a slide. "Any minute now, there'll be a campus-wide text saying that classes are off because of the murder. We can skip the optional counseling, I'm sure."

"Wake me up in two hours." I had to curl up small to fit on the sofa. As I pulled my jacket up to my chin, I caught Holmes's pale, considering eyes for the briefest moment before she looked away.

I WOKE UP TO A STALE TASTE IN MY MOUTH, SWEAT COOLING on my forehead. In my pocket, my phone let out the three-note sigh that meant that it was dying. For a horrible second I had no idea where I was. I looked up into the pleated ends of Holmes's riding crops, and remembered. It shouldn't have been as comforting as it was.

"That's been going off now for an hour," Holmes said from across the chemistry set. She was more undone than she'd been before: her jacket was rucked up to her elbows, and her hair was a spider web of frizz from the heat in our cramped quarters.

"And you didn't wake me up? What time is it?"

"You're wearing a watch."

"What time is it, Holmes?"

She looked blankly at me. "Seven?"

I swore, fumbling my phone out of my pocket. It was five till noon. I had a text from the school saying that classes were canceled and that grief counseling would be available in the infirmary. I also had thirteen missed calls. Ten of them were from my father, at least two were from England—*Unavailable*, read the caller ID—and one was a local number that I didn't recognize. I played the message on my voicemail.

"This is Detective Shepard, calling for James Watson. . . ."

At her chemistry set, Holmes peered into the bottom of an Erlenmeyer flask. "Yellow precipitate," she announced, more to herself than for my benefit. "Excellent. Absolutely perfect." Humming tunelessly, she poured the solution into a test tube and stoppered it, sliding it into her pocket.

I listened to the end of Shepard's message with a sinking stomach. "Is there a bathroom nearby?" I asked her blearily. "I need to wash my face."

She pointed wordlessly to the laundry sink in the corner, and I splashed myself with cold water. "According to the detective," I said, "they've all spoken to each other, and apparently my father is afraid I've hung myself from a tree branch, and we're all meeting in my room in thirty minutes. What am I going to say to him?"

It was a rhetorical question, and a confused one, at that, but she walked over to perch on the love seat's battered arm. "Your father?" she asked, and I nodded. She twisted her hands in her lap, and I noticed that the soft inside of one elbow was puckered with scars. *I heard it was going into her arm,* the redhead had said.

"I haven't seen him since I was twelve."

"Do you want to tell me why?" she asked. It was clear that she knew that this was what friends did—showed interest in each other's lives, offered a willing ear when the other was upset—and that she was doing her best to mimic it. It was also clear that she'd rather be pouring a gallon of water onto a live wire.

Then again, maybe she did that for fun, anyway. Who the hell knew.

"You could tell me," I said. "I'm sure you've already come to some deductions. Read some invisible bits of my past in my pinky finger."

"It isn't a party trick, you know."

"I know," I told her. "But it might be easier. For both of us."

"Easier?" Holmes sighed, and tossed me my jacket. "Come on, or we'll be late."

A sharp wind cut through the quad, but the sky above was mercilessly clear. Everywhere, students huddled in clusters of two or three against the cold. Quite a few were openly crying, I noticed as we walked past; freshmen who probably didn't even know Dobson were hugging each other.

But when they spotted me and Holmes, everyone just . . . stopped. Stopped talking, stopped weeping, stopped telling tearful stories. One by one, they turned to glare at us, and then the whispering started.

Holmes tucked her small white hand in the crook of my arm and powered me along. "Listen to me," she said rapidly. "Your parents are English, but you were raised in America; I know that from what my family has said about yours. Your accent isn't very strong, but how you stress your sentences is very specifically London. And you love London; I could tell from the look on your face when you first heard me speak, like you'd had a glimpse of home. You must have lived there, and at a particularly impressionable time in your life. Add in the fact that you said 'bathroom,' not 'toilet' earlier—and other times, you've shied away from using any slang at all, rather than make a decision to be English or American about it—and so you must have moved to London around age eleven or twelve. Am I correct?"

I nodded dizzily.

It was hard to hear Holmes talk, to learn that every one of my insignificant words and actions broadcasted my past, if one just knew how to look. But it would have been harder still to walk through the quad in silence while the rest of the school played judge, jury, and executioner. She'd known that, I thought. That's why she'd saved her deductions for this walk: two terrible birds, one stone.

"Your jacket wasn't always yours. It was made in the 1970s, judging from the cut and the particularly awful brown of the leather, and while it fits you well enough, it's a touch too big in the shoulders. I'd say you'd bought it secondhand, vintage, but everything else you're wearing was made in the last two years. So either you inherited it, or it was a gift." She slipped her hand into my coat pocket to pull it inside out. "Magic marker stains," she said with satisfaction. "I saw this earlier, on the couch. I doubt you were carrying Crayolas around last winter. No, more likely that it was around your house while you were growing up, and either you or your younger sister wore it, at one point, while playing at art teacher."

"I didn't tell you I had a younger sister," I said.

She gave me a pitying look. "You didn't have to."

"Fine, so it was my father's." It wasn't pleasant, being dissected. "So what?"

"You're wearing it," she said. "That's enough to tell me you don't hate him. No, it's not as simple as *hate*. This is veering into psychology, and I'm sorry, I *loathe* psychology, but I imagine you wear the jacket because, somewhere, deep down, you miss him. You left for London at twelve, but your father lives here. You call him that, 'my father'; you don't call him your 'dad.' The very mention of him makes you tense up, and since we've established he hasn't been beating you, I can safely say that it's dread built up from a long silence. The last piece of it, of course, is your watch."

We were nearly at Michener Hall, and Holmes paused, holding out her hand. I didn't really see another option: I unfastened the clasp and handed it over.

"It's one of the first things I noticed when I met you," she said, examining it. "Far more expensive than anything else you wear. A ridiculously large watch face. And the inscription on the back—yes, here we are. *To Jamie, On His Sixteenth Birthday, Love JW, AW, MW and RW.*" Her eyes glittered at her discovery—no, at the confirmation of what she'd deduced—and I understood then what it would be like to hate her.

"Go on," I said, so it would finally be over.

She ticked it off on her fingers. "Despised childhood nickname, so he doesn't know you anymore. Very expensive gift for a teenager? Long-standing guilt. But the key is in the *names*. He didn't just give you a gift from him; he made sure you knew it was from the whole family. His *new* family. Your mother's name is Grace, my aunt's mentioned it. So A stands for . . . Anna, let's say, and MW and RW would be your half siblings, then. Even his birthday present to you is a clumsy attempt to get you to love them. You haven't spoken for years because, most likely, he was cheating on your mother with . . . Anna? Alice? When your parents divorced, he stayed in America to start a new family. Abandoning, at least in your eyes, you and your sister.

"But your mother doesn't resent him: she didn't insist you box away a frankly ridiculous gift until you're older. This watch is worth at least three grand. No, she let you wear it. They're on good terms, even though they're divorced; perhaps she's relieved that he's moved on, as she'd already accomplished that feat before the marriage had ended. Either way, she'd be upset that you aren't on better terms with him—a boy needs his father, et cetera, et cetera. Your stepmother must be younger, then, but not so young that your mother disapproves."

"Abigail," I said. "Her name is Abigail."

Holmes shrugged; it was a small point to concede. Every other detail had been spot-on, gold star, perfect.

The cold wind chapped at my face. It blew her hair about, obscuring her eyes. "I'm sorry, you know," she said, so quietly I could barely hear her. "I don't mean for it to . . . to hurt. It's just what I've observed."

"I know. It was well done," I said, and meant it. I didn't hate her so much as I hated being reminded of what my father had done. How I couldn't seem to get over it. And I hated the dread in my stomach as I looked at Michener Hall's heavy wooden doors and thought about the people waiting for me inside. My father. The detective. *I'm not guilty,* I reminded myself.

I wondered why I felt like I was.

She took my arm again. "You also wear the jacket because you think it makes you look like James Dean," she said as we walked in. "The eyes are right, but the jaw's all wrong, and though you're handsome, you're no tortured artist. More of a wiry librarian." She thought for a moment. "I suppose that's not all bad."

No one else in the world would put up with this girl. "You are *awful,*" I said, and even then I was forgiving her.

"I'm not." Relief was written all over her face. "How am I awful? I want examples. Give me an itemized list."

"Jamie?" a hesitant voice asked behind me. "Is that you?"

I turned to face my father.

three

I'D BEEN TOLD ALL MY LIFE THAT I WAS MY FATHER'S SPITTING image, and after years apart, I could see it more than ever. The dark, unruly hair—though his was beginning to gray at the temples—and dark eyes, a certain stubborn set to the jaw. *Watsons might be stubborn,* he'd told me when I was younger, *but we temper it with a love of adventure.*

Well, here was my adventure: a dead misogynist jerk, me the prime suspect, and my estranged father waiting to sit in on my questioning. Detective Shepard hovered a few steps behind. Someone must've filled him in on my family history, and he'd decided to give the two of us a moment.

In the background, Mrs. Dunham fussed noisily with an electric kettle. A series of mismatched mugs were lined up on the front desk. "I'm making tea," she said unnecessarily. "So many English people. It seemed like the thing to do."

Honestly, she wasn't far off. "Cheers," my father and I said at the same time. Next to me, Holmes smothered a laugh.

My father's eyes lit on her, clearly casting around for something, anything to say. "So, Jamie, aren't you going to introduce me to your girlfriend?"

Her hand tightened on my arm—in horror, I assumed. I didn't dare look over at her.

"This is Charlotte Holmes," I said quietly. "She's not my girlfriend."

I'm not sure what reaction I expected. My mother would have gone thin-lipped and silent, saving up ammunition to barrage me with in private. *Isn't she a bit pale*, and *She seems very unfriendly, don't you think*, and, ultimately, *You know, she'll just bring you to grief in the end.*

My father was delighted.

"Charlotte! Wonderful!" he said, and to my shock and Holmes's, he pulled her into a bone-crushing hug. She actually squeaked. I hadn't thought she could even make that sound. "Do you know, I sent my son all your press clippings. You did such marvelous work with the Jameson diamonds—and so young! You remember the story, right, Jamie? She'd been eavesdropping on Scotland Yard briefing her brother Milo. From behind a sofa in the library, isn't that how it went? And then she wrote them a detailed letter, in crayon, telling them where to find the loot. Marvelous."

At that, he let her go, and she swayed a bit on her feet. "I never owned a set of crayons," she said, but he didn't seem to hear her. Clucking, Mrs. Dunham pressed a cup of tea into Holmes's hands.

"Wait a minute." Detective Shepard cleared his throat. "You mean that you're *that* Holmes? Which makes you—"

"Yes, yes," my father said, waving a hand. "That Watson. Let's go have a sit-down and clear this whole mess up. Where's your room, Jamie? Upstairs, I imagine." He strode off toward the stairwell, the detective at his heels.

"She was *ten*?" Shepard asked, and my father's laugh echoed down the stairs.

Holmes clutched her mug of tea in disbelief. "He hugged me."

"I know," I said, making to follow them.

"I think I might like him," she said miserably.

I went back and ushered her up the stairs. "Don't feel bad," I told her. "Everyone does, except for me."

THE FIRST THING THE DETECTIVE ESTABLISHED WAS THAT Holmes and I both had alibis for the night before, courtesy of our roommates. The second thing he established was that those alibis didn't really matter.

"We're exploring a number of options," he said, perched in my desk chair, "based on the forensic evidence. And we're not confining our scope to last night. I want to hear the full story of what happened between you two and Lee Dobson. After that, I want to hear exactly why, despite all reports to the contrary, the two of you appear to be thick as thieves." He looked at Holmes, then me, with narrowed eyes. "It wasn't my plan to interrogate you two together, and I don't think I can. Miss Holmes, since I don't have a parent present—"

"Check your email," she said smoothly. "You'll find a message from my parents giving permission for Mr. Watson here to stand in as my guardian."

As Shepard took out his phone, my father pulled a notebook and pen from the inner pocket of his blazer.

"I don't need you to take notes," the detective said, bemused.

"Oh, no. These are for me." He smiled. "I have an interest in crime."

Shepard glanced over at me for help, and I shrugged, sitting down on the bed. I wasn't my father's keeper.

It didn't take very long at all for Holmes to tell her side of it. How she had come here as a freshman, and how Dobson had gone after her almost immediately. (Understandably, she left out the bit about him calling her a junkie, but I watched her tug at her sleeves as she detailed what he'd said to her.) She hadn't been to school before this, and so, she told the detective, she wasn't sure how to handle his abuse. Others had witnessed it—Lena, she said, and her brother—if Shepard wanted to corroborate her account.

"It's important to note that I didn't want him dead." There was steel in her voice. "Of course I wanted him to stop. But quite honestly, I was fine. His actions didn't have much bearing on my life here."

I remembered her wariness when I first approached her on the quad. *Who put you up to this? Was it Dobson?* But then it was my turn to tell a few half-truths, so I guessed I couldn't blame her.

Yes, it was true that I'd punched Dobson because he was being disgusting about a girl, a family friend, and because no one was saying anything to stop him. Yes, there were better ways of solving my problems; yes, if I could do it again, I'd use words instead of fists. (A lie.) Holmes and I had fought, and very publicly, but I told the detective that I'd found her the next day to make sure there were no hard feelings. (A lie.)

As I talked, I watched my father struggle to contain his beaming approval. When I described my right hook to Dobson's chin, he took notes with a stifled grin. Really, with role models like him, it was surprising I wasn't already in jail.

For his part, the detective stuck to asking us simple questions and fiddling with the recorder he'd brought along; we'd given permission for him to tape our statements. After I told him that I'd snuck out of the dorm this morning to see if Holmes was okay (a half-lie) and that we'd hidden away in her lab to avoid our classmates (retroactively true), I came to the end.

Shepard made a show of shuffling through his own notes. "I think that's it," he said, and I reached for my jacket.

He held up a hand before I could stand. "Except for the part where, when we found Dobson's body, he was clutching your school library's copy of *The Adventures of Sherlock Holmes*. With one story in particular bookmarked. Or the part where you had sex with him. Dobson." He was facing Holmes, but his eyes were fixed on me. My father stopped writing.

Nothing could have prepared me for that.

I went cold all over, then hot, and I thought I might retch on the carpet. So Dobson had been telling the truth. Thick-necked, grunting Dobson, who I'd once heard brag about jerking off in the communal shower. I'd kill him. I'd hunt him down and strangle him with my bare hands, even if I had to resurrect him to do it.

Next to me, I felt Holmes go very still. "Yes, I did," she said.

Through that all-too-familiar blood-roar, I heard the detective say, "Is there a reason you decided to keep that fact a secret? Not just from me, either. It looks like even your friend here had no idea."

I shoved my fists under my knees. Was I breathing? I couldn't tell. I didn't care.

"Because I was using a rather large amount of oxy at the time," she said coolly, "and had that come to light, I would have been expelled. Your real question should be whether the sexual act was consensual. Which, considering my impaired state, it wasn't." She paused. "Do you have any more questions?"

Her voice broke on the last word.

At that, I had to leave the room.

I STALKED UP AND DOWN THE HALL, SHAKING. IF I DIDN'T already have a reputation for being a violent dickhead, I definitely had one now: Peter opened his door in a bathrobe, shower caddy in hand, but after one glance at me punching the wall, he ducked back into his room. I heard him lock the door behind him.

Good, I thought. The first person to look at me the wrong way would get the pounding that Dobson had deserved.

As for Holmes . . . it hurt too much to think about her. Of course the fact that she'd done hard drugs wasn't a huge surprise; even without the rumors, I knew about the Holmeses' long, storied history with cocaine and rehab. According to my great-great-great-grandfather's stories, Sherlock Holmes had always fallen back on a seven-percent solution when he was without a case. He needed the stimulation, he'd claimed, and Dr. Watson had only made cursory efforts to stop him. Oxy was just Charlotte Holmes's particular poison. Apparently, old habits died hard in this family.

But I kept *imagining* it, Holmes stretched out on that tattered love seat in her lab, one indolent arm over her face, the empty plastic pouch beside her. That image alone was enough to turn my stomach—her eyes sparkling with a false fever, the sweat on her brow. And then Dobson at the door, disgusting words on his lips. How did it unfold? Did he have to hold her down?

I was aware, then, of my breath, as hard and fast as if I'd been running. I thought about it for another half second. Dobson's face. The empty pouch. Then I slammed my fist again into the cinder-block wall.

My father stepped out into the hallway.

"Jamie," he said in a low voice, and it pushed me over the edge into tears.

I don't cry, as a rule. Nothing good comes out of fighting, I'll give you that, but crying? For a moment, you might feel a touch of release, but for me that's always been followed hard by waves of shame, and helplessness. I hate feeling helpless. I'll do anything to avoid it.

I suppose Holmes and I had that in common.

I half-expected my father to try to hug me, the way he did her, but instead he laid a hand on my shoulder. "It's the worst feeling, isn't it?" he asked. "That there's nothing at all you can do to make it better."

"I didn't kill him, Dad," I said, rubbing angrily at my face. "God, I wish I had."

"You mustn't blame her for this, you know," he said. "I imagine she's doing a good enough job of that herself."

I took a step back. "I'd never blame Holmes for this. It isn't her fault."

My father smiled at that, though sadly. "You're a good man, Jamie Watson. Your mother's raised you well." This was territory that I couldn't get into, not then, and he must've seen it on my face. I waited for him to insist that I sign off campus to go home with him—it would be a reasonable suggestion, after everything that'd happened—but he didn't.

"Come by for dinner next Sunday," he said instead. "Bring Charlotte. You still like steak pie, I'm sure." There wasn't a question there to say no to, and before I could find a way to protest anyway, he said, "It'll just be the three of us." No stepfamily, he meant. I found myself nodding.

Detective Shepard came out into the hall, ushering along an ashen Holmes. Her composure was eggshell-thin but intact.

I admired her self-possession, and still, I wanted to be a million miles away.

"Next Sunday, then," my father said, and fixed the detective with a look that said the interview was absolutely over.

Shepard stood there for an awkward moment. "Neither of you leave town without telling me. We'll talk again soon." He followed my father down the stairs.

Holmes and I stared at each other.

"You've been crying," she said, more hoarse than usual. She lifted a tentative hand to touch my face. "Why?"

I wanted to shout at her. I couldn't turn my feelings off like I was a machine, and as much as she pretended to be one—her spotless appearance, the precise way she spoke—I knew she couldn't either. Her emotions had to be roiling somewhere, deep below the surface, and I wanted to demand that she pull them out for my inspection. As if it were my right.

But instead, I covered her cold hand with mine. "I won't make you talk about it," I said.

"Yes," she said, withdrawing. "Don't."

"Okay." I took a deep breath to steady myself. "Did you give him whatever it was that you slipped into your pocket? That vial?"

"I did."

It was like pulling teeth. "Are you going to tell me what it was?"

She considered it for a moment. Considered me. "Watson," she said, "it looks like we're being framed."

MRS. DUNHAM WOULDN'T LET US LEAVE WITHOUT A PROMISE to go first to the infirmary. My knuckles were bleeding after I'd punched that wall, my fingers bruised and swollen. Holmes promised her we would, and she sat patiently as the nurse examined me. "You're becoming quite a regular," she said, tsking, and gave me bandages and an ice pack.

Holmes ducked into the dining hall to make us sandwiches while I waited by the door. I was surprised that she would remember to eat, as I'd been too upset to realize that I was starving. We were both, I think, too overwhelmed by our internal weather to pay much attention to what was happening outside. This time the stares and whispers as we crossed the quad didn't bother me. How could they? I had so much more to worry about. Up at Sciences 442, Holmes produced a ring of keys, and let us in.

"How did you con them into giving you a lab?" I asked, thankful for a neutral subject to discuss.

"My parents made it a stipulation of my acceptance," she said. Around us, the lab was as strange and dark as we'd left it. "Sherringford was quite eager to have me, and so they agreed. On my transcript, the work I do here is listed as an independent study."

I smirked. "In what? Murder?" She wrinkled her nose at me.

For those few minutes, I'd forgotten about Dobson, but the sight of the battered love seat brought it crashing back. I watched her watch me remember, and with a gust of energy, she slammed the door shut.

"It didn't happen here," she said matter-of-factly. "It happened in Stevenson. Yes, I generally do oxy here, when I do downers, so that was an exception. Yes, it was immensely upsetting; yes, I do get upset. No, I'd rather not tell you the details. I don't want you to *know* the details. I didn't kill him, and I didn't hire anyone to kill him. I had nothing to do with his death. As I've told you before, I can fight for myself. So stop looking at me like I'm an object for your pity."

"I don't pity you," I said, stunned. She turned to the wall, but I could still see her close her eyes, count backward silently from ten.

"No," she said, without turning around. "You just choose to feel all the things that I can't, or don't. It's overwhelming. We've been friends for less than a day." She paused. "Though I suppose we're neither of us very normal."

No one had considered me anything *but* normal, before this. Though I was sure that hadn't been the case for her.

After a long minute, I sat down on her disgusting couch. "Here is your lunch," I said, picking up the sandwiches from where she'd dropped them on the floor. "Normal people eat lunch, and so, for these five minutes, we are going to be normal. After that, you're free to tell me who's framing us for murder."

She flopped down beside me. "I don't have the *who* yet," she said. "Not enough data."

"Normal," I warned her. "At least try."

I wolfed my sandwich down, even though it was pastrami and lettuce on white bread, full stop. No condiments. It was the kind of sandwich only a posh girl with a personal chef and the appetite of a hummingbird would have made, and so maybe I shouldn't have been surprised. For her part, she ate a listless bite or two, eyes fixed on the middle distance.

"What do normal people talk about?" she asked me.

"Football?" I hazarded. She rolled her eyes. "Okay. Did you see that new cop movie?"

"Fiction is a waste of time," she said, pulling a shred of lettuce out of her sandwich and nibbling on its end. A snail. She ate like a snail. "I'm far more interested in real events."

"Like?"

"There was a positively fascinating series of murders in Glasgow last week. Three girls, each garroted with her own hair." She smiled to herself. "Clever. Honestly, I didn't even leave the lab as it unfolded, I was so taken with it. I called in some tips to my contact at Scotland Yard, and she wanted to fly me out to investigate. Then this happened."

"How inconvenient," I said.

She, of course, ignored the sarcasm. "It was, wasn't it?"

"Okay, normal lunch is an abject failure," I said, "so just get on with it. Why are we being framed?"

"You're asking the wrong questions," she said, tossing the sandwich on the floor as she stood. I picked it up and put it in the trash. "We're not on *who*, or *why*, Watson, we're still working out *how*. You can't theorize in advance of facts, or you'll waste everyone's time."

"I don't understand," I said, because I didn't.

I swear, she nearly stamped an impatient foot. "Fact one: Lee Dobson tormented me for an entire year before assaulting me on September 26. Fact two: you and Dobson got into an altercation on October 3. Fact three: Dobson was murdered on Tuesday, October 11, close enough to both incidents to link them all together. When his toxicology reports come back, they'll prove that Dobson was a victim of gradual arsenic poisoning, that it began the night you first punched him, and that the doses increased in amount until the night he died. I'm sure that his roommate and the infirmary will testify to the attendant headaches, nausea, and so on."

"Jesus Christ." I stared at her. "Arsenic? Don't tell me you have access to arsenic."

"Watson," she said patiently, "we're in the sciences building, and I have the keys."

I put my head in my hands.

"He was holding a copy of your great-great-great-grandfather's stories. They'll also find that, last night, Dobson was the victim of a rattlesnake bite, perhaps even shortly postmortem while the blood was still warm. Remember the scale that I found on Dobson's floor?" Stooping, she pulled a book from the bottom of her bookshelf and tossed it to me. I was startled to see it was *The Adventures of Sherlock Holmes*. "No? How about the glass of milk on his bedside table? Or the vent above his bed? Come on, Watson, think!"

I blinked down at the book in my hands, not quite believing what she was implying. "You can't be serious."

"Oh, I'm quite serious. They're re-creating 'The Speckled Band.'"

"The Adventure of the Speckled Band" is one of my

great-great-great-grandfather's most well-known stories; it's definitely the most frightening, and also the most riddled with factual errors. As so many of his tales do, "The Speckled Band" opens in 221B Baker Street, with a shaken woman asking for help. Her sister had died two years before in the middle of the night under mysterious circumstances, and now Helen Stoner, Holmes's client, has been moved by her patently evil stepfather into that same bedroom, weeks before her wedding. During their investigation, Sherlock Holmes and Dr. Watson find that the bed in that room is bolted to the floor. Beside it, a bellpull trails down from a vent above that opens into the stepfather's study next door. There, Holmes finds a saucer of milk, a leash, a locked safe, and, during their stakeout, an Indian swamp adder—the speckled band of the title—that Evil Stepfather is using to kill his stepdaughters, controlling the snake with a whistle and tossing it into the safe when he's finished.

John H. Watson might have been many things—a doctor, a storyteller, and by most accounts a kind and decent man—but he clearly wasn't a zoologist. There's no such thing as a swamp adder. And the idea that Sherlock Holmes deduced its existence from a saucer of milk is ridiculous—snakes have zero interest in milk. They also can't hear anything but vibrations, so they wouldn't hear a whistle. But they *do* breathe, so a snake couldn't survive in a locked safe.

When I was younger, my father and I liked to speculate about what actually happened on that case to drive Dr. Watson to that much invention. My pet theory is still that he slept late that day in Baker Street, missed both the client and the investigation entirely, and was only half-listening when Sherlock Holmes broke it down for him later.

At least, that sounds like something I would do.

"Whoever they are, they're taunting us," Holmes was saying, pacing the length of her lab like a caged cat. "The arsenic would have done Dobson in on its own. The snake is just a ridiculous flourish, there to send a message. Of course, our culprit couldn't find a swamp adder, because your great-great-great-grandfather made those up." I rolled my eyes at her clear disdain. "But honestly, Watson, why would Dobson have a glass of milk? There wasn't a mini-fridge in his room; he'd have to carry it back from the dining hall after dinner. And while I suppose it's possible that Lee Dobson had discovered a passion for folk music, having a slide whistle is too strange in the context of everything else. The presence of these items is *just* plausible enough that the police wouldn't see them as significant, and so, in planting them there, the killer must have known we would make our own investigation."

"We're being toyed with," I said. "But why would he want us to know he's after us?"

"*Us*, specifically." She arched an eyebrow. "Dobson was after me all last year, and nothing happened to him. Then you show up, and all this starts. We'll begin by investigating people who arrived in the area since the summer, or those who have a particular stake in bringing the both of us down."

Why would anyone be after me? Holmes, I understood. She was so clearly smarter than, faster than, braver than— there had to be someone on the other side of that equation to make it work. Maybe I was just collateral damage. Maybe there had been some mistake. Because, no matter how badly I wanted my life to be interesting, it wasn't. There was no reason for anyone to target me.

But if Holmes realized how unimportant a role I actually played in all of this, she might send me packing. Back to chemistry homework and Tom's dirty jokes and all the other trappings of my American exile. Back to dreaming about her at night while she went on, unmoved, with her life. But it would be worse this time, because I'd know exactly what I was missing.

I decided to keep my mouth shut.

Holmes stopped pacing to lean against the wall for support. I remembered that she hadn't slept at all last night. I had no idea how she was still on her feet.

"The police aren't going to let us help them, not if Shepard's any indication," she said. "Idiots. I suppose that they don't like that I tampered with their crime scene."

"We're also their prime suspects," I reminded her. "That sort of puts a damper on our working relationship."

She shrugged, as if that were beside the point. "That's it, then."

"What is?"

"That's all I have to tell you. I'll think on our next move."

It was a dismissal. Whatever use she'd had for me had expired, and our investigation was done for the day. I got to my feet, wondering if I'd made a misjudgment in thinking that I was starting to mean something to her.

Because it seemed that Holmes had already forgotten me. She brought down her violin case from its shelf and drew from it an instrument so warm and polished that it nearly looked alive. I remembered listening to a special on BBC 4 in my kitchen that past summer, in such a profound sulk at leaving that my mother had begun a campaign to cheer me up. That day, she was making cinnamon buns by hand, rolling out the dough in long strips that dangled off the edge of our tiny countertop, and I'd crept from my room, drawn by the smell of the sugar. She looked up at me with floured hands, a brown curl stuck to the side of her face, and before either of us could speak the radio presenter announced a feature on the history of the Stradivarius. Underneath his voice played the famous recording of Sherlock Holmes performing a Mendelssohn concerto on his own Stradivarius for King Edward VII. The music was scratchy and still tremendously alive through the static. I'd drawn nearer, and my mother had pursed her lips but didn't change the station, and so we spent the afternoon that way, icing the rolls she'd made as they cooled and listening to the announcer speak of the violin's shape, the density of its wood, how Antonio Stradivari had stored his instruments under Venice's canals.

The brown-sugar color of Holmes's violin brought it all back to me in a rush, and I stood there, transfixed, watching her run through a scale before beginning to play. The bow stood out against her dark hair; her eyes were closed. The song was both familiar and alien, a folk melody punctuated by bursts of gorgeous dissonance. Though I was standing only a few feet away, the distance between us stretched like the hundred years between Sherlock Holmes playing for the king and my hearing it—that remote, that distant.

I must have listened for a long time before she stopped playing, and I realized that I was standing frozen with my hand on the doorknob, like a fool.

"Watson," she said, letting the violin drop to her side. "I'll see you tomorrow." She turned away from me, and began to play again.

four

AFTER I AVOIDED ALL MY CALLS FOR ANOTHER DAY, MRS. Dunham came by my room and politely told me that if she had to speak to my panicked mother one more time, she would very publicly set herself on fire. So, that Thursday, I had to endure my mom's histrionics and my sister Shelby's thousand questions ("What happened? Are you okay? Does this mean that you can come home?"), a call that went on for hours. I told neither of them that I'd been invited to my father's house for dinner; I still hadn't decided if I would go.

Things settled down between Tom and me. Or rather, Tom's good nature won out over his suspicions, and after a day of uncomfortable silence, he came over to my desk while I was writing. I'd been scribbling down everything I could remember since Dobson's murder—times and dates, names of poisons, those things of Dobson's that Holmes had cataloged with her hands. I was thinking of making a story of it, and when Tom peered over my shoulder, it was easy enough to try it out on him.

Or to try out the version that wouldn't get either Holmes or me expelled.

Sherringford had released a statement referring to Lee Dobson's death as an accident—an "accident with a snake," which came off much more bizarre than terrifying. It was their attempt to reassure parents that our campus was safe, but students were still being dragged home in droves. Our hall, in particular, had an emptied-out feeling to it—for two days running, there was no line for the shower, no music blaring from behind closed doors.

Into that silence, the reporters appeared.

One day, they weren't there. The next, they were everywhere, crawling all over the quad with their cameras and flashbulbs and strident voices. They lay in wait after our classes, putting sympathetic hands on our shoulders and pointing the lenses into our faces. Most of the students ignored them. Some didn't. One day, during lunch, I watched the redheaded girl from my French class crying delicately into a camera. Her headshots, she sobbed, were on her website if they needed them. I guess I couldn't blame her for using the press; the press were using her, too.

That same reporter took a particular shine to me.

Following me from class to class, murmuring words of

sympathy before launching into questions like *Do you really think Lee Dobson's death was an accident?* and *Is it true you keep a snake in your dorm room?* From the logo on the cameraman's kit, I knew they were from the BBC. I would have known it anyway from the reporter's plummy accent and haughty chin, the very image of some grown-up Oxbridge wanker. He'd been sent across the pond to try to get some dirt on the Holmeses; I was sure by the way he kept turning the conversation back to Charlotte. Somehow, he'd gotten ahold of my class schedule, and for days he waited for me between classes, his cameraman always towering behind him.

The worst was the afternoon I thought I'd gotten away clean. The two of them were talking to a townie on the sciences building steps as I came out the front door. "Yeah, man," he was telling them, "I've heard the stories too. I have a lot of, uh, friends who say Charlotte Holmes is the head of this messed-up cult and James Watson is, like, her angry little henchman—"

I hurried past them, head down, but the reporter charged after me, calling my name, reaching out to pull on my arm.

I whipped around, ready to deck him. The cameraman stepped forward eagerly, training his lens on my face.

"See what I mean!" the townie said. I got a good look at him, this time. He was around thirty years old, with mean little features and thick blond hair. Tom had pointed him out to me as the campus drug dealer—I'd seen him lurking around campus at night.

Apparently these days he had more credibility than I did.

"Back off," I said quietly, and put my collar up. They let me walk on alone, but we all knew they'd be back the next day.

Except they weren't. Evidently, the reporters bothered enough of us that parents had begun to complain. Sherringford officially closed our campus to the public.

When I asked Holmes if she was relieved, she smiled politely. "My brother has an arrangement with the press," she said. "They've never bothered me."

Morale was low, and so it wasn't a surprise that the school decided to go ahead with our homecoming weekend despite all the commotion. Our school's green and white banners streamed from the chapel and the library; the dining hall announced they would be serving steak and salmon for dinner. In the days leading up to the dance, girls walked in droves to town and returned with long dresses in tied-off plastic bags. They had ordered them months before, from New York, and Boston, and one even from Paris. That was according to Cassidy and Ashton, who gossiped relentlessly through every one of our French classes. But it wasn't just girls who were preening in preparation. Tom was taking Lena, and he must have had his parents ship him his suit from Chicago. I had no idea how else he'd get his hands on a powder-blue jacket and vest.

It might have been a waste of time and money, but for once I understood it. Better to focus on pageantry than on death.

When I told Holmes that, she threw her head back in one of her rare laughs. "For a boy, you are massively melodramatic." I couldn't really argue with that. She had plenty of data to draw from, because I spent every spare moment I had in Sciences 442.

We had lunch there, and dinner—or rather, I ate in the ravenous way I always did while she made a series of deductions about my day. *You had Captain Crunch for breakfast,* she'd say, *and you've tried a new shaving cream you don't like,* the whole while pushing her food around her plate to disguise the fact that she wasn't eating. I bothered her about that, the way she picked at her food, and she'd eat a fry or two to appease me; ten minutes later, I'd bother her some more. One night, I mentioned that my favorite song was Nirvana's "Heart-Shaped Box," and an hour later, messing around on her violin, she played the opening measures of "Smells Like Teen Spirit." I don't think she realized she'd been doing it; when she caught my gaze, she jumped about a foot and slid directly into Bach's "Allemanda." (I learned the names of everything she played. She liked when I asked, and I liked to listen.)

The way we were with each other wouldn't have made sense to anyone else if I'd tried to explain it. I had a habit of volleying any ridiculous statement she'd make back over the net with top spin, and we'd ramp ourselves up into fierce arguments that way about beetles and Christmas plays and the color of Dr. Watson's eyes. We bickered over possible suspects: she was sure that our murderer had a Sherringford association, but I couldn't imagine why he or she wouldn't have acted the year before. I still couldn't imagine why I'd be a target. When I found a nest of prescription bottles hidden in her violin case, we had a pitched battle over the fact that she was still using oxy. "It's none of your business," she'd said, furious, and grew even angrier when I insisted that it, in fact, was. How could it not be? I was her friend. Maybe that's why the worst rows we had were about nothing at all. After we had it out one night about the way she always sprawled out on the love seat, leaving me to sit on the floor, I stormed from the lab to find, the next morning, that she'd brought in a folding chair. "For you," she said, with an idle gesture; it was all we really had room for in that small space.

But we didn't always egg each other on like that—more often, it was the opposite. Instead of yelling at her, I'd find myself sucked in by her hypnotic stare and unrelenting train of logical thought until I was letting her do something like pluck out my nose hair for an experiment. (To be fair, she did promise to do my chemistry homework for a month in exchange.) She taught me how to pick a basic lock, and after I'd finally maneuvered my pins into the right position and heard the telltale *click* and fallen back against the love seat in relief, she pulled a blindfold over my eyes and made me do it again. Later, after Holmes said she hadn't been allowed any when she was little, I bought a full-to-bursting bag of bulk candy from the union store and set it before her like an offering to a king. Deep in thought, she'd refused to try any of it, rolling her eyes at the very suggestion. When I returned from stepping out to take a call from my mother, I found her trying, very unsuccessfully, to bite into an everlasting gobstopper.

With all my time spent in Sciences 442, the outside world grew more and more strange. Sometimes, spending a day in Holmes's lab made it feel like a bunker we'd stocked against a nuclear apocalypse and moved into before it happened. When

Tom texted me to ask who I was taking to the dance, I found myself blinking hard in the lab's dim light, trying to remind myself that I could actually emerge into the unirradiated world and go.

But I didn't have a date, and told myself I didn't want one. When I thought about the dance, I kept imagining it taking place at some other Sherringford: one where spending an evening with the most fascinating girl I knew meant disco balls and shitty music, not Bunsen burners and bloodstains. One where going out into a sea of my classmates would be something other than absolute torture. There was no way to forget I was a murder suspect when people I didn't even know still stopped talking every time I walked into a classroom. Dobson's room was still roped off with yellow police tape. His former roommate Randall still tried to trip me in the hallways. My teachers all either handled me like glass or ignored me, except for whispery Mr. Wheatley, my creative writing teacher, who pulled me aside to say he was happy to listen if I ever needed an ear. I thanked him, though I didn't take him up on it. He was just offering because he was a nice guy. Even so, it felt good to have someone acknowledge, sanely, what was happening to me.

Because the truth of it was I was terrified. I kept expecting to wake up dead. Someone out there had it in for Holmes and me, and we had no idea who it was. More accurately, *I* had no idea who it was. I had the sinking feeling that Holmes did, but she sat on her suspicions with the smug languor of a cat on a pillow.

"I refuse to theorize in advance of the facts," was her response.

"So then let's go get some facts," I said. "Where do we start?"

She drew her bow over her violin, thinking. "The infirmary," she said finally.

Her plan was to see if Dobson, in the throes of arsenic poisoning, had tried to get help with his symptoms before his death. At first, I was a bit surprised that this was our next move. She'd done the tests and confirmed the poison's presence herself—why did she need to dig up more evidence that it had killed him? We knew it had.

But the more I thought about it, the more it made sense. Detective Shepard had completely dismissed Holmes's claim that we were being framed. Every time I stepped out of the sciences building, I saw the plainclothes policeman he'd stationed by the front door. I caught him going through the Dumpster outside my dorm. Holmes told me she'd woken one morning to find a team, on a ladder, examining her dorm room's window from the outside. She was more shaken than she seemed, I could tell. From her stories, and from the phone calls she still took regularly from her contact at Scotland Yard, I knew that Holmes wasn't used to working outside the law. Though she didn't say it out loud, I knew that she wanted to maneuver us back into the police's good graces. Having the school nurse corroborate our evidence would be a good first step.

"She likes you," Holmes said dispassionately as we walked toward the infirmary, a small, squat addition to Harris Hall, with a few overnight beds and a dispensary. Every time I'd been there in the past (cut-up hands, busted nose), I'd been taken care of by the same nurse. I'd never thought she was anything but businesslike with me.

"She likes me fine, I guess," I said. "So that's the plan? I fake some kind of injury, get her sympathy and her attention, and while she's busy, you go rooting around through her records?"

Holmes blinked at me. "Yes," she said, and pushed the door open.

The waiting room was empty. The nurse was finishing a game of Sudoku at the front desk. "Can I help you?" she said, without looking up.

"I'm back," I offered apologetically, holding up my hands. "These were hurting again, and I was kind of worried I might've broken something."

"Poor thing." She had a lilt to her voice that was oddly appealing. "And your girlfriend is here for moral support?"

I glanced over at Holmes, who managed a tearful smile. "I don't know if I can watch," she whispered. "I'm just so worried about him. I think I have to wait out here."

The nurse put a reassuring hand on her arm. "I won't do anything horrible to him, I promise. You can't leave him now. Come, come." She steered me and Holmes both back to the consulting room, where she poked at my hands (which did, in fact, hurt), said that they were healing just fine, handed me some Tylenol, and dismissed us. The whole visit took about five minutes.

"Well," Holmes said, scowling at the door behind us. "That usually works a bit better than it did."

I smirked. "You might have to work on your caring girl-friend routine. Is that it, then? No records?"

"No," she said. "I'll break in around midnight and get what I need. It's just tedious having to dismantle the security cameras again."

"Why didn't you just break in in the first place?"

Her smile flickered. "You seemed so eager to do something. I thought I might as well include you."

"Um, thanks?"

"But tonight I'll go alone. You're about as stealthy as a lame elephant. See you later." She patted me on the shoulder and took off down the path, leaving me behind, both charmed and insulted. The side effects of hanging around Charlotte Holmes.

When I arrived at her lab the next day after classes, Detective Shepard was stepping out of the door. I hadn't known that he could interrogate either of us without a parent there, but he must have found a way to talk to Holmes.

"Jamie," he said heavily. "I'll see you and Charlotte on Sunday night at your father's house. We'll talk then." With that, he fixed me with a pitying look and took off down the hall.

"Wait, you're coming to that?" I called after him, but he didn't respond.

Inside, on the love seat, Holmes was wrapped up in an avalanche of blankets. She looked like one of those Russian nesting dolls, like she was the smallest Holmes in a series.

Whatever words she'd exchanged with Shepard, they'd left her in a mood.

"Why did you let him in? What was that about, exactly?"

"Nothing."

"Nothing," I repeated. "I thought you were giving him Dobson's infirmary records."

"He already had them, of course," she said. "He chided me for breaking and entering, and left."

"So Dobson *did* go to have his symptoms treated."

"He went to the infirmary often," she said. "Mostly rugby-related injuries, Shepard said. He said they'd tested his hair for arsenic and found it, and didn't need any of my proof. Then he asked me to identify all the vials on my poisons shelf. And then he left, saying he'd see us soon, in a voice I think he thought was threatening. Amateur."

"Wait, back up. You let the detective in here. You let him look at your poisons shelf."

"Yes."

"Poisons."

"Yes."

"And there's arsenic on that shelf?"

"Yes."

"And he's interrogating us again this Sunday," I said, feeling sick.

"Yes," she said, drawing the word out like I was an idiot.

I stared at her for a long minute. She had to know something she wasn't telling me. "Right. We need to make a list of possible suspects. We need to find something we can give them. Anything to make you—us—look less guilty."

Turning away, I taped a sheet of butcher paper to the side of her bookcase and wrote "suspects" at the top.

"Watson," she said, "you don't have any suspects."

I glared at her. She brought her cigarette to her lips and took a long drag. We'd reached an unspoken agreement: she'd dump the pill bottles, and I'd stop checking for them. That's how I chose to read the new and constant presence of a lit Lucky Strike in her hand—that she was trying out a drug that wouldn't kill her, at least not as quickly.

But all that smoke meant the unventilated lab was starting to resemble some toxic back room of hell, edging me ever closer to my breaking point. And still Holmes sat, and smoked, and told me nothing.

"What about the person who checked out that copy of *The Adventures of Sherlock Holmes* from the library? There have to be records."

"Correction. That particular copy was new and had never once been checked out from the library. Someone stole it off the shelf," Holmes said. "Currently, the library database has it listed as 'missing.' And as the physical copy is in police possession, I have no way of examining it."

"What about enemies? We could list Dobson's enemies."

"Go on, then. Put down every girl at the school." Her eyes went dark. "Though I can tell you that, from the research I did last year, I know I'm the only one who had a . . . run-in with him."

I swallowed. "We could list our enemies, then."

"You haven't got any enemies."

"I've got ex-girlfriends," I countered. "English ones. American ones. Scottish ones. I could so see Fiona with some sort of tartan apothecary box for her poisons . . ." Although it was hard to actually imagine Fiona doing anything but dumping me in front of my entire class.

Holmes raised an eyebrow. "No," she said, and exhaled.

I kept myself from pulling the cigarette from her hand and grinding it out on the floor.

"I haven't been sleeping," I told her, "because I am worried that either you, or I, or some innocent lunch lady will bite it now that we've gotten ourselves a murderous fan club. So give me a hand, will you?"

Her eyes narrowed in concentration. "The Marquess of Abergavenny," she said, finally. "I set fire to his stables when I was nine."

"Fine," I said, and then, in a smaller voice, "Can you spell that?"

She ignored me. "I suppose you could add Kristof Demarchelier, the chemist. The Frenchman, not the Dane. And the Comtesse van Landingham—Tracy never liked me. She didn't like my brother Milo either, for that matter, but then he did break her heart. Oh, and the headmistress of Innsbruck School in Lucerne, for beating her so often in chess, and the champion table tennis player Quentin Wilde. I suppose you might as well add his teammates Basil and Thom. Thom with an 'h,' of course. Though I can't remember their surnames. Strange."

"Is that it? Or are there peers and MPs that you're forgetting? Maybe a crowned head or two?"

She took a puff that sent her into a coughing fit. When

she regained her composure, she said, "Well, there's August Moriarty," as if that shouldn't have been the first name out of her mouth.

"What," I asked her slowly, "were you doing picking fights with a Moriarty?"

Professor James Moriarty was Sherlock Holmes's greatest enemy. In some ways, he was almost as notorious as the Great Detective himself. Moriarty was the first criminal mastermind of London, who famously died after fighting Sherlock Holmes at the Reichenbach Falls in Switzerland. After that fight, Sherlock faked his own death in order to hunt down the rest of Moriarty's agents in disguise. Even Dr. Watson thought Sherlock was gone for good. Though the official story says differently, I have it on good authority that when Holmes waltzed back into his consulting room three years later, my great-great-great-grandfather delivered one hell of a punch to his former partner's jaw.

Like I said before, I haven't had the best role models.

But then neither had Charlotte Holmes.

She dashed her cigarette out in the ashtray with a delicate, vicious hand. "It's irrelevant." There was smothered hurt in her voice, but I couldn't afford to drop the subject.

"Professor Moriarty still has fans, Holmes. Followers. Did you know that some English serial killers still list him as their greatest inspiration? And they've never recovered all the art he stole. Not to mention the rest of his family actively attempting to live up to his legacy." I drew a line under his name. August. I had never heard of an August Moriarty. "I mean, I know it's been more than a hundred years, but—"

"I'd prefer to think," Holmes said, cutting me off, "that we aren't all so mercilessly bound to our pasts." She rose, shedding her blankets. Underneath, she wore a short pleated skirt, rolled at the waist to appear even shorter, and her white oxford was undone to the fourth button.

Had she dressed this way for the detective? Or for something else? What was she playing at?

I cleared my throat awkwardly. In one of her mercurial shifts of mood, she flashed me a smile and hauled a box out from underneath the love seat.

Inside was a collection of wigs. Dozens of them, stored in soft mesh bags and arranged by color. Holmes drew a hand mirror out from the box and peered at herself for half a second before smoothing her hair up into a knot.

"So this conversation is over," I said, but I might as well have been talking to the air. It was no use; I'd been outplayed. She didn't want to talk about August Moriarty, and so she wouldn't, and nothing I could say would change her mind.

Getting to watch her transform herself helped soften the blow. She did it with all the cool efficiency of a violinist tuning her instrument. A stocking cap went over her hair, followed by the wig—long blond hair, curled at the ends—and makeup that she applied with an expert hand, balancing the small mirror between her knees. I didn't know the terms for what she did, but the face that looked up at me was doe-eyed and glimmering, her cheeks pink, her lips smudged with sticky gloss. She spritzed herself with perfume. Then, without a hint of modesty, she pulled a pair of plastic inserts from a bag and slid them, one at a time, into her bra.

I turned away, my cheeks burning.

"Jamie?" asked a bright American voice as she stepped in front of me. "Are you okay?"

She was like textbook jailbait, all curves where there used to be straight lines. I hadn't registered before that Holmes had perfect posture, but I noticed the absence of it now, as she stood indolently in—dear God, knee socks. The blond wig and makeup lit up her gray eyes, imbuing them with a friendliness that I hadn't thought they could have. And the look those eyes were giving me was *criminal*.

"I'm Hailey," she said, her pronunciation lazy and Californian. "I'm a prospective student? For next year? My mom's in town but I wanted to, like, see the campus for myself. Is there a party tonight?" She touched my chest with a finger. "Do you want to take me?"

I'd never been so turned off in my life.

I stepped back into her chemistry table. The beakers rattled against each other; one crashed to the floor and shattered. And then there Holmes was again, underneath all the false wrapping, severe and mysterious and . . . pleased.

"Good," she said, in her usual hoarse voice, rapidly tossing things into a backpack. "If you hate Hailey, she'll do just fine for my purposes."

"Which are?"

"Be patient," she said. "I promise I'll tell you everything later." She glanced at the suspects list, at the name at the bottom. *August Moriarty*. "Everything, Watson. But not now."

"This is completely unfair," I pointed out.

"It is." Holmes smiled to herself. "We can talk more at the poker game tonight. I'll be there as myself."

"No one's going to come. Everyone thinks we're murderers."

"Everyone will come," she said, correctly, "because everyone thinks we're murderers."

"Well, you'll be lucky if I'm there."

"Yes," she said simply. "I will be."

"Fine," I said, throwing up my hands. Because she'd won, check and mate.

She was already at the door, and, having taken those five steps, she wasn't Holmes anymore.

With a coy wave over her shoulder, Hailey said, "Bye, Jamie."

And then I was alone, with nothing to do but sweep up the shards of the beaker from the floor.

I WASN'T SURE IF IT WAS OUR DUBIOUS CELEBRITY, OR JUST brewing excitement for homecoming weekend, but Holmes had been right about the crowd. When I arrived at Stevenson at half past eleven, the basement kitchen was already overflowing with people. Some freshman boys had spun off a satellite game of five-card stud in the common space, and I had to push past a group of giggling girls to get through the kitchen door. Instead of going silent at my presence, the way everyone else did, they giggled louder. Gritting my teeth, I finally got through to the card table at the back.

Holmes wasn't anywhere to be found, but Lena was holding court in an improbable top hat. I'd seen her around, but I hadn't paid much attention to her before. There wasn't any doubt that she was beautiful, in a way I'd heard Tom wax rhapsodic about late at night: long straight hair, inky eyes, brown skin. Tonight, she was flushed with excitement and something else—probably vodka—and she'd stacked her mountain of chips into a neat pyramid. When she spotted me, she waved me over.

The boy sitting next to her wasn't Tom, and he didn't look happy to see me. "Hey, killer," he spat. I ignored him.

"Hi, Jamie," Lena said, ignoring him too. "Do you want to play? We're out of chairs, but I can totally deal you in if you want to stand."

"Actually, he can have my seat. I need another drink." The girl on her other side—Mariella, I think her name was—pushed herself to her feet and tottered over to the counter, where I spotted a handle of Vodka-brand vodka and some dubious-looking pineapple juice. The freshman girl that had asked me to homecoming was playing bartender. I avoided her eyes, too. Was there anyone I wasn't avoiding?

"I'm happy Mariella left," Lena told me conspiratorially. "At least fifty bucks' worth of this haul is hers. Was hers, I guess. Oops."

If she were anything like the other Sherringford students I'd met, Mariella wouldn't miss her money in the slightest. I thought of the thirty-five dollars left in my checking account that I couldn't afford to lose and turned Lena down when she offered to deal me in, telling her I didn't know how to play.

"I'll try to pick it up, though," I lied. Really, I just wanted to keep my seat until Holmes arrived, since I didn't know anyone else here.

"Oh my God," Lena said, putting a hand to her chest. "You're British, too? You two are adorable, I love it."

In England, I was an American. Here, it was the opposite. "Actually, I was born here," I said.

"Are we going to play or not?" the guy next to Lena asked.

"Not," she said, pushing back her chair. "Or whatever, you guys play. I want to talk to Jamie." She stuffed her chips into the pockets of her dress and pulled me aside. I didn't bother to correct her on my name; I'd just about given up on asking people to call me James.

"I just want you to know," she said, over-enunciating each word, "that I don't think you and Charlotte killed Lee. Look at you! You're adorable, and now you're *blushing*, that's even more adorable. It's like you were invented to get her over that whole August thing. I totally refuse to believe you guys have gone all Bonnie and Clyde on Lee." She frowned. "He sucked, anyway."

"August?" My voice caught on his name, and I winced. "Um. I don't know any Augusts. Who's that?"

"Hold on," she said. "Let me take another shot."

I may have been a terrible liar, but Lena was drunk.

"Oh, you know. *August*. The guy back home. She was pretty upset about it when she got here last year. I mean, she didn't say she was upset but I heard her talking on the phone about him. You know, through the door? Then her brother came to visit and they were all like CIA about it the whole time. I kept hearing his name, which is a weird name, so I remembered it. Anyway, Milo left, but before he left, he was all like, *Rrr, I'm going to do something about this,* and she was a lot happier after that." She put a hand to her mouth. "Shit. Oh, shit. I probably shouldn't have told you that. Girl code."

I wanted to ask her what, in fact, she *had* told me, except maybe about one of Milo's drone hits. "It's fine," I said, drawing from the sane, imaginary place in my head, where no one was brutally killed down the hall and my only friend deigned to tell me the barest facts about her life. "I know all about it. Failed love. Tragic, really. And that house fire, with . . . with all the puppies."

"Exactly!" She pressed her hand against my arm. "You guys are going to homecoming, right? I ordered this dress from Paris—you know, we go there every summer, my family does—but then it didn't fit right, and no one does alterations here. Not good ones, anyway. Charlotte has this beautiful black dress that I asked if I could borrow—Tom would totally flip out—but she said no, so I figured that she had a date."

Holmes probably had that dress made specifically for some Norwegian gala where she beat a foreign minister at chess, stole a French-Yugoslavian treaty, and then smuggled herself into the hotel clothes hamper so that she could escape through the laundry chute. I wondered what it looked like; it had to be pretty spectacular if Lena wanted it that badly. A long dress, I imagined. Black and slinky, something a Bond girl would wear.

But Lena was wrong about Holmes having a date. The only boy she'd ever consider taking was—

I cut off that line of thought. Where was she, anyway? It was past midnight.

"Yeah," I said, craning my head to look over the crowd. "Er, no. No. I don't think Holmes does dances. Is it okay if I step outside and look for her? I can throw out your drink if you're finished." Lena was beginning to look a bit sick. As I eased the cup from her hand, a thought occurred to me.

"Um, Lena?" I said. "Why did Holmes start having these poker nights? She doesn't seem to like"—I was about to say *anyone* before I caught myself—"crowds. Isn't it kind of weird for her to host them?"

"Oh," Lena said, surprised. "You know, her parents don't give her any spending money or anything. And Charlotte burns through a lot. I think she does a lot of online shopping, she always has packages at the front desk." I coughed to cover my laughter. I was positive those packages contained something more sinister than designer clothes. Lena really was the perfect roommate for Holmes, I had to give her that. "Anyway, you know. She always knows when people are lying, so I guess it makes sense for her to play poker for cash. I think it's funny."

Tom snuck up behind Lena and put his arms around her. "Baby, you're drunk," he said, leaning in to kiss her on the cheek.

"Baby, stop. I gotta poker. Charlotte's not here, and I'm making a killing. I think I'm going to get a Prada purse."

"Better split it with me before you cash out." Tom kissed

her again, and she wrinkled her nose. "Since I'm your muse and all."

"Her poker muse," I said, as seriously as I could manage.

"I bet you Charlotte's his," Tom stage-whispered.

"Oh my gosh, that's *so cute*." Lena touched my cheek and turned back to the game, depositing her chips on the table in handfuls. When she looked away, Tom filched a few and slipped them in his pocket.

I pitched Lena's drink in the trash and set off in search of Holmes.

Since I was already in Stevenson, I snuck up to check her room first. It wasn't hard at all to get past the hall mother, asleep on her pillowed arms at the front desk. I quickly found Holmes's door on the first floor: Lena had covered it in paper flowers, and there was a notecard bearing her name in curly purple script. Holmes's name was hastily scribbled in black ink below it. The door was unlocked—Lena's fault, I was sure—so I let myself in.

Unlike the room Tom and I shared, which could've won awards for its messiness, theirs was as neat and orderly as only a girls' dorm room could be. Lena's side was a riot of color, big pillows and bright tapestries, the shut laptop on the desk covered in stickers. She had photos of young Cary Grant pinned to her corkboard, nestled between song lyrics that she'd copied out onto sticky notes. She'd left her keys on the desk. More or less what I'd expected.

I was much more interested in Holmes's side, but it seemed that she had scrubbed all traces of herself from her room, saving her brilliant oddness for Sciences 442. Her desk was bare and clean, except for a digital clock, and the corkboard above boasted a single bright-blue Post-it that read *luv u girlie xo Lena* and had curled a bit with age. (That Holmes had left it up that long was surprisingly endearing.) On the shelf above her bed, her textbooks were all in a neat line, and on the bed itself was a navy coverlet—and below that was a sleeping Charlotte Holmes, wig askew, mascara already beginning to rub off below her eyes.

I shut the door softly behind me. "Holmes," I whispered, and before I could say it again, she sat up like a shot had gone off.

"Watson," she croaked, and reached blindly for her clock. "I just meant to lie down for a moment."

"It's fine," I said, sitting at the edge of her bed. "You're probably still catching up on sleep. It's not healthy to go three days without it, you'll start hallucinating."

"Yes, but the hallucinations are always fascinating." She stacked her pillows behind her back. "So?" she asked, in a *Why are you here* voice.

"So," I said, "how did it go? Did you learn anything? Who were you targeting?"

She heaved a sigh, pulling off her wig and stocking cap. "Watson," she said again, "really."

"I'm a murder suspect too," I reminded her, "and I thought we were partners in this. You dress up in this whole ridiculous *thing* and then you don't tell me how it went? Spill."

"I didn't learn anything. Anything at all. I must've spoken

to at least fifteen first-year male students—statistically, murderers are more often men, and anyway Hailey is useless with girls, they generally want to drown her in the nearest river—and none of them showed the slightest sign of being responsible." She said it all in a rush, like she wanted to expel it from her system. "And I'm starving. I'm never starving. I ate *yesterday.*"

"You had to have learned something," I said, choosing to ignore that last part. In my short experience with her, Holmes had treated her body like an inconvenience, at best, and at the worst of times like an appendage she was actively trying to destroy.

"*No,*" she said petulantly. "It was an utter waste of my time, and I used the last of my Forever Ever Cotton Candy perfume to do it. Which means I have to order more, and they only sell it on the Japanese eBay, and it's not cheap for something that smells that foul. And God, the humiliation of getting those boxes in the post." She stuck a hand under her pillow, producing a trio of wallets. "I was mad enough to pick three of their pockets, which should at least cover the cost, if not the emotional damage."

"Holmes," I said slowly, taking one from her. The wallet itself was worth more than my mother's flat, and it was stuffed with cash. "You can't do that. We have to give these back."

She cocked an eyebrow at me. "These were the ones who tried to get me drunk so they could have their sordid way with me."

"Well then." I pulled out five twenty-dollar bills and tossed them on the bed. "That's more than enough for your perfume. Do you know what we're going to do with the rest?"

"Give it all back to appease your sudden fit of conscience?"

"No," I said. "There's a car key on Lena's ring. We're going out for midnight breakfast. And then giving the rest to, like, charity."

"I'LL HAVE TOAST," HOLMES TOLD THE WAITER, HANDING HIM her menu. "Two pieces, whole wheat. No butter, no jam."

"No, she'll have the silver dollar special, with her eggs sunny-side up and . . . bacon, instead of sausage." I fixed her with a scathing look. "Unless there's something else on the menu she'd rather have. That isn't under 'side orders.'"

She snorted. "Right, then. He'll be having the same thing, except he wants sausage, not bacon, and please do keep on giving him decaf instead of regular. It's a mistake on your part, but it works to my advantage. He's quite cranky when he doesn't sleep."

The waiter scribbled down our orders. "Happy fiftieth anniversary," he muttered, and moved on to the next table.

"Ignore him. He hasn't had a girlfriend in three years," Holmes said. "Did you see his shoes? *White* laces. That alone should tell you."

I couldn't help it; I started snickering. Holmes graced me with one of her quicksilver smiles. She'd wiped most of the mascara from under her eyes and taken off her wig, but she was still done up like a Christmas tree. It was disconcerting, being able to see the thin gauze of persona laid over the real thing.

"There are at least fifty people in this restaurant eating breakfast at two in the morning," she said, sipping at her water. "All under the age of twenty. And forty-eight of them didn't have it this morning, including Will Tillman, the freshman across the room who is never at breakfast and who is, in fact, most likely here to buy drugs. Why on earth is this place so popular? I don't understand."

"That's because you're a bit of a robot," I said fondly, and she rolled her eyes. "So, are you the only one who can go incognito, or do I get to wear the disguise next time?"

"Do you have one in mind?" she asked, clearly struggling to take me seriously.

"I don't get to pull a Hailey on the new girl students?"

She snorted. "Even if I wasn't done pursuing innocent fourteen-year-olds, you really are just not pretty enough for knee socks."

"Well, I do a really good impression of a mindless rugger."

"No, you don't," she said. "Thank God. You should tell your therapist that rugby does nothing whatsoever to alleviate your very real anger issues."

"Not my therapist. My school counselor."

She hid a smile. "All the same. You really should take up boxing, or fencing—"

"Fencing? What century are you from?"

"—or solving crimes."

"Are you prescribing me your company, Doctor?"

"Detective, you can read me like a book." She lifted her glass, and I clinked mine against it.

I was suffused with a sense of well-being. The restaurant was warm, and warmly lit. Someone in the kitchen was making us pancakes. And I was sitting across from Charlotte Holmes.

I felt at home enough to ask her something that had been nagging at me for a while. "Right, so I have a question. Tell me if I'm out of line."

She tipped her head.

"My parents . . ." It took me a minute to find the right words. "Well, my grandfather very notoriously sold his inherited rights to the Sherlock Holmes stories to pay off his gambling debts. We're just not important anymore. At least, we're not in the public eye. We might be trotted out for the occasional press op, but my father does transatlantic sales—which is a lot lamer than it sounds—and my mum works in a bank. The Holmes family, though . . . I mean, you guys have been Yard consultants for generations. So why aren't they helping us? Where are they?"

"In London," she said. Before I could protest her flip answer, she held up a hand. "In London, where they'll stay. They won't interfere."

"But why not?" I asked her. "Have you told them not to?"

"No." Holmes slumped against the back of our booth, rubbing the crook of her left arm. "Do you remember when I told you I'd been taught at home until I came to Sherringford? Did you ever find it strange that I came here in the first place?"

"I didn't, actually," I told her. "I assumed your family had tossed your room for drugs, found out about your habit, and sent you to America to do penance. When Lena told me tonight that your parents had cut you off, it more or less confirmed it."

Holmes blinked at me. Then she started laughing, a rare and surprisingly unwelcome sound. The waiter brought our food, and I'm sure we made quite the sight: Holmes giggling into her hands, me glaring at her across the table.

"Tell me the funny part isn't my solving a mystery on my own," I said, stabbing at a sausage.

She managed to compose herself. "No," she said. "I'm laughing because I was a fool to think you wouldn't. You're entirely right, of course."

"And they cut you off because they thought you'd use the money to buy drugs?"

"No," she said again. "They cut me off because I wasn't fit to be their daughter." She dipped a finger into her water, tinkling the ice cubes. "In their eyes, my vices got in the way of my studies."

I looked at her, so thin and angular and sad, so surprised at herself every time that she laughed, and I wondered what it would have actually been like to grow up in the Holmes household. Long velvet curtains, I thought, and libraries filled with rare books. A hushed fight always happening the next room over. Charlotte and her brother made to wander around the house in blindfolds, listening at doors for practice, scolded for any emotional attachments except to each other. It sounded like a movie, but it must've been hell to live it.

"Eat," I said, pushing her plate at her. To appease me, she took a single bite of bacon. "Did you even want to be a detective?"

"That was never the question. I've been solving crimes ever since I was a child. I do it well. I take pride in how well I do it, do you understand?" I nodded quickly. There was a fire in her eyes. "But I was the second child. Milo has always done everything they've ever wanted him to. I can't say it hasn't paid off—he's one of the most powerful men in the world, and he's twenty-four years old. But I . . ." She smiled a secret, pleased sort of smile. "I'm not interested in doing anything I don't want to do."

"And so they sent you to America to cool your heels."

Holmes shrugged. "The *Mail* had a field day with all that. Will you look it up?"

"No," I said, and it was true. I'd always been afraid to shatter my fantasies of her by researching the real thing. "Unless—do you want me to?"

"There's no point. Milo had every word of the scandal scrubbed from the web. And I don't want you to know all about it. Not yet." Her smile faded. "Anyway, it was awful. They printed my middle name."

She was trying to change the subject, so I let her. "Regina? Mildred? Hulga?"

"None of the above. And to answer your original question, I've got to solve this mess myself. I'm sure that if I rang my family up and said, *Look, I'm about to be chucked in jail, will you help,* they would. Because they don't believe I can do it without them, anymore."

"I believe you can," I said. "Though that might just be a necessary delusion. Otherwise, I'm forced to believe that this Sunday, Detective Shepard will say that after a thorough investigation, it's clear that we are the guiltiest guilty murderers in the world."

"That's not what he's going to say." She took another bite. "How did you know I wanted bacon? Did you deduce that as well?"

"I guessed," I said, and watched the smile come back to her face. "Try the pancakes. They're good. My father used to bring me here when I was in grade school."

"I know," she said. "You ordered without looking at your menu."

We sat in companionable silence for a long time. I'd long since finished my own food, so I watched Holmes cut her pancakes into tiny slivers, dropping each one in a bath of maple syrup before putting it in her mouth. It was nice to linger somewhere. I hadn't been comfortable anywhere at Sherringford outside of Holmes's lab. Still, we were closing in on three in the morning by the time she'd finished eating.

"What's our next move?" I asked. "If we've ruled out the new male students, that's at least a start."

"Exotic animal licenses," she said. "Private owners first, then the zoos. You can begin digging in the morning to see who around here keeps deadly snakes. Surely one has to have been stolen. There's no doubt the police have already looked, but then, I'm able to see things they can't. And everyone's falling over themselves to prepare for homecoming tomorrow, so we should be relatively free to move around."

It was good to have a concrete plan. I felt myself relax a little bit further.

Holmes cleared her throat. "Watson," she said in a funny voice, "you weren't going to ask me to the dance, were you?"

"No," I said, maybe a little too quickly. I tried to imagine Holmes under a disco ball, jumping around to some Top 40 song. It was easier to imagine a whale dancing, or Gandhi. Then I imagined some slow song, one that wasn't complete shit, and the lights down low, and what it'd be like to have her in my arms, and I drank down my glass of water in one go. "Did you want me to? Because I had the impression you didn't."

"Watson," she said again. I didn't know if she meant it as a warning or an endearment. But then, I never knew, with her.

This was a subject I didn't want to touch without full body armor and a ten-foot pole. She'd warned me away from it the first time we ever spoke.

"Right," I said, picking up Lena's keys, "we should go before your hall mother wakes from her thousand-year nap."

I held the door open for her. The parking lot was almost empty. I squinted, waiting for my eyes to adjust, and just then, at the far end of the parking lot, a black sedan started up.

It kept its lights off as it peeled out of the parking lot.

"Holmes?" I said, frozen. "Did that just happen because he saw us?"

But she was already running for Lena's car. "Come on," she barked.

I fumbled to unlock the car, to back out of the space, to

maneuver us out of the lot. Holmes was almost cross-eyed with impatience, but to my relief, she didn't say anything. I hadn't exactly done a lot of driving back in London. I mean, I'd driven my mum's car through a parking lot. Once.

But my life dictated that the first night I was on the road, I'd end up in a car chase. It wasn't like the movies, I thought grimly, as we pulled out onto the empty street. The sedan was only a pair of lights in the distance, speeding toward town. It was almost impossible to stay on its tail. The dark was stripped away by a series of streetlights, and ahead of us, the sedan burned through one red light and then another, leading us away from Sherringford and toward the coast.

Holmes had pulled a pair of folding binoculars from God knows where. She leaned forward, peering through the windshield. "The driver's alone. He has a black coat and a black hat down over his ears. Blond hair under it. I can't see his face. There's—there's a case in his front seat, the kind my old dealer used to carry his—"

"Dealer?" I asked tersely.

She shot me a look from behind the binoculars. "Yes."

I thought about the pinched-face man talking to the BBC reporter. *Charlotte Holmes is the head of this messed-up cult and James Watson is, like, her angry little henchman.* "I think I know who it is. But if he's a dealer, why the hell is he running from us?"

"Watson," she said, in a warning tone, as I bore down on him. We cleared seventy miles an hour. Eighty.

"You're not going to tell me to slow down, are you?" I asked, clutching the wheel.

"No." I heard the smile in her voice. "I was going to tell you to go faster."

We blew past dark farmland and stands of trees, past hints of civilization—a bait shop, a crappy motel. My brain was racing as fast as the car. If the police pulled us over and hauled us back to school, we'd be expelled for sneaking out after hours. If the car in front of us braked or even slowed down—

We'd be dead.

My hands tightened on the wheel. I wasn't going to let up, not this close to finally learning something concrete. *Give us a clue*, I thought, *a real one. Let us get just a little bit closer.*

At the next intersection, he jerked into a hard right turn, trying to take us by surprise. Which is when he lost control. Under the bright streetlights, his car spun out down the center of the road, finally beaching itself on a curb outside a shuttered gas station.

I slammed on the brakes, and we fishtailed after him. Holmes's binoculars flew out of her hands and into the windshield with a sharp crack.

We shuddered to a stop two feet from the sedan.

If I didn't know it before this, I knew it now. I wasn't like Charlotte Holmes. I wouldn't ever be. Because while I was still unbuckling my seat belt with shaking fingers, trying to remember how to breathe, she'd freed herself, cleared our car, and was wrenching open the door of the black sedan.

While he was escaping through the passenger side.

"Holmes," I yelled, stumbling outside. *"Holmes!"*

We were in the middle of nowhere. Trees crowded the

two-lane road, dense with underbrush, and I watched her crash after him into the pitch-black wood, shouting for him to stop.

I took off after them.

It was like a nightmare. Branches lashed back at me as I ran, leaving stinging welts across my face, my arms. More than once, my foot caught on a tree root and sent me sprawling, and when I picked myself up, they were that much farther away. I remembered, suddenly, being a kid in a wood like this one, playing a game of ghost tag in the dark. I'd hidden myself in a burned-out tree trunk, and I remembered the hand reaching in to tag me, a white flash in all that darkness. I'd screamed myself hoarse.

Tonight didn't feel all that much different.

Holmes pulled farther and farther ahead of me. She didn't trip. She didn't fall. She moved like a cat through the night.

And then I couldn't see her anymore.

"Come back!" I shouted, finally skidding to a stop. "Give it up!" I could hear him, faintly, still crashing through the bushes. We weren't going to catch him. Besides, what would we do with him if we did? I didn't have any weapons. I didn't know how to threaten someone with anything but my fist.

In the far distance, I heard sirens.

"Holmes!" I shouted again. "Someone called the police!"

"Jesus, Watson," her voice said a little bit ahead of me. "I'm right here."

She'd stopped to catch her breath. In the dim light, she looked as terrible as I felt, scratched and grim, but I saw her eyes gleaming with the thrill of the hunt.

"We have to get back to the car," I said. "Now."

When we got back to the road, the cops were still out of sight, though the sirens were getting louder. We were a long way from anything, out here.

As I started Lena's car, Holmes quickly rummaged through the dealer's sedan, taking pictures with her cell phone, touching everything through the cloth of her shirt. Careful, I knew, not to leave fingerprints.

"Come on," I hissed.

As she climbed back in, she tucked something small into her pocket. "Pull around to the back of the petrol station. Park next to the owner's truck, turn it off, and duck down."

I did as she said, and not a moment too soon. Red-and-blue lights flooded in through the rear window. I held my breath as the cop car circled the gas station, slowing down behind us. A door opened, closed. Footsteps padded up to our back window.

If he shone a flashlight in—if he even glanced in—he'd see us. I thought I might throw up.

And then a sound of something big thunking onto metal, as if he'd dropped his bag onto the trunk of our car.

"I need to get my gloves out," the cop said, his voice muffled. "I know they're in here somewhere."

"Well, hurry up," the other cop replied.

"My hands are ass-cold, man. Give me a second."

"We've got a single-car crash and a drunk wandering somewhere in these woods, Taylor. We better get to it."

Taylor must've found his gloves, because there were

footsteps again. Retreating. The cruiser ambling back out to the road, and the officers getting out to look again at the sedan.

Holmes turned to me with a look of morbid satisfaction. She had been right. We hadn't been found. Crouched below the steering wheel, I rubbed my face with my hands. One way or another, this year was going to kill me.

I could hear the pair of officers talking as they examined the black car, though I couldn't make out their words. An endless hour passed while they dickered about something. Their lights kept flashing; I fought to keep my eyes open. Holmes had folded herself down to the foot of her seat, still alert, somehow. Our wild chase hadn't exactly been subtle, and if someone had called it in to the police, they would know there was another car. What if they came back around again, searching for us? I dug my hands into the seat, trying to steady my nerves.

Then finally, *finally*, we heard it. The unmistakable groan of a tow truck as the sedan was hauled away. The cop car following after.

When I shut my eyes, I could still see the flashing lights pulsing against the darkness.

It was another half hour before Holmes gave the all clear. "We should wait longer," she said, her voice even hoarser than usual, "but the petrol station will be open any minute now, and I don't want us to get caught back here."

Every joint in my body cracked as I climbed back into the driver's seat. I caught a glimpse of my face in the rearview mirror, scored here and there by the sharp fingers of branches.

"Jesus," I said, with feeling. Holmes cracked her neck. "All that for the campus dealer. Some paranoid freak who probably just ran because we were chasing him."

"Not a dealer," she said. "Something worse."

My heart hammered in my chest. "Like what?"

"It doesn't add up. If he's sampling his wares, as it seems from the powder spilled on the driver's side seat, why is he in such terrific shape? Why was he was wearing four-hundred-dollar shoes and running like an Olympic sprinter? If he's a dealer, he's unlike any I've had contact with. I'd be shocked if he was Lucas, the townie who deals on campus."

"Why?"

Holmes's face twisted. "He ran like one of my brother's men."

"Did you see his face?"

She shook her head.

"Then how—no, wait. Your brother has *men*?"

"Several thousand, at last count. It's the most rational explanation. He has a tail or two on me most of the time. I imagine we ran into one, and he panicked."

I let that sink in. "All that was because your brother was trying to check up on you? Your brother. Who's a *good* guy. It doesn't add up."

"It's likely that Milo wanted to assess you. Find out where your loyalties really lie. My friends . . . well, I haven't ever really had one before."

"Oh," I said.

She considered me for a moment, her eyes bloodshot. "I don't want my brother on your tail. You don't deserve that. You haven't done anything wrong."

"And you have," I said softly. *My vices got in the way of my studies.*

We looked at each other. She bit her lip, took a breath—she was on the cusp of saying something—and then she turned away.

"What did you find?" I asked, finally. "What was that thing you put in your pocket?"

She didn't look at me. "Let's get back," she said. I tried not to look at the square outline of the thing in her jacket, and started the car.

We didn't talk. Instead, I turned on the radio as Holmes peered silently out the window. The passing streetlights washed her face blank and bright.

I couldn't tell you what was in her head. I couldn't even guess. But I was beginning to realize I liked that, the not knowing. I could trust her despite it. If she was a place unto herself, I might have been lost, blindfolded, and cursing my bad directions, but I think I saw more of it than anyone else, all the same.

five

I SPENT THE NIGHT OF THE DANCE CATCHING UP ON HOME-
work.

After Tom finished telling me how appalled he was at
my decision—this took several hours—he got ready. Out of
the corner of my eye, I watched him preen in the mirror. He
managed to pull off his baby-blue suit from sheer force of
will; I think it would have made me look like Buddy Holly's
deranged cousin. After asking me one more time if I wanted to
go ("Mariella doesn't have a date, and she doesn't even think
you're a murderer!"), he finally cleared out to go pick up Lena,
leaving me to write a poem for Mr. Wheatley's class. I traded
my contacts for my horn-rimmed glasses in an attempt to get
myself in the proper mood.

Pen hovering over the page, I wondered, not for the first time, what I was doing.

For one thing, I used to like dances. That is, I liked taking girls to dances. Well. I supposed I just liked *girls*. I liked getting shy looks from them in class, and the way their hair smelled like flowers, and how it felt to walk along the Thames on an overcast afternoon, talking about which teachers they hated and what they were reading and what they'd do after we finished school. But in my head, all those memories had begun to run together. I couldn't tell you if it was me and Kate at the chip shop the night it snowed, or Fiona; if Anna was allergic to strawberries; if Maisie was the one my sister Shelby had adored. Even Rose Milton, the girl of my daydreams, with her softly curling hair and endless string of awful boyfriends . . . I can't say that I would have left my room, that night at Sherringford, even if she'd asked me to be her date.

Even if Holmes had asked me to be her date.

I wondered if her misanthropy was beginning to wear off on me.

I'd left her in Sciences 442, after a long, trying day. The spectacularly bitchy text war she pitched with her brother wasn't even the worst of it. She didn't show me the original message she sent him, but I saw the ones he'd returned. *No, you didn't find my spy,* he insisted. *He's obviously still at large. For instance, I can tell you right now that you're wearing all black, and that Jamie Watson is annoyed with you. I have eyes watching you right now.*

THAT IS NOT SPYING THAT IS SHODDY AMATEUR

DEDUCTION AND IT IS INCORRECT, she replied furiously.

She was, of course, wearing all black.

"Can we do some actual research, please?" I finally asked, trying to keep the irritation out of my voice.

We'd spent an unsuccessful afternoon running down rattlesnake owners in Connecticut. Even after we extended our search to Massachusetts, and then to Rhode Island, we drew a blank. No one was missing their pet snake—at least, no one who would admit it to me, in the guise of a chipper cub reporter researching a book on deadly animals and the owners who, goshdarnit, loved them anyway.

Holmes, still fuming from her conversation with her brother, sat and watched me work.

I scratched the last name off our list. "So maybe we should start calling the zoos—"

"This is unbearably tedious," Holmes snapped. "Do you know, if I had my Yard resources I'd have this case solved. God, in England, even my *name* would be opening us doors. Instead, I'm sitting here while you try to determine down the phone if these small-minded idiots with pet jaguars are *lying* to you, which you're not at all equipped to do." She flung herself down on the love seat, cradling her violin to her chest like a teddy bear.

"Right, then," I said, standing. "What was that thing you pulled out of that car last night? The thing you wouldn't show me?"

She stared at me evenly.

I threw up my hands. "Fine. I'll just go pack my things. You know. For jail."

When she realized I was waiting for her to reply, she picked up her bow and began sawing out a Dvořák concerto so savagely that it quite literally drove me out the door. We had no leads, no real information, and tomorrow we'd have to account for whatever Detective Shepard had dug up to indict us with.

And if I wasn't arrested, I still had homework.

Which left me in my room, with my blank journal page. I tried to push the rest of it from my mind and get to work. Our assignment for Mr. Wheatley's Monday class was to compose a poem that was difficult for us to write. The prompt didn't help me much, since all poems were difficult for me to write. They were like mirrors you held up to a black hole, or surrealist paintings. I liked things that made sense. Stories. Cause and effect. After an hour or two of agonizing cross-outs, I dropped my head down onto my desk.

There was a rap at the door. "Jamie?" I heard Mrs. Dunham say. "I brought you a cup of tea. And some cookies."

I let her in. She looked a bit dotty, as usual, with her crooked glasses and frizzy hair, but the cookies were chocolate chip and still warm.

"You're the only one in the dorm that stayed in tonight," she said, handing me the steaming mug. "I thought I'd come say hi. I know things have been hard for you lately."

"Thanks," I said, embarrassed. "I needed to finish some homework. Writing a poem."

She made a sympathetic noise. "Any luck?"

"Nope." She'd brought me English breakfast, and the steam fogged up my glasses. Right then, I wasn't sure who was more of a cliché, me or her. "Any advice?"

She hummed, thinking. "I've always liked that Galway Kinnell poem. 'Wait, for now. Distrust everything, if you have to. But trust the hours. Haven't they carried you everywhere, up to now?'" She had a fine voice for reciting poetry, deep-timbered and slow. "Doesn't that just make everything better?"

"It does," I said, and wished it were true.

Behind her, in the doorway, a girl appeared.

"Are you ready, Watson?" It was her strange, fantastic voice, even smokier than usual, and Holmes stepped into my room.

I blinked rapidly. She'd done something with her hair. Instead of its usual glossy fall, it was tousled, in unfinished-looking ringlets. Her dress looked nothing like I imagined. It looked, in fact, like the night sky. I could see why Lena had coveted it: the cut of it brought my eye to certain places I'd tried to avoid looking at.

"You look very nice," I said. It was true. She also looked disturbingly like a girl. Hailey had been made from plastic and wet dreams, and everyday Holmes was all exact angles, but this . . . whatever this was, it was something else entirely. I wasn't sure if I liked it. From the way she shifted her weight from one heel to the other, it seemed Holmes wasn't sure either. What plot was she brewing?

"Hi, Charlotte," Mrs. Dunham said. "Jamie didn't tell me you were coming."

"Yes, I'm sure he forgot," she said. "We're in a bit of a hurry.

The dance is nearly halfway done."

"We are, and I—ah—" I was wearing my glasses and a pair of Highcombe sweatpants.

With an expressive sigh, Holmes began rifling through my drawers. "Braces," she muttered. "Or as they say here, suspenders. I know you own the ridiculous things. Here." She tossed them to me, and kept looking.

"So you want me to wear them? Or you don't?"

"Oh, do, it's your thing, with the leather jacket and the— yes, here we go, a skinny black tie, and your nice shirt, and the trousers you wore on the fourth day of school but that haven't reappeared since then. Dark wash. There. Socks, and your oxfords." Mrs. Dunham scurried out of the way as Holmes buried me in a pile of my own clothing.

I looked down. "You're trying to make me into a hipster."

"I don't have to try." Holmes tapped her wrist where the watch would go. "Time, Watson."

"You really can't be here while he's changing," Mrs. Dunham said.

Holmes put a hand over her eyes. "I am counting down from one hundred."

"Thanks for the heads-up," I said, sorting through the clothes she'd given me.

"Ninety-nine. Ninety-eight."

We were out the door with three counts to go.

From across the quad, I could see the union all lit up for the dance. Each time the doors opened, I heard a bit of a song I couldn't quite place. On a bench sat a boy and girl holding hands; he was whispering in her ear. Nearby, a cluster of shivering girls admired each other's dresses.

"Are you going to tell me why we're here?" I asked Holmes, holding the door open for her.

She paused on the threshold. "Not yet," she said, and went in.

Sherringford was a small enough school that we could all fit into the union's alumni ballroom. (Apparently, the school went bigger and fancier for prom. Tom was sure that this year's would be on a yacht.) The theme had something to do with Vegas; the first thing I saw as we entered was a string of blackjack tables, manned by real casino dealers in green-and-white livery. Holmes sidled over, only to make an affronted noise when she saw they were playing with Monopoly money. I was more interested in the chocolate fountain that burbled in the corner, crowded by people holding out skewered marshmallows. Otherwise, there were all the usual trappings: a punch table, strobe lights, a DJ. Bored-looking teachers were "chaperoning," which meant they mostly chatted together in pairs. Out on the dance floor, girls swayed in dresses the colors of Christmas ornaments. We'd won the football game earlier, so the mood was victorious. As I took it all in, Cassidy and Ashton from my French class brushed past us. Cassidy looked lovely, and Ashton looked exactly like one of the Thundercats. I'd never seen such a radioactive-looking tan.

What I noticed most of all was how many students had been pulled home. There couldn't have been more than a hundred of us on the dance floor. Still, everyone seemed like they were having fun—no one thinking of the murder, or their safety, or anything except for the ABBA song that had just begun.

It felt, disconcertingly, as though I stood with one foot in a novel and one foot in a shopping mall. I might've belonged here, but Holmes very much didn't. I turned to ask exactly what her plan was, when I caught her mouthing the words to "Dancing Queen."

"Oh my God," I said as she startled. "Oh my *God*. You just wanted to come here to—"

"There are excellent opportunities for observation and deduction here," she said hurriedly. "Look at the specimen pool! Everyone with their guard down, probably a good few drinking—the girl next to you has a flask of peach schnapps in that little bag of hers—and perhaps that dealer is here, somewhere, and—"

"—to dance." I was trying very hard not to laugh. "Would you like to?"

"Yes," she said, and fairly dragged me out onto the floor.

Holmes, for all her strange and myriad skills, proved to be a terrible dancer. But what she lacked in skill she made up for in absolute abandon. Under the kaleidoscope lights, her hair went blue, then red, then blue again, the music so loud that my head throbbed in time, and she flung her arms straight up as the chorus came, throwing her head back to mouth the words. She knew the words to the next one, too, and the song after that, and she sang them all with her eyes shut, shuffling her feet like a grandfather. For a glorious twelve minutes, I orbited her, and when she grabbed my hand and said, "Twirl me," I spun her around as she laughed.

A slow song came on, some treacly number by an English boy band my little sister liked. All around us, people slipped into each other's arms. Across the room, I saw Tom, resplendent in his ridiculous suit, dip Lena while she giggled.

Holmes and I stood there, in the middle of the floor, trying not to look at each other.

I struggled to hide my panic. From the corner of my eye, I could see that Holmes's cheeks were still pinked from dancing.

"Um," I said.

There was a tap on my shoulder. The wispy blond girl that had asked me to the dance stood there, her dress a dramatic red. "Hi," she said shyly. "I thought you weren't allowed to come."

I watched Holmes rapidly catalog my reaction. After a moment, the girl turned to look at her, too.

"Oh my gosh, I'm sorry. I'm in your way." A little line appeared between her eyebrows, and I thought, for a moment, that she was going to cry. I was sure Holmes noted that too. Her brain was like a bear trap: nothing escaped alive.

This had to be a nightmare. I'd look down, and I'd be naked, and the dance floor would become my math classroom, and then I'd wake up.

I didn't.

"We're not— I'm not— I need something to drink," I managed, and darted away like the coward I was.

The thing was, I didn't know if I wanted to slow dance

with her. Holmes. Or maybe I could just imagine it a bit too readily, how it would feel to have my hands on the small of her back, to have her uncertain breath hot on my neck. Her soft laughter as the boy band sang *I wanna kiss you, girl.* How I'd drop my hands to her waist, pull her even closer to me.

But if I squinted, I could see that blond girl in my arms just as easily. Honestly, it wasn't very fair to any of us. I knew myself pretty well; I could be so easily taken in by the now, not thinking much about the after. But with Holmes, all I could think about was the after. Silent drives at dawn, wildfire conversations, sneaking into locked rooms to steal away evidence to our little lab—I wanted those things. I wanted the two of us to be complicated together, to be difficult and engrossing and blindingly brilliant. Sex was a commonplace kind of complicated. And nothing about Charlotte Holmes was commonplace.

Even the way she filled out her dress.

No. I wasn't going to think about that. Our track record proved that we were too volatile to survive that sort of shake-up. Just this morning, she'd chased me from her lab, wielding her violin like a weapon. Tomorrow night we might be sharing a cell. Tonight?

Tonight, I was getting punch.

Mr. Wheatley, my creative writing teacher, was manning the refreshments table with a pretty-ish woman around his age. He looked deathly bored, but brightened a bit when I made it to the front of the line. It wasn't long. Not many of us were too lame to have someone to slow dance with.

"Jamie," Mr. Wheatley said, though I could hardly hear his

voice above the music. "What'll it be?"

"How's the punch?" I asked.

"Horrible." He leaned in to the woman next to him. "This is one of my best students," he said, pointing to me. "Jamie, this is my friend Penelope. She's keeping me company tonight."

I didn't know that Mr. Wheatley had even liked my writing. Everything I'd turned in, my poems especially, came back to me in a mess of green ink. But I'd been working hard to revise them into something better, and it was nice to know my work was paying off.

"It's lovely to meet you." I shook hands with Penelope. She had a sort of standard art teacher look to her, with her curly hair and loose-fitting dress. A nice counterweight for Mr. Wheatley, I thought, who always buttoned his shirts up to his collar.

"She's a writer friend from New Haven," he said. "A poet. She teaches at Yale. Jamie might be someone you'd want in your freshman workshop, in the not-too-distant future."

"Oh, is this the one you were telling me about?" she asked Mr. Wheatley, who went a bit pale. "The murder investigation? Dr. Watson's descendant? So, do you write mysteries too, Jamie?"

"Not really," I lied, as I processed the rest of what she'd said. She'd heard about the police's suspicions about me. "You've been watching the news coverage?"

Mr. Wheatley pulled at his collar.

"Oh, the media's moved on by now," she said. "But Ted's on top of it. He knows details they haven't even released to the press!"

While I was trying to make sense of this, Holmes appeared, proffering a pair of chocolate-covered marshmallows on a fondue stick. An olive branch, I thought. She seemed to have forgiven me my awkwardness, so I took mine with a thank-you smile.

"Hello," she said to the adults. I made a round of introductions.

"Penelope was just saying that Mr. Wheatley's in the know about all that Dobson stuff," I said, a bit obviously. I wished we'd set up hand signals for this kind of situation, or that she was actually telepathic. There was a good chance that she could have deduced my suspicions just by looking at me, but I didn't want to take the chance.

"Oh?" she asked, her face perfectly blank.

"Yes, ah"—Mr. Wheatley cleared his throat—"I should do another walk around the room. Penelope?" She smiled politely at us, her interest already elsewhere, and the two of them glided away.

"Well, you cocked that up rather badly." Holmes drifted back onto the dance floor. So much for an olive branch. I pulled the second marshmallow off the stick and bit into it hatefully.

I WANDERED THE BALLROOM FOR A WHILE, FLOPPING DOWN finally at an empty table. The dance was coming to a close, and the DJ had put together a long set of slow songs to end the night. The floor was thick with couples that would be social-media official by the morning. I was surprised, and then less surprised, to see Cassidy and Ashton swaying together, so close their foreheads touched. Randall, Dobson's roommate, danced the whole set with the little blond freshman. He kept his hands low, grabbing at the fabric of her red dress. In his giant arms, she looked as small and inconsequential as a snack cake.

I felt vaguely sick.

"Okay." Lena plopped down next to me. "Jamie. You look, like, super pathetic."

"Where's Tom?"

"Playing poker." She pursed her lips. "Go talk to her."

"She's dancing with Randall," I said, being difficult on purpose.

"Jesus, come on. Charlotte's sitting outside, alone. You guys are just *sad* without each other. There's like this obvious empty space next to you." It was poetic, for Lena. She stood and offered me a hand.

"Are you asking me to dance?" I asked.

She cocked an eyebrow. I let her haul me to my feet. And she dragged me all the way across the ballroom and out the front door, where she gave me an unceremonious shove into the night air.

"Bye," Lena trilled, and disappeared.

Holmes sat on a bench by the entrance, staring out across the dark quad at a particular copse of trees. It was where I'd faced down Dobson, I realized. It was the last time we'd talked before he died.

She was shivering. I took off my jacket and draped it over her shoulders.

"Thank you," she said, not looking at me.

A little notebook was open on her lap, her fingers splayed across its pages.

"Is that the thing you took from the sedan last night?"

Holmes nodded.

"And you brought it with you?" I sat down next to her cautiously, the way you'd sit next to a bomb. I had questions. I didn't want her to hide the notebook away before I got a chance to ask them.

To my surprise, she didn't. "I didn't think I'd get to it," she said, and went on, her voice strange (was Holmes *nervous*?), "I played a few rounds of poker, but it wasn't sufficiently distracting. It was me and Tom and one of the chaperones—the school nurse. Tom spent the entire game staring at Lena's butt across the room. So obvious. Everyone is so obvious. For example, that school nurse? She wishes she were a doctor. She misses her boyfriend, who has blond hair and an earring, whom she's been with since high school, and who doesn't like her as much as she likes him."

"How could you—"

Holmes smiled a relieved sort of smile. Better to be making deductions, I supposed, then answering my questions. "She couldn't take her eyes off the dance floor. Her eyes teared up when 'I Luv U Girl' came on. Why would anyone react like that? Especially to *that* song? Nostalgia is the only answer. She's attractive enough, but not a knockout—that is to say, not so attractive to have been popular enough in high school that she pines to be back there. And every time a tall blond boy walked by, her eyes trailed after creepily. She's wearing an ugly tennis bracelet on her left wrist that could only have been chosen by a man, but not one who cares enough to pay attention to her actual taste. And she wishes she were a doctor because she tried to diagnose the cause of my shaking hands three separate times over the course of our game."

"Why were your hands shaking?"

"Exhaustion. I haven't slept since that nap you woke me from. She thought it was pneumonia at first, and then she implied it was from mental illness, the cow. And the whole time I had to pretend to *like* her just in case we need to question her again. So I cleaned her out. It was satisfying, even if it was Monopoly money."

I couldn't help it. I laughed. "You're a terrible person."

It derailed her completely.

She stiffened and put her hands up to her mouth. I looked down reflexively at where they'd been, covering the pages of the notebook.

I got it, then. Why she was nervous.

In her lap was a madman's journal. Its pages were thick with handwriting, the same five words scrawled again and again. Each time they were written in a markedly different style, as though a group of schoolboys had each been made to copy down a line from the chalkboard all into the same notebook. Here, the stark black capitals of a military general. Here, the rounded letters of a high school girl. Here, the elegantly dashed scrawl of a Victorian gentleman.

Every line said the same thing.

CHARLOTTE HOLMES IS A MURDERER
CHARLOTTE HOLMES IS A MURDERER
CHARLOTTE HOLMES IS A MURDERER
CHARLOTTE HOLMES IS A MURDERER

I snatched the notebook off her lap. She didn't try to stop me. She watched in aching silence as I turned one page, another, another, every single one striped with those same five words.

As I stared down uncomprehending, the doors burst open with a bang. The dance was over.

"Holmes," I said, my voice almost drowned out by the people streaming by, "what the hell is this?"

"I have the same book at home," she murmured. "Mine is green. It's a forger's notebook. I was made to practice in it until I could imitate nearly anyone's handwriting. Real people's, those of archetypes, characters I'd made up. You're given a phrase to work with, one that represents most of the alphabet. But this . . . this one is terrible." She reached out to touch the words. "It uses many of the same letters."

"It says you're a murderer. A *murderer*. And that dealer had it," I said. "He can't work for your brother. He's something else, some kind of maniac writing crazy things in the dark. He's probably not a dealer at all. He has to be responsible for Dobson—for framing us—God, and we let him get away—"

"How do we know that man wrote this? We don't. He could have picked it up; someone could have given it to him."

"Why did you wait to show me this?" I demanded.

Something snuffed out behind her eyes.

"Holmes—"

"Do you know that I dusted it for prints? I did, it's clean. Do you know that Professor Moriarty carried a little red memoranda book? He did; I've seen it. My father keeps it in a drawer. Did you know you can buy this particular model that I'm holding from seventy-two different online shops, not to mention innumerable bookstores and gift shops? You can. I ran down the license on that black sedan. It doesn't exist. The car itself was stolen from a Brooklyn street corner five years ago. Why does it reappear now? Watson, there's no *pattern* here. I can't figure this out. *I don't know.* Do you know what it's like to not know?"

I did know. She was the one who kept me in the dark.

"You still could have shown it to me," I said, getting to my feet.

Across the quad, a girl let loose a long, laughing scream as a boy grabbed her around the waist and lifted her over his shoulder.

"What if it read 'Jamie Watson is a murderer'? Would you have shown it to me?"

She set her chin, avoiding my eyes. "You wouldn't, for one single moment, worry that I might believe it?"

There was an unnerving quaver in her voice. I stared down at her, at her thin shoulders, the dark lines of her dress under my jacket. Just last night, I was sure I knew her better than anyone else in the world.

What had Charlotte Holmes really done to get herself sent to America?

"You didn't kill Dobson," I said.

"No," she whispered. "I didn't kill Dobson."

"So then—" I swallowed. "Did you—is August Moriarty still alive?"

At that, she stood and fled into the quad.

I picked up the notebook and followed, pushing past the clusters of shrieking girls, the boys surrounding them like black flies in their suits. Some chaperone's voice shouted for us to get back to our dorms, that night check would be in ten minutes, but Holmes plunged through the crowd, not toward Stevenson Hall, but to the sciences building. As if it were her safe house. Her panic room.

The place where she could hide away from me.

I called for her, hoarsely, as she cut through the small stand of trees in the middle of the quad, and though people turned to look, she plowed straight on ahead. I put on a burst of speed and with a lunge caught her by the arm and whirled her around.

She shook my hand off with a snap. "Don't you *ever* touch me without my explicit permission."

"Look," I said, "I am not saying that you killed him. I'm saying that someone wants me to think that. Wants the world to. Why can't you just tell me if he's dead? Is August dead?"

"You thought it," she said. "I watched you think it. That I killed him."

"Why can't you just *tell* me—"

I must've stepped forward; she must have stepped back. I was pressing her farther into the trees as if every step brought

116

me that much closer to the answer. I was so caught up in *finding out* that I missed what was written all over her face. I was so used to her fearlessness that I couldn't recognize her fear.

But she was afraid. Of me.

Dobson had loomed over her too.

Holmes took another step backward, and stumbled over the little freshman girl's body.

SIX

SHE'D BEEN DISCARDED LIKE AN AFTERTHOUGHT THERE IN THE dark grass. Stretched out on her back, her red dress pooled around her like blood.

God, I thought, *it's starting again.*

I was so used to Holmes taking charge that I stopped and waited for her orders. But none came. Her eyes were fixed on a point somewhere over my shoulder, her hands shaking. *Exhaustion,* I remembered her saying, though I thought now that it was something else. Distress, maybe. Uncertainty. Whatever it was, she didn't know how to master it.

It was down to me, then.

Gently, I knelt down beside the freshman. Her eyes were half-closed, as if she were just falling asleep. *She didn't ask for this,* I thought. *None of us did.*

I realized that I didn't even know her name.

Steeling myself for the worst, I pressed my fingers to her throat. There. A pulse.

"She's still alive," I said, leaning down to hear the girl's breath. It came in agonized rasps. "But she's having trouble breathing. We need to get help."

Holmes nodded, but made no sign of moving.

"Hey," I said to her, gently. "I need to keep an eye on her. Can you call an ambulance?"

She shut her eyes for a moment, collecting herself. Too long a moment. Beneath me, a shudder ripped through the girl's body.

I had to get someone else's help, then. "Hey!" I shouted to some girls cutting through the quad on their way back to the dorms. "There's been an accident! Someone's hurt! Call 911!"

They ran over. One girl pulled her phone out of her purse and dialed. The other saw who I was kneeling next to and began to scream.

"Elizabeth," she sobbed. She put herself between me and the girl on the ground as if to protect her. "That's my room-mate! Elizabeth! What did you *do* to her?"

"I didn't do anything," I said, shocked. I hadn't realized how this would look: the darkness, the body, the pair of us. "I found her like this. She was dancing with Randall and then . . . we found her here. Charlotte and I. We were . . . we were just walking."

We were beginning to draw a crowd. Behind me, I heard

murmurs. Angry ones. The sound of feet running toward us.

Elizabeth's roommate turned her tear-streaked face to me. "Murderer," she snarled. "*Murderers.*"

Behind us, the murmurs built to an angry roar.

I think it was that word that did it. How it'd been leveled at Holmes—and at me—in the weeks after Lee Dobson had died. How it was written down thousands of times in the notebook I had in my pocket, each stroke of the pen damningly precise. How, somewhere deep down, I knew there was the possibility that it was true. That Holmes had been sent here for killing a Moriarty. And she had read my thoughts from a glance.

No matter what the reason, Holmes reacted as if she'd been hit with an electrical shock.

She knelt down next to Elizabeth. "You need to go get an adult," she said to the roommate, who stiffened. "Look, believe what you will about my motives, but either way, this crowd will make sure I don't hurt your friend. Okay? So go get help and let me work. I've been trained for this kind of situation."

"CPR?" the girl asked unsteadily.

Holmes's smile was mirthless. "Something like that."

"What do you need me to do?" I asked.

"I need you to hold her mouth open." She tilted Elizabeth's head back. "Keep her steady. Do you see it there, in her throat?"

The skin of Elizabeth's neck was raised and ridged, the unmistakable sign of an object lodged there. With gentle hands, I pulled her chin down until her lips fell apart.

This girl had asked me to the dance. Maybe she'd even wanted something like this: the pads of my fingers against her lips, the shallow breathing, the two of us hitched up in the dark. My stomach roiled. All this—all this was so completely wrong.

"Her body's in shock," Holmes said calmly, reaching down into the hollow of Elizabeth's throat with pincer-like fingers. I shut my eyes against it. The girl thrashed and gurgled under my hands.

"Good girl," Holmes murmured, "good girl," and when I opened my eyes again, she was holding a gleaming blue diamond up against the moonlight.

It gleamed because it was covered in Elizabeth's blood.

I swallowed down bile. Behind me, someone threw up into the grass.

"It's 'The Adventure of the Blue Carbuncle,'" Holmes murmured.

"I know," I said as Elizabeth took a jerking breath.

"You." Holmes tossed the diamond to a boy in the crowd. "Take this thing. It's plastic, so don't bother stealing it, but I'm sure the police will want to see it anyway, and as you're all so keen to cast suspicion on me I'd rather not be held responsible for its safekeeping. Where's Randall? You. Fetch him. Can't you see that this girl has been manhandled by a rugby player? Look at those footprints. Look at her *dress*. I saw them dancing. *Find him.* I need to know if this was consensual. The sex, you idiot, not the paste diamond stuffed down her craw—yes, of course she's had sex, or at minimum a very athletic snog. Look at the marks on the ground, are you blind? And where on earth are the chaperones? What about that bloody nurse?"

"Here," a harried voice said. It was the first time I'd seen Nurse Bryony outside the infirmary; her party dress fit her so tightly that it looked painted on. She smiled reassuringly at me, but I looked away. I didn't deserve reassurances.

"Tend to her, will you?" Holmes told the nurse, straightening. "Where *is* that ambulance?" She shaded her eyes against the nonexistent light.

"Holmes."

"Not now, Watson." She plucked another boy's phone out of his hands, dialing 911 as he sputtered at her in protest. "You talk, then," she said to him, handing it back. "Be of some use."

"Holmes," I said, more urgently.

I'd caught a glimpse, at the very edge of the crowd, of the drug dealer's thick blond hair.

She followed my gaze and made a startled noise. "I didn't think we'd see him again."

"Well." I got to my feet. "What now?"

"Don't look at him directly." But it was too late. As she spoke, he turned in a way he must've thought unobtrusive, beginning to melt into the darkness.

"We're going to have to chase him again," I said. God, my legs hurt at the thought.

That quicksilver smile. "On your marks."

The dealer threw a glance behind him, and took off at a run.

We bolted through the crowd. Some ducked out of our way; others tried to pull us back, thinking we were fleeing the crime scene. We were, but not in the way they thought. There:

he was pelting across the flat green expanse, headed straight for Stevenson Hall. Lots of the underclassmen girls lived there—Holmes did, and Elizabeth did too, and I couldn't think of any reason why he'd be heading there except to do more damage. Guilty people ran. He had to be guilty. I pushed myself to run harder, but I was already topped out. Sirens wailed—the soundtrack of my ridiculous life—and Holmes's dress ahead of me caught the red-and-blue light, strangely beautiful. She was faster than me, smaller, leaner. She was just beginning to gain on him when three cruisers and an ambulance pulled off the road and onto the grassy quad beside us.

"Some help here," Holmes yelled as a group of policemen clambered out. The EMTs were already unloading a stretcher from the ambulance.

"Is that Charlotte Holmes?" It sounded like Detective Shepard. I spared a look and spotted a lone man not in uniform. "Stop! What are you doing? James! Jamie Watson!"

Neither of us slowed down in the slightest. So Shepard took off after us.

The policemen gave confused chase behind him, cursing and breathing heavily. Up ahead, the dealer rounded the corner of Stevenson Hall and disappeared from view.

"The access tunnels," Holmes called. "There's an entrance, there—it's that half door; it has a key code—"

I pushed the building's tangled ivy out of the way as she tapped out the code.

"You have about two and a half seconds," I said, "before the police brutality begins."

She gave me a feral look. "I only needed one."

The lock clicked open. She jerked me inside. The door slammed shut behind us.

WHEN HOLMES HAD FIRST MENTIONED THE SCHOOL'S TUNnel system to me, I'd had trouble wrapping my head around it. A network of passages below campus, connecting Sherringford's buildings underground? I'd done some digging to find out more.

By digging, I mean that I'd turned around in my desk chair and asked Tom, my personal font of useless information, what the deal was.

Legend has it the tunnels had been built at the end of the nineteenth century, back when Sherringford was still a convent school. When the grounds were under a few feet of snow, the nuns used these heated passages to get from their quarters to prayers at dawn and vespers. These days, Tom said, the tunnels were used by the maintenance workers who took care of our dorms. There were boilers down there and supply closets. Every entrance to the tunnels was only accessible via key code, and those codes changed every month. I'd told Tom about how disappointed I was that the tunnels weren't used as Cold War bomb shelters or by moonshine smugglers or something equally interesting, and he'd grinned at me. Even better, he'd said. The codes changed so often because students were always bribing janitors for them—the access tunnels were one of the only private places to hook up on campus.

Holmes, I knew, used the tunnels to practice her fencing.

"They're the only space long enough and private enough at this school," she'd said, bright spots of color on her cheeks, "and if you continue to snicker at me, I swear that I will tell your father you want a weekly lunch date with him to talk about your *feelings*."

Tonight, the tunnel in front of us was empty. Our man was nowhere in sight. As I crept down the hall behind her, the lights above us flickered. Holmes's shoes clicked against the floor, sounding like an insect tapping its legs together. The hair on the back of my neck stood up.

"He'll have holed up here somewhere," she said, a breath of sound.

"Should we start trying doors?"

She shook her head, putting up a finger. There were footsteps ahead of us, creeping ones. We were shifting gears from a chase to a slow, deliberate stalk, and I followed her as she slunk along, her eyes fixed on the ground.

She was following a trail he'd left on the linoleum floor, one I couldn't make out through the dirt tracked in by that week's workmen, the ragged lines from carts and trolleys. What was she tracing, I wondered, straining my eyes to see—and then I remembered. *Why was he wearing four-hundred-dollar shoes?* she'd asked the other night. Looking again, I saw the narrow tread of a dress shoe on the floor.

Silently, we followed his trail through the labyrinthine halls. The shouting of the police outside became a dull echo. Soon, I knew, they'd get ahold of the key code, and they'd be hard on our tail. Holmes knew it too. She roved the halls like a hunting dog. We were under the quad, now. The concrete walls were spotted with damp, and there was a smell in the air I knew from rugby practices. Mud. Wet earth. My mind wandered back to Highcombe School and its rugby pitch, to Rose Milton's shining hair in the stands, her hands clasped together, my cleats tearing into the grass, and the sense that just this once, I was doing what everyone wanted me to do and doing it *well*—

Holmes flung a hand across my chest. "There," she mouthed.

The door at the end of the hall, where the footprints ended.

Behind us, the unmistakable sound of a steel door slamming shut. The detective's voice bellowing Holmes's name.

"After you," she said, with the smile of a hunter closing in on its prey.

She couldn't have known what was behind that door.

She couldn't have.

As I walked inside, Holmes followed on my heels. She let the door shut behind her, cutting off what little light we had. I groped for a switch, a cord, anything to help me see better, but all I found were shelves, rows of shelves, and the cool cinder block of the back wall. I pulled out my phone and clicked it on, using its dim light to sweep the room.

We were alone.

Somehow I'd known from the moment I stepped into the room that our man wasn't going to be in here. Maybe I'd been unconsciously listening through the door for his breath, for some movement; maybe I knew enough about the way our luck worked. Maybe, deep down, I was relieved to not have to confront him. Whatever the case, it was only Holmes and me in there, and I was unsurprised to find us that way. Unsurprised, but not relieved. Not exactly.

We were alone in the killer's lair.

Photographs of Dobson, before and after the fight we'd had—someone had taken a shot of him across the quad with one of those paparazzi cameras, so sharp that you could see the bruises I'd given him. A map of the tunnel system, blueprints for Michener Hall and Stevenson Hall. Dobson's class schedule with classes highlighted and others crossed off, little notations written in beside them in Holmes's crabbed, angry handwriting, and—Jesus Christ—pictures of Elizabeth laid out across the floor, a thick file with her name on it. I stooped to pick it up but stopped; Holmes had trained me too well to leave stray prints.

"Holmes," I said. "That's your handwriting."

"I know." Through the cloth of her dress, she lifted a T-shirt from the pile of clothes on the bare mattress on the floor. I realized that I recognized it; she recognized it too.

"That's yours," I said.

She nodded. "It's a duplicate of one I own."

"Is this your . . . your . . ."

"My lair?" She still held the shirt between her pinched fingers. "Someone certainly wants you to think so, don't they."

I had questions for her. Questions I didn't really want an

answer to. Questions I'd have to ask later, because as we stood there, the police were kicking down doors all up and down the hall. In a minute, they'd find us.

All the while, they were shouting Holmes's name.

WE WERE HAULED DOWN TO THE STATION, WITH SHER-ringford's explicit blessing.

"So much for their protecting minors. But I imagine finding a television-styled murder den changes things," Holmes said next to me in the back of the police cruiser. She wore her handcuffs with a kind of elegant disdain, bringing both hands up to tuck her hair behind her ear. "We're going to be fine, Watson. Do you trust me?"

I didn't say anything. I didn't want to lie.

Detective Shepard cleared his throat in the front seat. "I usually don't warn people about this after I've read them their rights, but you're kids, so. You two don't want to say anything that incriminates you." A pause. "Not like either of you listen to me."

When we got to the station, Shepard separated us. I was put into a poorly lit interrogation room, with a mirror that I knew from the movies was actually one-way glass. There was a chair, a glass of water, and a piece of paper and pencil. For my confession, I imagined.

Really, it was all just like the movies, except in the movies, they don't show you the waiting. And there was so much waiting. For almost two hours, I sat in my desperately uncomfortable chair, jerking in and out of sleep, waiting for someone to come in and ask me to talk about what happened.

What would I even tell them? Well, officer. First, this asshole died after I punched him, but not *because* I punched him. He was poisoned, and also a snake got him. A snake that apparently appeared from thin air, because no one on the eastern seaboard is missing a snake. Then a drug dealer followed us to the diner and ran from us in the woods. I went to a dance, and thought about kissing my best friend, but didn't, and another girl wanted me to dance with her and maybe kiss her instead, but someone shoved a plastic diamond down her throat, so nobody kissed anyone, except maybe her and Randall. In a room underneath the school, I found a whole bunch of evidence that my best friend, who I didn't kiss, is a psycho killer. And now I guess you're questioning me about all these crazy crimes that I haven't committed, but someone wants you to think I've committed, and they've done such a good job of it that I almost believe I committed them too.

That's good, I thought blearily, and started writing it down.

Above my head, a speaker crackled to life. I blinked up at the pair holstered high up in the corner. I'd missed them. I couldn't now: they were speaking with Holmes's voice.

"All last year, I bought from a senior named Aaron Davis," she was saying.

"Hey!" I yelled. "There's something wrong with your sound system!"

No reply. Nothing but Holmes's voice droning on.

"He delivered in packages to my dorm, and I'd put the money in his mailbox. It was all very straightforward like that, when it was pills. But last May, I wanted something harder, and he took me down to that room to—to use in front of him. To make sure I wasn't just buying to rat him out."

Shepard's voice, then. "So that dealer, the one you took it on yourself to chase—"

"I've never even seen him before. In fact, I still haven't even seen his face clearly, and for that reason alone, I thought he worked for—" I heard her about to say *Milo*, or *my brother*, or maybe even *Moriarty*. "I don't know. I don't know what I thought." *Not your best save*, I thought with a wince, and then remembered I wasn't on her side. Not tonight.

"We found your prints there, Charlotte."

"Aaron used to *deal* out of that room. Why aren't you listening to me? If you found my prints there, anywhere, I'm sure it was on the inside of the door or on the wall, not actually on any of the fake-serial-killer things pinned to it, and that they're at least several months old."

"So is that why you were down there? Trying to destroy the things you forgot to touch with your gloves on? Innocent people usually don't give as many excuses as you do."

"You're asking why you found me in the room I went directly to, knowing you were following me—the room that only the most wretched Sherringford students have reason to know about. The room that I decided to style like a network television art director. So that I could destroy *paper records* that I left there in my own handwriting." She snorted. "I won't insult your intelligence, Detective Shepard, by reminding you who my family is. Not to trade on my blood, but on my training. I am not an idiot. And I didn't kill Lee Dobson, or attack Elizabeth Hartwell. I'm sure that when she's fit to speak, she will tell you exactly that."

"She's suffered a traumatic brain injury," Shepard said gravely. "We don't know yet how much she remembers. But with all your *training*, I'm sure you knew that would be the result when you clobbered her with that tree branch."

"Fine. Call my parents. Call Scotland Yard. I have contacts there. They'll tell you that I *help* people."

"You should have called us, Charlotte." The sound of a chair scraping back. And then a final blow. "By the way, what was Jamie Watson's part in all this? Your accomplice? He's clearly not the brains of the operation."

"Hey!" I yelled again. I did *not* want to hear this. "Hey! Anybody!"

"Don't cater to my vanity," she snapped. "You'll find I do that well enough on my own."

"Your accomplice," he said again, louder, "until you needed a fall guy. Someone to stay and swing for all of this when your rich mommy and daddy smuggle you out of the country on a private plane."

At that moment, I was in the awful position of thinking something that I desperately didn't want to believe.

Thought: The police set this up, this weird, "accidental" eavesdropping, so that when Holmes admits she's been using me all this time, I'll flip out and confess to her doing everything. I'd seen *Law & Order*. I knew how this worked, how they divided suspects, got them to tell on each other. But they were wrong. There was nothing to tell.

Except.

What if the police were right?

What if she actually did kill Lee fucking Dobson and decided, for a lark, to drag me along, pretending to solve the crime that she committed? What if Holmes was so unnerved by someone calling her a murderer because she was, in fact, a murderer? What if, in the time between stomping away from me and Mr. Wheatley at the punch table and when I found her on the bench, she clobbered Elizabeth Hartwell on the head and stuffed that plastic jewel down her throat? What if she really did elaborately off Dobson in an act of cold-blooded revenge? What if—oh God—what if our friendship was just a sick footnote in her sick reenactment of these stories? Holmes and Watson, together again, playing out "The Blue Carbuncle" on the dark Sherringford quad. Only, instead of hiding the stolen gem in a goose's craw, we stuffed it down a girl's throat to make her choke to death.

"Jamie Watson," Holmes said evenly, "is far smarter than you think. He isn't my accomplice. He's no one's accomplice. And he isn't guilty of anything."

He isn't, she said. Not the both of us.

I didn't feel any better. Not even when the door swung open to let in my haggard father, who took one look at my face and said, "Right, we're going home."

ON THE WAY OUT, MY FATHER TOLD ME THAT NEITHER Holmes nor I were being charged with a crime. The police didn't have enough evidence to hold us; everything they had right now was circumstantial, so the best they could do was question us. "It's good they didn't get around to you," he said, then looked at me hard and told me, like he was imparting great wisdom, to always remember to request a lawyer.

Usually, I hated that my father didn't act like a father. Most days, I would've traded him and his enthusiasms for the most boring authority figure on the block, but tonight, I was just happy to be spared a lecture and tears.

My father is picking me up from the police station in the middle of the night, I thought, *and he mostly just seems kind of excited.*

"I'll pull around the car," he said at the entrance. "Once we get home, you'll need to sleep. I could only get you a day's reprieve. They want you back for more questioning after dinner. Shepard's keeping his Sunday-night appointment."

I swayed a little on my feet, not thinking much of anything. Not until I felt her creep up behind me on cat feet. I refused to turn around.

When my father pulled the car up, Holmes opened the passenger door and climbed in without a word. Fuming, I got into the backseat, pushing aside a small avalanche of toys and snack wrappers that belonged, no doubt, to the half brothers I'd never met. I tried to fight the feeling that I was a guest star in my own life.

As we drove, my father kept up a steady stream of chatter that Holmes replied to in monosyllables. I couldn't manage any response at all. My brain had roared back to furious, nervous life. When he stopped at a Shell station outside town, I tipped my head against the cold window and tried to steady my breathing. In a few hours, I'd be arrested for a crime I hadn't committed. I wished I'd never come back to America. That I *had* killed Dobson, just so I'd have something to confess to. A way to get this all to end. I thought again about my pathetic fantasy, the two of us on that runaway train. Maybe this was the sensation of it crashing.

Without a word, Holmes reached back, fumbling for my hand, and when she found it, she grasped it firmly in hers. I thought about taking it back. I reminded myself that I was maybe holding the hand of a killer, but I decided I was too tired to care. The three of us drove the rest of the way in silence.

Really I'd been so distracted by what had happened at the station that I'd forgotten to dread the rest of it. Then it came into sight, my childhood house in the country, and I remembered all at once learning to ride a bike down this street, my father holding on to the seat even after I told him he could let go. He did, finally, with a great laugh like a shout, and I went a full three feet before I hit a bump and flew head over handlebars.

Today, despite the cold weather, there was a bike fallen on its side in the yard. It wasn't mine. I watched my father notice it, how his eyes flickered to me in the backseat. I noted the worry there, his own dose of dread. It was the first time I ever felt sorry for my father.

"Abbie and the boys are at her mother's for the weekend," he said with false cheer as we pulled into the garage. "So we'll have the place to ourselves. I made a steak pie that I'll put in the oven for dinner. But right now, you two need to get some rest."

Holmes stumbled into the house and over to the living room couch. Without taking off her shoes, without saying a word to either of us, she stretched out in her homecoming dress and went immediately to sleep.

"There's a guest room," my father said as I folded myself up into the armchair beside her.

"I know," I said to him. "I used to live here."

He didn't have anything to say to that.

The truth was that, for many varied, contradictory reasons, I didn't want Holmes out of my sight. Even as I fell into a dreamless sleep, I kept an ear open. Listening in case she ran, and left me there alone.

When I woke, it was dark again, that sort of fall-evening gloom. The clock on the wall said 6:07. I'd slept the whole day, and from the state of the couch, so had Holmes.

There was a rustling in the kitchen. Inside, it was as well lit as I remembered, and the table and chairs were the same. But the dark cabinets had been given a coat of white, the walls painted a farmhouse blue. A ceramic rooster presided over the sink. Abigail's additions, I was sure. When my father offered, I turned down a tour of the rest of the house.

Holmes had hoisted herself up onto one of the stools at the counter, and she sat there, swinging her legs while her eyes roved around the room. I watched her put together the story of this house, of my childhood, the way a soldier assembles a gun in the dark. At least one of us knew how to behave normally—though for the record, this may have been the first time it was her, and not me.

"Hi," I said to her.

"Hi," she said back. "Did you sleep well?"

"I slept fine."

We avoided each other's eyes.

"Well," my father said as the oven heated up. "Let's get down to it. That Shepard fellow arrives in"—he consulted his watch—"an hour. What have you got for him? To clear yourselves?"

"Nothing," Holmes said. "Well. The fact that we didn't kill anyone, for starters."

"You haven't killed anyone," I repeated. It was the first time she'd admitted it.

She lifted an eyebrow. "We haven't attacked a single person at this school. We've never killed anyone."

She was choosing her words carefully, I could tell.

"And that—that serial killer den wasn't yours."

"That serial killer den wasn't mine." Unexpectedly, she grinned at me. "It wasn't yours, was it? It's a bit rude not to share."

I wrinkled my nose at her, and she hit me in the arm. God help me. I couldn't stay mad at her, even if she did turn out to be a cold-blooded killer. I was in way, way too deep.

"Right," my father said, confused. "I had sort of thought all of that was a given. Do you have any actual proof that clears you?"

"Enough witnesses to prove that we weren't the people who attacked Elizabeth. Elizabeth herself, when she wakes up. But that's moot, anyway. In about an hour and fifteen minutes, I'll have the leverage we need to clear our names and get Shepard to involve us in his investigation."

I didn't know anything about this. "What?"

She tucked a lock of hair behind her ear, and said nothing. Across from us, I swear my father's eyes were sparkling.

I stared at him. "Shouldn't you be, you know, worried?"

But he was already pulling a bottle of champagne from the refrigerator. "A toast is in order, I think. A little glass couldn't hurt at this point."

The cork popped, and steam fizzed out. Holmes and I exchanged a startled glance. She hadn't expected him to believe her. Very few people had the ability to surprise her, but apparently my father was one of them. I didn't care. I had a glass of champagne, possibly my last as a free man. I slurped the foam off the top of my glass.

Holmes, being Holmes, looked at my father and decided to investigate. "Oh, this is lovely, thanks much. But tell us why we're celebrating! You can't trust me *that* much. There has to be something more to it." She leaned on one hand, drawing on the vast reserves of charm she kept hidden away for just this purpose. "That pie smells tremendous," she added. "Can't think of the last time I had good comfort food."

If my father noticed the show—and really, how couldn't he?—he didn't mind it. "It's Jamie's grandmother's recipe. I haven't had a chance to make it in a long time." He beamed.

"I'm happy this worked out for you two. I'd worried it wouldn't."

"What worked out?" Wherever this was headed, I was sure it was a bad, bad place. "If you're about to tell me you killed off Dobson to get me some detective practice, I swear to God—"

With a wave, he cut me off. "Jamie, don't be so melodramatic. Of course not."

"Of course not," Holmes said, under her breath. The machinery in her head was whirring to life. "It began before that."

"Yes," my father said, delighted. "Go on."

She looked me over the way you might do a horse. I shifted uncomfortably in my seat. "And sport. It has to do with rugby."

"Excellent." He lifted his glass to her. "I'm sorry, Jamie, but I still can't believe you bought it. A rugby scholarship? Yes, you're a perfectly adequate player, no doubt, and certainly good enough for their team, but you have to admit that the idea was a bit far-fetched." He took a meditative sip. "No, it was all something that we plotted up in our cups, last summer."

"We?"

"You and my uncle," Holmes said to my father, bypassing me entirely.

"What?" I said faintly. I was still trying to process the fact that I wasn't, in fact, a genius rugger, and that no one had told our poor captain. "Wait. You're going to solve *this* mystery. Not the Dobson-Elizabeth-drug dealer mystery. This one. And you're going to solve it now." I stifled a semi-hysterical laugh. "When I didn't even know there was a mystery. God, what could I possibly have done in a past life to get stuck with someone like you?"

"Go on," my father was saying happily. It was good that one of us was enjoying himself. "Tell me how you know."

She ticked the deductions off on her fingers. "You were born in Edinburgh like the rest of your family, but you have an Oxbridge spin on your words. When you opened your cupboard to fetch these flutes, I saw a mug, top shelf, with the Balliol College blazon on. Oxford, then."

My father spread his hands, waiting for her to continue.

"You hugged me with a surprising amount of familiarity when we met, but you didn't hug your son. Even with your difficult relationship"—my father's smile faltered for a moment—"if you were so prone to hugs, you would have made an attempt on him anyway. No, you felt you knew me. You must have heard of me, then, and not in the papers—or there would have been polite pity and no hug—but from someone who spoke highly of me, and with warmth. The first rules out my parents; the second, most of my relatives. My brother, Milo, doesn't believe in friends, and anyway, you'd have no reason to chat to a pudgy, secretive computer genius who leaves his Berlin flat only under extreme duress. My aunt Araminta is nice enough, which means she's glacial by society's standards. Cousin Margaret is twelve, and Great-Aunt Agatha is dead, and that's the *tour de monde* of the effusive members of my family.

"Excepting, of course, my dear old uncle Leander, Balliol College '89, who gave me my violin, and is the first Holmes in known memory to host a party of his own free will. Of course you're friends." She peered at him for a second. "Oh. And flatmates. For at least a year, no more than three."

I poured another glass of champagne and drank it straight down.

My father, smartly, put the bottle away. "You're as clever as he is, Charlotte, and a great deal quicker. Though Leander, bless him, is lazy enough to solve a crime and forget to tell his client for months.

"He came to your seventh birthday party," my father told me. "Don't you remember?" My seventh birthday party had been held at one of those roadside amusement parks with a go-kart track and a half-dozen arcade games. "He brought you a rabbit as a gift. Giant thing. Big floppy ears. Your mother, being your mother, sent it immediately to a nice home in the country."

"Harold," I said, piecing it together. That had been the rabbit's name. I had an impression of a towering man with slicked-back hair and a lazy smile.

"I roomed with him back before I met your mother," he said. "Bachelor days, before I was lured away to London. Leander had set up as a private detective, and I was . . . well, I was very bored. We were introduced at an alumni event at a pub; I'm sure you've noticed how keen everyone is to introduce a Holmes to a Watson. He was chatting up the bartender. I think he brought him home in the end. Could turn on the charm, Leander, when the situation called for it." He raised an eyebrow at Holmes, who didn't blush but looked like she might've liked to.

"And you're still friends?" I asked.

"Yes, of course," my father said. "The two of us, we're the best kind of disaster. Apples and oranges. Well, more like apples and machetes." He studied my face for a moment. "I thought you could use a little shaking up, Jamie. That school in London was too expensive for what a bloody toff factory it was, and even with what I could contribute, we couldn't afford to keep you there. I told Leander about my frustrations, and he mentioned that Charlotte here had just been deposited, friendless and alone, only an hour from my house. Did you really think this was a coincidence—the two of you winding up here, in America, at the same boarding school?"

I was fed up with all these ridiculous bombshells and rhetorical questions. "Yes," I said pointedly. "Also, your pie smells like it's burning."

Holmes sniffed the air. "It smells quite good, actually," she said, and took it out to cool. I scowled at her. She made a helpless gesture.

"The tuition . . . well, Leander offered to pay it. When I said no, he told me that otherwise he'd just buy another Stradivarius. I tried telling him that he'd have to put an entire town through Sherringford to come close to the price of a Strad, but he held firm. I gave in. And so Leander arranged some sleight-of-hand with the board of trustees and offered you a 'scholarship.' You didn't wonder why you didn't lose your scholarship when you were suspended from the rugby team?" He grinned. "That's why. The whole thing was quite fun. I think he enjoyed it immensely."

"Yes," I said, thinking of all my violent resentment at being sent away, of having to leave London, my friends, my kid sister. "Fun."

"Well then." My father clapped his hands together. "You've met! You're friends! You've found yourselves a murder! I couldn't have asked for more. Come, let's eat before the detective arrives."

Holmes's phone buzzed. "I have to take this, excuse me." She stepped out the back door, and I watched her through the glass as she paced in her dress, speaking rapidly to someone.

"Who could possibly be calling her?" I wondered aloud. "It must be her brother."

My father kept slicing the pie. "I hope you're not terribly mad at me."

"I'm not," I said. "I'm furious."

"It seemed to have worked out rather well, though, you have to give me that." He handed me a heaping plate. I wished, badly, that I wasn't starving.

"*Well?* This worked out well?" I choked. "God, I don't have to give you anything."

"Jamie. Please don't be like this." He was avoiding my eyes. "Aren't you happy you met Charlotte? She's lovely, isn't she?"

"Will you please stop side-stepping the point? This isn't about Holmes, it's about the strings you pulled to get me here. God, you don't even know me! I hadn't seen you for years! How can you not understand that being bored isn't an excuse to reach in and fuck with my life for fun?"

"Language," my father warned.

"You don't get to do that." I heard myself getting loud. "You don't get to deflect every response you don't like. I'm in a horrible mess that you, for whatever reason, have decided to find *charming*."

With shaking hands, he set down the knife. I was shocked to see his eyes glossed in tears. "You're right, Jamie. I don't know you anymore. God help me for wanting that to change."

The doorbell rang.

"He's early," my father said, and hurriedly plated some pie for Holmes. "I'll get it."

When he left the room, I let out a ragged breath I hadn't known I was holding.

Holmes slipped back into the house. "Well, that looked rather brutal," she said, eyeing me. It was an observation, not an attempt at sympathy, and so I didn't have to respond to it.

"Sit," I said instead, pulling out a stool. "Who called you?"

My father walked in, Detective Shepard behind him. Holmes read something in their faces that I didn't, because her posture, always impeccable, went ramrod-straight.

"Jamie. Charlotte." I noticed that Shepard had dark circles under his eyes. "I'd like to get you back down to the station. Now."

"What are you charging us with?" I asked him.

"I'd like to get you back down to the station," he repeated, a patented non-answer.

"You'll need to wait for my lawyer," Holmes said coolly.

"He'll be representing both of us, but as his office is in New York, it could be several hours until he arrives. Do you mind if I phone him?"

The detective nodded, and she placed the call right there.

I felt a rush of relief. The worst possible outcome was happening. I could finally, finally stop dreading it.

My father, being my father, chose that moment to begin to worry.

"Do you mind if they eat in the meantime?" he asked, a plea in his voice. "I don't know how long they'll be down at—at the station, and dinner's on the table. You're welcome to join us, of course."

Shepard hesitated. He took in Holmes's too-thin frame, the steaming plate in front of me, and I watched him give in. "Fine. They can eat, since we'll have to wait for their lawyer anyway. But be quick about it." He set his bag down, and took a seat.

I made an effort with the pie, though I pushed it aside after a few bites. Shepard's scrutiny made me too uncomfortable to eat. For her part, Holmes decided to develop an appetite. Slowly, fastidiously, she picked the carrots from the crust one by one. Once removed, she sliced them into quarters and then halved them again. After spearing each piece with her fork, she dipped it into the mashed potato and transferred it to her mouth. She chewed each morsel seventeen times. And then she repeated the process. Across the table, my father watched her, one hand gripping the table hard.

I wondered if he was still enjoying himself.

Silence reigned. After twenty minutes, Holmes hadn't even

gotten to the steak, and the detective began to shift unhappily in his chair. I took the chance to catalog him, to try to draw some Holmesian deductions. He was in his late thirties, I decided. Clean-shaven, but in rumpled clothes. He clearly hadn't gotten home to change or shower since interrogating Holmes last night. There was a wedding band on his left hand. I couldn't tell if he had kids of his own, but his decision to let us eat dinner made me think he did. What I couldn't account for was the reluctance that radiated off him, the way he projected unease in his posture, in his frown, his furrowed brow. Like my father, he'd lost his eagerness.

"I understand why you did it. To Dobson," he said quietly, watching Holmes eat. She didn't look up. "Every account I get says that kid was a bastard, and he was fixated on you. But what I don't get is why you didn't just tell the school about his abuse and get it to stop. And I don't get why the two of you would attack Elizabeth Hartwell. Bryony Downs, the Sherringford nurse, told me that you, Charlotte, had been behaving erratically at the dance all night—"

"Way to make friends," I said to her.

"—and then the two of you chase some other guy down into these underground tunnels I've never even *heard* of, where we find you in a room straight out of a TV procedural, just *waiting* for us. I found these in there." He dug a pair of trousers and a black shirt out of the bag, and shook them out for her inspection. "Yours?"

The clothes from the mattress.

She looked up uninterestedly. "Yes," she said. "Though if

you've examined them, you'll see that they've never been worn."

Shepard nodded. She wasn't telling him anything he didn't know. "I examined them, Charlotte. I made a lot of calls this morning. One of those was to your mother."

My father leaned forward. "And?"

Shepard rubbed at his temple, thinking, and then he pulled a binder out of his bag, laying it open on the table. "Jamie, do you mind pointing this purported drug dealer out to me?"

I pushed my plate away. The twelve men in front of me were uniformly blond and ugly. They ranged in age from a few years older than me to forty. One sported an eyebrow scar. Another smiled, missing teeth. The third one from the top looked the closest to what I'd remembered. I racked my memory.

"Him," I said, sounding slightly more confident than I felt.

"That man turned himself in this morning," he said, tapping the photo. "Said that Charlotte has been dealing for him for years. Gave me a record, in her handwriting, of transactions he said she'd done for him. Said he was sorry, that he'd seen the error of his ways, that he just wanted the kids to be safe, now, from *her*." Shepard shut his eyes for a pained moment. "The records are immaculate, you know. They perfectly match the sample of your handwriting, Charlotte, that I got from your biology teacher."

"What's his name?" Holmes asked, showing a glimmer of interest.

Shepard raised an eyebrow. "He gave it as John Smith."

Wordlessly, Holmes left the room, returning a second later with the little red notebook. She flipped through it there at the table until she reached a page near the end. CHARLOTTE HOLMES IS A MURDERER, it read, in her own spiky hand. "Believe me or don't," she said, "but we found this in John Smith's car." She went back to her dinner.

"We're going to follow up with the students that Charlotte sold to," the detective told us. "We'll find out the truth of it then."

"He forged those records," I said, looking at her. "All of them. The ones in that room—"

"Look," Shepard said, interrupting. "One of my calls this morning was to Scotland Yard. Everyone there vouches for you, Charlotte. Okay, some of them might not like you much, and they weren't surprised that you were mixed up in a crime, but to a man, they swore up and down you wouldn't hurt anyone. Annoy them to death, maybe."

One corner of Holmes's mouth turned up, but she stayed silent. The detective rubbed his eyes. "I was also reassured that if you *did* do it, I wouldn't have you on my list of suspects at all." He turned to my father. "Apparently she's that good. Then I talked to Philly PD about Aaron Davis, Sherringford's last dealer, and apparently the kid is doing time down there for dealing oxy at UPenn. I have a buddy down there who owes me a favor, asked Aaron some questions. He remembers Charlotte. Confirmed her story, that he sold to her down in that room last year. He also said she didn't have enough friends or enough patience to ever deal on her own. We'll follow up, like I said. Aaron's a con, so his word isn't golden, but . . ." Shepard shrugged expressively. "But a kid's dead. Another is in the hospital. You two just look too good for it. Charlotte has a private chemistry lab where she keeps a whole bunch of poisons. And you"—he pointed at me—"you could easily get into Lee Dobson's room at night. You were flirting with Elizabeth Hartwell. It looks, for all the world, like the two of you are in some kind of lovers' pact gone wrong. Someone might be doing their best to set you up, might be throwing absolutely everything at the wall to try to find something to stick, but the much more *rational* answer is that Charlotte Holmes isn't half as good as everyone thinks she is. I might not like it, but until I have a better answer—"

Holmes looked up, and a beat later, Shepard's phone rang.

"Hold on." He put it to his ear. "Shepard. Slow down. She *what*? No. No, that's fine. Yeah. Is she—good. Yeah, I'll be there as soon as I can." Glancing over at us with something like relief, he said, "I just need to finish up something here."

"This pie is delicious," Holmes said to my father. He looked back at her helplessly. "Is there any more?"

SOMEONE HAD TRIED TO KILL LENA.

That's how Shepard put it to us. Unbothered by Holmes's absence, Lena had spent the day after homecoming holed up in bed, reading magazines and working her way through a care package of cookies from home. She'd been playing music loud enough that when there was a knock at her door, she wasn't sure, at first, if she'd imagined it. But when she finally got up to check, there it was on the threshold: a parcel, and inside the parcel, a sliding ivory jewelry box.

Though she unwrapped the paper, Lena didn't open the box. With the roommate she had, she'd gotten used to seeing some weird things, and in the past, when mysterious packages had arrived, they'd always been for Holmes. ("I do a lot of online shopping," Holmes told Detective Shepard without batting an eye.) So she'd set it on her roommate's desk and taken a nap.

She woke up twenty minutes later to a man in a ski mask looming over her, one hand at her throat, as if he were about to check her pulse or strangle her. Lena screamed. The man ran. And she immediately called the police, surrendering the mysterious box to their custody. As we spoke, they were examining it at the station.

Something about all this was naggingly familiar, but I couldn't put a finger on what.

"When did this happen?" Holmes demanded, hands shaking. I hadn't realized that she'd cared about Lena so much. "Just now? I spoke with her not twenty minutes ago."

The detective took out a notepad and paper. "What about?"

Holmes's mouth twitched. "She'd spilled punch on me at homecoming and wanted to know if I was still angry. I told her I was over it, and we'd get my dress to the cleaners. No harm, no foul."

So it had been Lena on the phone, earlier. I'd never seen Holmes take one of her roommate's calls before. She always sent them, and everyone else's, straight to voicemail to screen at her leisure.

"Does she know that you went down to the station? Did she know where you were today?" he asked.

"No," she said. "The only person I really talk to is Jamie. I doubt anyone at the school knows I'm gone, unless they saw you haul us away in the cruiser. But it was dark."

My father was taking notes in a chair in the corner. "Dark," he muttered to himself.

"But Lena's okay?" Holmes asked. Her lower lip trembled. "I'm sorry, I just—this sounds awful, but I really do think that man was there to hurt me, not Lena. And that weird box . . . Jamie, doesn't it ring a bell for you too?"

She wasn't acting like herself. She was acting *normal*. Like she'd have any reaction other than swift and extreme mobilization at hearing that that she'd missed a crime in her own dorm room. Like she wasn't . . .

I put it together in a flash.

Oh, she was brilliant. Like a hurtling comet you couldn't look at dead on without burning your retinas right off. Like a bioluminescent lake. She was a sixteen-year-old detective-savant who could tell your life story from a look, who retrofitted little carved boxes with surprise poison springs early on a Saturday morning when everyone else, including me, was asleep in their beds.

She'd set herself up to be the target of a fake crime to get us off the hook for the real one. And she'd used Lena, and some mysterious guy, to do it.

"Culverton Smith," I said, piecing it together aloud for Shepard's sake. "It's from a Holmes story. We're being set up. Jesus Christ, tell your policemen to wear gloves when handling that box. Thick ones."

To his credit, he took me seriously. "Making a call. But I want an explanation as soon as I'm back." He stepped outside.

"You," I said to her, "are a genius."

Across the table, Holmes slipped from false concern into very real satisfaction. "It's quite a good story, you know. 'The Adventure of the Dying Detective.' Pity that Dr. Watson smothered what should have been an exercise in logic in all that sentimental garbage about his partner."

"The Adventure of the Dying Detective," for me, has always been the hardest of the Sherlock Holmes stories to read, and not because it isn't brilliantly done. It's 1890. Dr. Watson, who's living with his wife away from Baker Street, is urgently called to Sherlock Holmes's bedside. The detective has caught a rare, highly contagious disease that, as he tells Dr. Watson, can only be cured by Culverton Smith, a specialist in tropical illnesses living nearby. The catch: Smith hates Holmes because he correctly accused Smith of murder. His victim was infected with, and died of, this same disease. But Holmes insists that Watson bring Smith anyway, that Smith is their only hope. While Holmes rattles off a series of ridiculous-sounding orders on how Watson is to go about fetching this specialist, Watson idly picks up a small ivory box that's been resting on the table. Out of nowhere, Holmes insists that Watson put it down and not touch it again.

All the while, Watson thinks his best friend is dying. It's wrenching to read, and even more so as we watch Watson follow Holmes's orders—the clear product of a hallucinating mind—to the letter. From trust, or affection, or old habit, we're not sure, but either way, the last of these insane directions has Watson hiding himself in the closet in preparation for Smith's arrival. Smith comes in. The gaslight is low. Holmes is sweating in feverish agony on the settee. The specialist begins to gloat, thinking he and the detective are alone. That little ivory box? He'd mailed it, fitted with an infected metal spring, hoping to catch Holmes with it unaware. After Smith has confessed everything to Holmes, who he believes to be a dead man, Holmes asks him to turn up the gaslight. It's a signal: in bursts Inspector Morton of Scotland Yard, who's been waiting at the door, and Watson, who's witnessed the whole conversation from the closet. Smith is hauled away to jail.

And Holmes? Not sick at all. He faked his symptoms. Starved himself for three days until he was skin and bone, then applied a convincing coat of stage makeup to make himself appear at death's door. As for the box—well. He wasn't in any danger. He reminds Watson that he always thoroughly examines his mail.

Charlotte Holmes had stripped the "Dying Detective" for details and rearranged them to make her own narrative, pulling Lena in on her scheme to sell the story. I wondered who the man in the ski mask was. Tom? Unlikely. Still, it was just the sort of story that our Sherlock-obsessed murderer would've seized on and used against us.

The part I couldn't get over, that distracted me from even this show of Charlotte Holmes's powers, was remembering how much my great-great-great-grandfather had trusted hers. Oysters, I remembered. Between the instructions he'd given

Dr. Watson, Sherlock Holmes had been ranting, in his "hallucinations," about oysters.

And his partner had still followed his directions exactly.

I thought about the piped-in interrogation in the police station. About the little notebook that still lay open between us on the table. About how my own doubts about Holmes's innocence ran alongside my doubt that she could get us out of this mess.

She *had* just gotten us out of this mess. And no matter what my head wanted to tell me, I knew in my bones that she wasn't a killer.

"I'm sorry I didn't trust you," I said to my Holmes, in a low voice.

She shook her head. "I needed your shock to be genuine for me to sell it."

"I don't mean about the details. I don't need to hear the details." I reached across the table to put my hand on hers. "I meant to say that I won't doubt you again."

I watched her catalog me. The planes of my face, the tilt of my head, how I sat in my chair, my fingers' heat and the ruck of my hair: she took it all in, deduced from what she saw, and came up, in the end, with something she hadn't expected.

"You won't," she said with flat surprise. "You really won't, will you?"

Next to me, my father cleared his throat. I didn't spare him a glance.

When Shepard returned from speaking to his team, we gave him the background on the Culverton Smith story. And he told us what we already knew. They had, in fact, found a spring loaded into the ivory box, poised to strike when it was slid open. That spring was coated in an infectious tropical disease; the police lab weren't sure of its exact origin, but they guessed it to be Asia. Samples of this kind were tightly controlled, and so far, their search into local scientists who had requested access to them had ended in an absolute null.

(I asked Holmes, much later, how she got her hands on the sample. She said something about Milo, an ex-girlfriend at the CDC, and "catching as catch can.")

"This blows my list of suspects wide open," Shepard said. "So we're back to option one. Someone trying their damnedest to frame you two. We'll need to talk about who out there in the world wants to get you. And I'll have to notify the station that I won't be needing a pair of cells. At least not tonight."

So his plan *had* been to arrest us.

"Let us help you," Holmes said. "I'm an official informant for Scotland Yard, and between Watson and me"—I was gratified to be back on a last-name basis—"we're experts on the killer's MO. Sherlock Holmes stories? We're the obvious choice. Not to mention that we can informally question anyone at Sherringford without arousing suspicion, or that you're getting an excellent chemist and a relatively fearless pugilist in the bargain. We're not a bargain. We're luxury goods."

"No," he said. "Absolutely not."

Holmes shrugged; she'd anticipated this response. "Then I'll conduct my own investigation, and deal with the culprit, after I catch him or her, as I see fit."

"You actually think that threatening vigilante justice will make me want to take you two on?" Shepard demanded. "You're a *child*. I don't know how desperate the police are across the pond, but we play it by the book here. Isn't it enough that you're not suspects anymore? I don't see any reason to put you and Jamie in the line of fire."

"Really. Then perhaps call Scotland Yard again and ask them about what transpired after I sat through this exact conversation with DI Green. If she's reluctant to speak to you, tell her you know all about the deep freezer, the meat hook, and how I found her two minutes before the killer returned. Honestly, I might've gotten myself there sooner if she hadn't been such a cow about it. Just the year before I'd recovered three million pounds' worth of jewels and given her all the credit." She yawned. "Do it in the morning, though. I'm knackered."

"But—"

"Mr. Watson, this was a lovely dinner. Would you mind taking us home now?" Without waiting for a response, Holmes disappeared into the garage, her gown trailing after her.

In her flair for the dramatic, she'd left behind my jacket and her phone. I collected them, trying not to feel like her valet.

"That girl is a piece of work," Shepard said, somewhere between admiration and despair.

"Holmeses." My father laughed, and reached for his car keys. "Would you know she's one of the nicer ones?"

seven

IT TOOK SHEPARD LESS THAN A DAY TO AGREE TO HOLMES'S terms.

"You have until Thanksgiving break," he said to us; I had him on speakerphone. He'd spent all that morning sleuthing in Holmes's and Lena's room, and come up empty-handed. I wasn't surprised. Holmes, of course, had been thorough. "That's a little less than a month. We'll share information. *Share* it, do you understand me? DI Green warned me about how you like to play the magician so you can do the big reveal at the end. That won't fly here." A long, scratchy pause. "The only reason I'm allowing this Encyclopedia Brown business is because I don't want any more hurt kids. You two are included in that. So, Jamie, I need you to keep an eye out for her. I've heard you're a brawler. I'm okay with that."

"Do you honestly think I can't take care of myself?" Holmes asked, draped over the love seat like a boneless cat. "I'll have you know I'm an expert at singlestick and baritsu."

"Yes, and sometimes a pair of fists is much more useful," I said, "if less dramatic. I'll keep an eye out, Detective. Will you clear us publicly?"

"Terrible idea," Holmes put in. "It might lead to escalation on the murderer's part if they think they need to reconvince the police of our guilt. No, tell the school privately, but don't let anyone release a statement."

"Fine." More crackling. "I'll send over what we have so far on the snake."

"And a copy of *The Adventures of Sherlock Holmes*," I said.

"Fine. You should know that we found the ski mask the intruder used in a garbage can outside Stevenson Hall, but we weren't able to lift any prints off it."

"These people are too good for that," Holmes said. I coughed. "But yes, send over the bit about the snake. And I want access to the personnel files of all of Sherringford's students and employees, including any EU immigration information."

"I'd lose my job."

"You'd lose your job anyway when they find out you're letting us help."

Static.

"Done," he said finally. "Charlotte, Jamie—just keep your mouths shut."

"Yes, yes," Holmes said, "thank you," and hung up on him.

It was Monday at lunch. I'd hidden away in Holmes's lab in an attempt to finish writing my poem for Mr. Wheatley's class that afternoon. It was already going badly, but then I watched Holmes finish her calculus problem set in the ten minutes between concluding some frothy, smelly experiment and picking up her violin for a spin through Beethoven's Kreutzer Sonata as if it were "Twinkle, Twinkle Little Star."

She threw her bow down. "I have to wait until the school day is over to investigate. Two hours!" she said. "Do you think, if I set fire to the maths building—"

"No."

"But—"

"Still no. Why don't you help me with this poem?" I asked, an attempt to derail her. "It needs to be one that's 'difficult for me to write,' whatever that means."

"What do you have so far?" she asked.

"'The.' Or maybe 'A,' I'm not sure."

"I'm bad with words." She sat down next to me. "Too imprecise. Too many shades of meaning. And people use them to lie. Have you ever heard someone lie to you on the violin? Well. I suppose it can be done, but it would take far more skill."

"Speaking of lying," I said. "Who played your masked man, the other night?"

"One of Lena's on-and-off hookups. I knew I needed a failsafe, and Lena was willing to play along. We'd laid the groundwork up a week ago. All she needed was the go-ahead. She'd been telling him she loved scary movies, and being afraid sort of turned her on, and asking him if he had a ski mask—that sort of thing. All she had to do was mention that I'd be away on Sunday night. He didn't question it at all when she screamed and chased him out, and after, I had her put a fresh mask I'd taken from the athletics shed into the bin outside. Really, it's a good thing she's so completely insane. It means she can get away with anything."

"And how is she holding up, after her 'scare'?"

"Oh, fine," she said airily. "I think she's counting the days until her new handbag comes in the post."

I put my pen down. "I thought you might pay her off. With what money?"

She bit her lip. "She wouldn't take any. Which, to be honest, makes me nervous."

"The fact that she likes you enough to help you for free? *That* makes you nervous?"

"I'd rather deal in quantifiable transactions," she said. "But she said she'd made a killing at poker and reminded me that her allowance is staggering. After that, she sat me down in front of her laptop and made me help her pick out something called a minaudière. It looks like a bejeweled toad."

"Oh," I said, wondering what it meant that Holmes had never once offered to pay me.

"I have a rainy-day fund, you know," she said, not quite looking at me. "Until recently, it was raining . . . rather a lot. But I . . . I've been trying to use an umbrella."

"See, and you say you're bad with words. I'm stealing that." I scrawled it down.

She drifted over to her bookshelf and lit a cigarette. With the toe of her shoe, she tapped her copy of *The Casebook of Sherlock Holmes* before she leaned down to pick it up. I could tell I'd lost her to her thoughts.

It seemed as good a time as any to do the thing I'd been avoiding.

The hospital corridors were empty when I arrived, carrying a bunch of flowers. It wasn't hard to find the right ward. They had it guarded like Fort Knox. Thankfully, Detective Shepard had had the wherewithal to put my name on the visitor list, and after showing my ID to two separate policemen, I was allowed into her room.

I'd been told that she was awake, but her eyes were closed when I came in. She looked terrible. Her blond hair was matted to her head with sweat, her arms wound in tubes and tape. Strangely enough, she was clutching a whiteboard to her chest in the way you would a teddy bear. As quietly as I could, I put the flowers on the table beside her bed and debated writing her a note. Was that what the board was for?

While I stood there, Elizabeth opened one eye, then the other.

"Hi," I said. "I hope you don't mind that I came."

She shook her head no, though I wasn't sure if it was *No, I don't mind,* or *No, actually, leave.*

"May I sit down?"

A nod.

"How long until you get your voice back?" I asked. When Detective Shepard said that Elizabeth had been unable to speak to the police, I hadn't thought he meant it literally.

Slowly, achingly, she pulled a marker out from the folds of her blanket and scrawled something down on the board. I peered over at what she was writing. *Don't know*, it said.

I didn't mean to interrogate her. That wasn't why I'd come. Besides, Shepard had told us that Elizabeth's parents had asked the police for a few days' grace for their daughter. They said that she had been through enough without being forced to relive it all.

"I'm sorry," I told Elizabeth, looking down at my hands. I'd come to apologize. It was why I hadn't brought Holmes. Apologizing was the kind of thing that made her break out in hives.

A scribbling sound. *For what?*

"For what happened to you. You didn't deserve this. Any of it. I'm sorry."

I don't remember all of it. But the detective told me you found me and got help. Thank you. Her exhausted eyes met mine. Exhausted, and gentle. I didn't deserve that gentleness.

"I hope you feel better soon," I said, standing to leave.

Scribbling again. *Detective said "blue carbuncle" to my parents. He thought I was asleep. Explanation?*

I sat back down. "Do you know the story?"

A headshake. She scrubbed her board blank with her hospital gown and wrote *Talk fast. My parents went to get takeout. They won't tell me anything but I need to know.* She furiously underlined the last four words.

I understood what it was like, being kept in the dark.

"It's a Sherlock Holmes story," I began, "about a rare missing diamond. A blue carbuncle. One that a policeman finds in the throat of a dead Christmas goose on the street. Holmes and Watson trace the goose back to its breeder, and from there, to the breeder's brother. He'd stolen the gem from a countess and hidden it in a goose's craw."

It was the quick and dirty version, the boring one—all facts, no flair. It left out all the details that made the story something I loved. But Sherlock Holmes's strategies and Dr. Watson's observations didn't have a place in this guarded hospital room.

Even so, Elizabeth listened avidly. When I'd finished, she held up her whiteboard. *So I guess I'm the goose.*

I hesitated, and she lifted her eyebrows in a challenge. "Guess so," I said.

Fucked up.

"Yeah." It was, impossibly so. "How much do you remember about that night?"

Not much. Seeing you. Making out with Randall. They showed me the thing that was in my throat.

"Did you recognize it?"

No. Her eyes were imploring. *Do you know anything about it?*

"The police are trying to solve this as fast as they can." I took a deep breath. "Did Randall do this to you? Do you remember?"

She shook her head, blushing a little. *I don't remember his face, but I DO remember what the guy said. "Give my regards to Charlotte Holmes." I don't think Randall would say that.*

There was a commotion outside the door. "Who did you

let in to see my daughter? A friend? What's his name?" I didn't hear the police officer's reply. Hastily, Elizabeth rubbed her board clean and then started writing something else.

Elizabeth's mother barged into the room, her arms full of Chinese food. "Don't tell me," she said in a dangerous voice. "You're Jamie Watson. You're the one that found her."

She might have said *found her*, but it was clear what she meant was *attacked her*. Elizabeth's eyes seized on mine.

"No," I said, extending a hand. "I'm Gary. Gary Snyder." He was a poet we were reading in Mr. Wheatley's class, one I vigorously hated.

"And what exactly are you doing here, Gary Snyder?"

Elizabeth tugged on her mother's sleeve. She held up her whiteboard: a half-completed tic-tac-toe game.

Charlotte Holmes would have been proud.

Her mother deflated. "We've just been so worried, sweetie," she said, and burst into tears over her daughter's bed.

I took that as my cue to leave. *I think I have some leads,* I texted Holmes in the elevator.

Somehow, I wasn't surprised to find Detective Shepard waiting for me on the sofa in Sciences 442.

"So, next time, *tell* me when you're planning on pulling something," I said, hanging up my jacket. "Her parents were conveniently gone? Oh, Elizabeth couldn't talk to the detective, but she could easily talk to *me*. What, did you wait until I stepped out the door and then had the hospital cafeteria closed?" The last was directed at Holmes.

Across the room, she poked at her vulture skeleton until

it spun in circles. "For the record, I merely waited until you left and then had Emperor Kitchen offer free takeout to all the families in the ICU. I'll make Milo pay for it. I told you he'd go either today or tomorrow," she said to Shepard. "You should trust me more often, you know. I *am* the world's foremost Jamie Watson scholar."

"Look, I'm happy to question her, but next time, I want to be in the loop. Otherwise I'm just going to build my own chessboard and let you move me around it."

"Stop being dramatic, and tell us what happened," Shepard said, sounding like he wanted to get out of 442 as quickly as possible. I couldn't blame him—Holmes had lit up her jar of teeth from behind, probably in anticipation of the detective's visit. It was, I thought, her version of hanging fairy lights.

I filled them in. Shepard made a low growling noise. "'Give my regards to Charlotte Holmes,'" he repeated, shaking his head. "I need to talk to John Smith again. He won't confess to the attack. Only to dealing drugs, and then he only gives me information he wants me to use against *you*, Charlotte."

Holmes touched a finger to the skeleton's nose, stilling it in its orbit. "Something else is going to happen if our attacker doesn't get what he wants," she said. "Someone else is going to get hurt."

"What does he want?" I said. "Us locked up, no key. I don't see how he's going to get that. Unless Shepard puts us away for show."

"No." She frowned. "I need unfettered access to the campus, not to be rotting away in some cell. We need to figure out the connection between the man you're holding and the man he claims he is. I need to make a plan."

"*We* need to make a plan," Shepard said.

So we did.

Holmes and I began by retracing our steps through the access tunnels, back to the police-cordoned storage room. John Smith's footprints still ended at its door, a literal dead end. But Holmes refused to give up. We covered what felt like miles of territory that night, her coursing ahead, me yawning clandestinely behind my hand.

When we returned to her lab, we stayed up even later examining the school library's copy of *The Adventures of Sherlock Holmes*. It was a brand-new school edition of the stories. The bookmark the killer had placed inside was one of the Sherringford ones they left on the circulation desk, and it was clean of all but the school librarian's fingerprints. But that was to be expected. Besides, Mr. Jones had no conceivable connection to either me or Holmes. The book itself was completely unremarkable: intact spine, intact pages. The only remarkable thing about it was that the killer had tucked it into Dobson's cold hands. At dawn, when Holmes began going through it page by page with an actual magnifying glass, I curled up on the floor to go to sleep.

I spent the next few nights even more tired, wading through all the BBC America footage that had been shot after Dobson's murder and put online. The police had requested everything that wasn't on their website, and there were hours and hours to contend with. I ran through it all frame by frame, looking for a still shot of the dealer's face. I needed to know if the man Shepard had in custody was the same one I'd seen around Sherringford. It took hours. I found a lot of talking-head speculation about boarding school life, about how privileged kids consider murder to be just another game. I found a number of interviews where our classmates slagged off Holmes, slagged off me, cried for show. I ate a lot of jalapeño-flavored cheese puffs. And I didn't see a single hair of the man we were looking for. After I slept through my French class three days in a row, Monsieur Cann cheerfully suggested that I would perhaps prefer to take Spanish, *n'est-ce pas?*, and I decided to give the solo research up as pointless.

While I'd been chained to my laptop, Holmes had done the legwork, pulling up security footage closer to home. Sherringford didn't have any cameras of their own, so she'd done a circuit of the businesses whose storefronts faced campus, getting the lowdown on their security systems. Then, she told me, it was just the simple expedient of hacking into their feeds, using this particular spring-code that her brother had taught her, which, of course, she had modified herself using the blah-blah differential, and then something else that sounded like conversational calculus, and my eyes began to cross.

She poked my shoulder with her shoe, and I trapped it neatly with my hands. "What?" I asked.

"Since you don't care about the more complex workings of tonight"—she shook her foot free—"do you want to be in charge of the snacks?"

"Snacks are complex," I said. "How do you feel about tasty, tasty puffed corn?"

More footage. More cheese doodles eaten in the dark of Sciences 442, one more long, dreary, wasted weekend. Still no sign of the man we were looking for. Could he make himself go invisible? Did he even exist at all? I fell asleep with my head on a bag of Jiffy Pop and woke up nauseous and pissed off to the dim light of the screen against Holmes's face. My watch read 2:21 in the morning, but her eyes were still wide open.

There was nothing else to do but ask Shepard to let me talk to his prisoner. I was sure that I'd remember his reedy, obnoxious voice even if I couldn't exactly place his face. Shepard dragged his heels on it for days, but when it became clear that neither he nor we were making progress, he agreed to let one of us in to see him. Holmes, tight-lipped, agreed that it should be me; I'd had the clearer look at him, after all.

The night before I was to go to the jail, the prisoner hung himself.

It took another three days before we persuaded Shepard to let us into the morgue.

"You're part of the forensics club," the medical examiner said doubtfully.

I shifted my weight from foot to foot. "Detective Shepard is our adviser," I said. It was true. Sort of. You could look at this semester as the weirdest independent study anyone had ever had.

"I thought forensics was the school speech team." She

blinked at us through her glasses. "Not the science club."

"Huh. I haven't heard that," I said, straight-faced.

Though it was a Saturday, Holmes was wearing her school uniform, her ribbon tie pressed and perfect. She'd found a pair of glasses somewhere, black-framed ones that dwarfed her features, and she'd drawn on her eyebrows to make them seem thicker. Holmes usually looked like a weapon. Today she looked like a teen movie's idea of a dork, the one that could take off her glasses, shake out her hair, and instantly be elected prom queen.

She looked, in short, like the kind of girl that adults found themselves confiding in.

"Can I tell you the truth?" she asked the examiner in an American accent. She sounded eager. Bright. "I mostly wanted to come here because I heard you had an amazing microscope. I have some samples from my bio class in my bag. Could I take a look at them? I'm working on a project for the national Intel contest. Cancer research."

The examiner's face softened slightly. "That's fine," she said, and laughed self-consciously. "For a second, I thought that you wanted to look at a *body*."

Holmes laughed too, her pretty-girl laugh. "Oh my God, I don't know if I could handle that. How do you even get used to it? You must be so brave."

"Practice," the examiner said. It was clear that she didn't get this kind of glowing admiration every day. "Practice, and patience."

"Are they . . . are they scary? Do you still feel like they're people? Or does it change for you depending on the body?" Holmes shook her head. "Wow, thinking about this would keep me up at night."

The examiner pursed her lips philosophically. "It should. These are important questions you're asking, Charlotte. I think about them every day."

I nodded to hide the fact that I thought she was full of shit.

As always, Holmes was better at this than I was. "Wow," she said. "Just—wow. And it's like you run this whole place by yourself. That's awesome. How many do you end up dissecting in a day?"

"It depends, really. I only have one intact body right now." The examiner walked over to the wall of morgue drawers. "Are you feeling brave?"

Game, set, match.

Holmes looked over at me with wide eyes. "Oh my God," she said, a perfect imitation of the bright, well-adjusted girl she'd never been. "Maybe? Yes! Okay, yes, I am."

We put on gloves and masks, and the examiner put on her best fortune-teller voice, saying "John Smith!" as she pulled the drawer out of the wall with a flourish.

I won't describe his face. It's enough to say that his death by hanging left him bloated and bruised and unrecognizable, far past the point where I could positively identify him. But his height was about right, his shoulders. I stared for a moment at his throat, wishing that I could hear his voice to be sure.

"Can I?" Holmes asked, reaching for the corpse's forearm.

A small line appeared between the examiner's brows. "I guess," she said.

Swiftly, Holmes turned it over. The man had a tattoo near his wrist in the shape of a compass. Underneath, the word "navigator."

Holmes looked at me. *Do you remember this?* her eyes were asking. I shook my head no, and said aloud, "That's the kind of tattoo you could hide under long sleeves." At the examiner's sharp look, I coughed. "Um, I've been thinking of getting one."

"The navigator," Holmes said to herself, lifting his arm to examine his fingernails. She checked his fingers one at a time, lifted his chin to look at the veins of his neck. Then she ducked her head to look up the man's nostrils. "Moriarty means 'seaworthy.'"

The examiner stared at us furiously.

"Etymology," I said. "It's really popular. With the kids."

Our grace period was up, and Holmes knew it too. "Manual labor," Holmes said, quickly deducing. She pulled out a folded sheet of paper and an inkpad and took down the man's prints while the examiner sputtered. "Look at those finger callouses. Look at the state of his ankles. He's all muscle, but it isn't from the gym. These are a working man's muscles. Do you see the rope burn on his arm?"

"He's not a dealer," I said. "It's not him."

"It's not him," Holmes said, in the voice that was ragged and wild and hers. "Jamie—it's a Moriarty."

"Get out." The examiner jerked her head toward the door. "Now."

On Monday, I'd skipped all my classes—my grades were falling, lower now than they'd ever been—to be alone, to make my half idea into a project without her peering over my shoulder. I pulled from the resources Shepard had given us access to and from the files we'd put together on our own. Flight passenger lists. Family trees. Moriartys with criminal records and lists of their known aliases. I took down the riding crops from the wall and pinned all of this up in their place, then began the long and arduous task of cross-referencing. I needed to know which of the Moriartys had come into this country and when. If John Smith wasn't a member of the family, he was definitely on their payroll. The trick was to find out who hired him.

In the back of my mind, I knew there was a good chance that I was blowing all of this out of proportion. The simplest answer was almost always the right one, and the idea that the entire Moriarty family was out to get me and Holmes was a big, complicated leap from where I was standing. Even if there had been a conflict between Holmes and that family, it was probably small and contained, nothing like the sprawling conspiracy that I was charting up on the wall.

But I kept thinking how the Sherringford killer was insistently re-creating the Sherlock Holmes stories. Those past wrongs that Sherlock and Dr. Watson had made right were being pushed into our present, and the details of the good deeds they'd done were being used to hurt us and the people we knew. Sure, maybe the killer had a personal vendetta against Holmes, but it felt to me like it was something bigger than that, something older, something reaching back more than a century.

Anyway, I couldn't ignore the way the word *Moriarty* made my skin crawl.

I focused on four of them. The four Moriartys whose whereabouts weren't dictated by respectable jobs, who'd been sloppy enough to have their shadier dealings dragged into the public eye. Whoever was doing this to us was sloppy, there wasn't any doubt of that, and I meant to use it to my advantage.

Hadrian and Phillipa were a brother-and-sister pair of art collectors whose fortune, rumor had it, was used to buy favors from dictators in countries they wanted to plunder. Lucien was August's older brother, an adviser for some of the more scandal-ridden members of the British Parliament. I read a profile of him in the *Guardian* that had hinted strongly that Lucien Moriarty knew how to throw his money around to clear just about anyone's name.

And then there was Lucien's younger brother: August.

For this, I didn't have to look through Shepard's records. It was as easy as plugging August's name into Google and clicking a button.

The first article that came up was from his college at Oxford. August had presented some complicated theorem at an academic conference in Dusseldorf. The reporter took special care to mention his age: he'd been doing his doctorate in pure math at twenty. He must've been a genius to be doing that work so young. The article described his dissertation (fractals, imaginary numbers) in layman's terms, and I still couldn't begin to understand it.

But it was dated two years back. I needed newer information, to know if he was still at Oxford, if he'd graduated or been hit by a car or moved to, I don't know . . . Connecticut.

The rest of the search results linked to academic journals and fellowship competitions, all dated that same year. Not a word about his personal life or about him dating Charlotte Holmes. Just a list of his achievements: August, recipient of a prestigious Institut Zalen grant. August, publishing on vector spaces and the cosmos in *Mathematics Today*. August, flown to the Arctic Circle to collaborate with scientists studying something called "ice fractals."

After that, there was nothing. Not a word had been written about August Moriarty in the last two years.

I put it all up on the wall anyway.

At three o'clock precisely, Holmes swung open the door to 442, humming something under her breath. "Hello, Watson," she said before she'd even seen me, "you're here early," and then she stopped in her tracks, staring at the wall.

I realized, too late, that I'd pretty much re-created the murder den we'd found in the access tunnels.

"Oh," she said.

I waited for the explosion.

She sighed, dropping her backpack on the floor. "It's a place to start. I came to tell you that Milo ran down John Smith's prints in some of the more . . . unusual databases. He's worked as a domestic for the last five years."

"A domestic?"

"A servant, Watson. He was Phillipa Moriarty's driver until his disappearance four months ago. There's our link to the family, sorted. The question is if he was doing all this alone, or . . ."

"You don't think he was. So, Phillipa then?"

We looked at the wall, side by side.

"Have you ever heard of a rat-king?" She reached out and touched the corner of Hadrian's photo. "The Moriartys—their disgusting tails are all tied together. Let's not try to separate them just yet. We'll start by finding out which of them came into this country, and when."

On her direction, ship manifests went up onto the wall, freighters that had traveled from England to Boston and the names of the sailors who manned them. ("Seaworthy," she muttered, taping them up.) We went through lists of private airstrips and private jets. Helicopters. Rowboats. We scrolled through records in New England and in England both. Moriarty was a horrifyingly common last name, but things became even worse when we began running known aliases. Our series of papers grew, day by day, until they engulfed the wall.

Phillipa spoke at a gallery opening in Glasgow. Lucien was photographed with the British prime minister. Hadrian showed up on some German talk show to chat about the Sphinx. How could it be any of them? Were they taking care of business in Europe, flying by night to Connecticut to ruin our lives? It seemed absurd, even by our standards. I spent every moment in 442, working like a madman. (I was even growing the beginnings of a madman's scratchy beard, which I secretly thought was kind of awesome.) And she worked right beside me with a fury I hadn't yet seen. Almost everything else went out the window.

Especially for Holmes.

She'd stopped battling me on August Moriarty. Every time I tried to learn something, anything, about what happened between them, she regarded me with a weary tilt of her head, like I was a fly she couldn't quite get rid of. I was relatively sure she wasn't eating or sleeping. But it wasn't just her attitude. Her eyes were somehow both glassy and dry, and as she scratched absently at her scalp, going over her millionth passenger manifest, her hair made a crackling sound that hair really shouldn't make. I kept stifling the urge to ask her if she was okay, to touch her forehead to see if she had a fever. To take care of her.

I brought her food, but it stayed untouched on the plate no matter how I tried to cajole her into eating. When I caught her taking twenty minutes to eat a single almond, I began wondering if there was some kind of Watsonian guide for the care and keeping of Holmeses.

When I sent my father an email to that effect (subject line I Need Your Help, postscript *Still haven't forgiven you and won't*), he responded that, yes, over the years he'd written down an informal series of suggestions in his journal; he'd do his best to adapt and type them up for me.

When the list arrived the next day, it was twelve pages long, single-spaced.

The suggestions ran from the obvious (*8. On the whole, coaxing works rather better than straightforward demands*) to the irrelevant (*39. Under all circumstances, do not allow Holmes to cook your dinner unless you have a taste for cold unseasoned broth*) to the absurd (*87. Hide all firearms before throwing Holmes a surprise birthday party*) to, finally, the useful (*1. Search often for opiates and dispose of as needed; retaliation will not come often, though is swift and exacting when it does—do not grow attached to one's mirrors or drinking glasses; 2. During your search, always begin with the hollowed-out heels of Holmes's boots; 102. Have no compunctions about drugging Holmes's tea if he hasn't slept; 41. Be prepared to receive compliments once every two to three years; 74.* (underlined twice) *Whatever happens, remember it is* not your fault *and likely could not have been prevented, no matter your efforts*). I wondered if I should create some kind of subclause for when the Holmes in question was a girl and her Watson was a guy who liked girls. *It's not your fault if you care too much about her. If you want impossible things. It couldn't have been prevented, no matter your efforts.*

I had to employ rule #9 (*sometimes for your own sake you must leave Holmes to his own devices, even if you return to find he's set himself on fire*) when real life began to creep in. The rugby team had asked for permission for me to rejoin in what should have been the last week of my suspension, and gotten it from the school. Holmes had insisted that I go. A number of Dobson's friends were on the squad, and she'd decided I should ask them, in a roundabout manner, about his last weeks alive. If he was seeing anyone unusual, leaving campus at late hours, taking strange calls. If some blond man had sold him any drugs, and what he'd said. That sort of thing. I'd figured that I could manage well enough.

Holmes disagreed. "You're a terrible liar," she said, perched on her lab table. I stood before her, like a schoolboy about to recite his lessons. "More specifically, I can read your thoughts as if they were printed in block letters on your forehead. Really, sometimes you think so loudly that I can hear you in the next room. There's no way you can approach your teammates in an innocent manner. We need to fix that."

"I'm so sorry to hear about your unfortunate telepathy," I snapped.

"See, just there? You're frustrated, and think I'm being rude."

"Oh, well done," I told her. "Really fine detective work. Why are we doing this now?"

She ran a hand through her hair. "Watson," she said, "we've hit a brick wall. We've come up with nothing new. Just let's get you into shape, okay?"

"Okay." I deflated at the pleading note in her voice.

She smiled. "Let's start with the basics. How to recognize when others are lying to you, so you can begin to police your own habits."

She walked me through it—where someone looks when they're recalling a memory, and when they're fabricating one; how an honest man stands, and a lying one, how they hold their shoulders (slumped), their hands (behind their back, to hide fidgeting), if they'd prefer to stand or sit (to stand, probably with nervous feet). All of it she rattled off as though reading from a book.

"How young did you learn all this?"

"Five," she said. "My mum was cross with Milo for teasing me. He kept telling me Santa Claus was real."

"I'm sorry," I asked, "was? Don't you mean wasn't?"

"No." She ran her finger down the agenda in her lap and sighed. "Right, so it's eight o'clock already and you're tetchy because you have history homework for tomorrow—I can tell by your feet, stop shuffling—so do a practice run or two and then we'll be finished."

I stuffed my hands in my pockets to keep myself from fidgeting. "Do you want me to try to lie to you?"

At that, I watched Holmes fight back a laugh. "God, no, that would be pointless. No, I'll make a series of statements and you can tell me which are true. Thumb up for truth, thumb down for a lie."

"I'm pretty good at reading you, you know," I told her.

"That might be true," she said gamely. "But did you know that my father worked for the M.O.D. for fourteen years before the Kremlin got wind of a scheme of his and tried to have him assassinated? Or that, growing up, I had a cat called Mouse? She's white and black and very fussy, and once the neighbor boy tried to drown her in a bucket. My mother hates her. Milo joined up with MI5 at age seventeen. No, that's false, Milo runs the world's largest private security company. Or no, actually, he's an *enfant terrible* preparing a hostile takeover of Google. He's unemployed. He's a complete tosser. For years he was my favorite person in the world."

I held my hand out rather stupidly between us; my thumb

hadn't moved. I'd spent too much time imagining what her life was like, before me, so I drank in all these facts—even the contrary ones—as if they were water.

"Pay attention to my face, Watson. Not my words. Listen to my tone. How am I sitting? Where am I looking?" She snapped her fingers. "I own three dressing gowns. I dislike guns; they cheapen confrontations. I first took cocaine at age twelve, and sometimes I take oxycodone when I'm miserable. When I met you, my initial thought was that my parents had set it up. No, it was that you were *dreamy*." Grinning, I put my thumb up; she pushed it back down. "No, I thought, finally what someone wants from me, I can give them. I know how to play to an audience. I liked you. I thought you were another chauvinistic bastard who thought I couldn't take care of myself."

"All true," I said, quietly, before she could continue. "All of it. At one point or another, including the business about your brother. He's done all those things, been all those things. You thought all those things about me."

"Explain your method." Holmes pulled a cigarette out of her pocket and lit it.

"Because, somewhere in that brain of yours, you've decided I should know more about you, but you don't want to do it outright. No, it can't be simple, you're Charlotte Holmes. You have to do it sideways, and this is the most sideways approach you could dream up."

She exhaled in a long stream, head tipped to the side. I suppressed a cough. "Fine," she said, finally, and I chanced a smile. Grudgingly, she returned it. "But none of those deductions were *methodical*, Watson. That was all psychology. I *loathe* psychology."

"It's okay," I told her. "I hate losing at games, too."

The next day, she put me through another session, this time with a new test subject. I shouldn't have been surprised that she brought in Lena.

We met on the quad after classes, shivering and stomping our boots. Lena's hair hung in a braid down her back, and her hat had a knit flower that drooped down over her brow. She had a date with Tom in town that night, she told us, so she couldn't stay too late. It was odd to watch her next to Holmes in her trim black coat, hands stuffed into the fur muff strung from her neck. When the wind nipped at us, Lena huddled against her roommate with a familiarity that was almost shocking. I wondered what they talked about together. I couldn't imagine it.

For two hours, until the tips of my fingers were literally blue from the cold, I practiced reading Lena's tells. (In the process, I learned her down to the ground. I really didn't need to know that much about her sex life.) By the end of it, I was so exhausted from shivering that I wanted nothing more than to go to bed with a cup of something warm. Thankfully, when I went a full ten minutes without mislabeling one of Lena's statements, Holmes let us call it a day. We ducked into the Stevenson Hall lobby for warmth.

"You guys are up to secret things, I can tell. How are your secret things?" Lena asked, unwinding the scarf from her neck.

"They're about to go much better." Holmes discreetly

stuffed a roll of bills into Lena's coat pocket. "Run the poker game as usual tomorrow, will you? I don't want anyone to note a change in my behavior."

Lena pulled the money back out and pressed it into Holmes's hand. "Keep it," she said. "I kind of like being your test subject."

Holmes froze. "But—"

"Ugh, don't be weird about it. We're friends. And I don't, like, need the money." Standing on her tiptoes, she kissed me on the cheek. "Thanks, Jamie. That was a lot of fun, but I want to get to ask *you* inappropriate questions. Maybe we could have pizza in town sometime."

"You're having pizza in town with Tom tonight," Holmes said.

"Sure," I said, ignoring her. "I'd like that."

Holmes had on the kind of scowl toddlers get when their favorite toy is stolen away. "We're done here," she announced, and dragged me off by my elbow.

When I arrived at practice the next day, Kline was surveying the rugby pitch, fists on hips like a taller, dumber Napoleon. He was mad, and not without cause—their record stood so far at a predictable 0–7.

"We're starting in ten! Look alive!" he shouted. It was true, the team did seem dead. Our fly-half was actually sleeping, on his side, at midfield. Larson, our eight-man, trotted by and kicked him in the small of the back. Without a flicker of interest, Coach Q looked up from his director's chair and then back down at his copy of *Men's Health*.

"We're down to fourteen players, so many students have gone home. I don't think the school would've let you back on if that wasn't the case." Kline looked me over. "So, have you been staying in shape?"

"Running five miles every day," I lied. "But I'll do whatever. I'm happy to be back on the team." Another lie, delivered smoothly. I'd been practicing. "Where's Randall? I haven't talked to him since Elizabeth . . . you know . . . and I wanted to make sure we were on decent terms."

Kline pointed. "He's getting ready to drill with the backs. If you want to talk to him, make it quick." He cupped his hands around his mouth. "We're starting in five!"

When I caught up with him, Randall was even redder-faced than usual. I wasn't sure if it was from exertion or anger.

"Oh hey, the jackass is back," he said, shoving past me on his way to the bench.

A bit of both, then.

"Randall, wait." He slowed down slightly and I pulled up even. "Look. I wanted to say I'm sorry about Dobson. I didn't know him that well, but I know he was your friend."

"You have some issues, dude. That was fucked up. Going after him for saying what's on his mind? He was just messing, and you jumped on him. Then he shows up dead. Fucked up," he repeated, and dug his water bottle out from his bag.

I counted backward from five. "Charlotte Holmes is like my sister. Okay? He said the absolute worst thing he could have said. But I didn't kill him, I promise that."

"Then why do the police keep hauling you in? Why were

you the one who found Elizabeth?"

"Wrong place, wrong time," I said.

"Bullshit," he countered. "I've seen that detective with you like a million times. You got hauled down to the station after Lizzie got hurt. Why does he suspect you, if you're so innocent?"

"Same reason why you would, if you were them." The words came out bitterly. That fear of winding up in an orange jumpsuit hadn't entirely gone away—a bit of it lingered at the edges of everything I did, really—and I pulled from the truth of that feeling, laid it under my words.

Randall eyed me. "I don't know, man."

"Think what you want," I told him. "But you should know I feel like shit about all of it. I've heard all these rumors that Dobson hung himself, and I can't sleep, thinking I somehow drove him to it."

A lie, of course, but I was baiting my trap. Holmes taught me that: people would much rather correct you than answer a straightforward question. Randall wasn't an exception to the rule.

"Dude, you weren't *that* important to him," he said. "No, I heard that he was poisoned. I don't know which one's true."

"Poisoned? From the dining hall food?"

"Maybe." Randall shrugged. "But other people would probably be sick then too. I don't know, he'd been eating these cookies his sister sent him, and they looked nasty. Maybe it was in those. Or that weird protein powder he had. That stuff was the wrong color. He said it was from Germany and expensive, but I didn't buy it. Maybe your little friend slipped something into it."

"Out on the pitch," Kline hollered.

"All right," Randall said, "later." The venom was gone from his voice. I was happy about that, at least.

"You good?" Kline asked.

"Yeah," I said. "Hey, so, he said something about protein powder? Do you . . . do you know a good brand?" I bent to lace a cleat so he couldn't see my face. I wasn't sure I could pull that one off: I wore cable-knit jumpers and read Vonnegut novels and had a girl for a best friend. I was about as likely to build up giant biceps as to build a colony on the moon.

"Talk to Nurse Bryony at the infirmary," he said. "She has some prescription stuff she gets from Europe."

I reached in my bag, ostensibly for my water bottle, and sent Holmes an urgent text. I just hoped her phone was on this time, and not pickled in formaldehyde or in pieces across her chemistry table.

Practice crawled by at a snail's pace, especially once we began running plays. When Kline announced the last of them, I gritted my teeth and waited for my opportunity. Then I threw myself up for a catch in the most insane possible position, sprawling out like a diver going into water. I let myself go limp. My head bounced once, twice, three times against the frozen ground.

No one could say I wasn't dedicated to my game.

I heard Kline holler, "That's *it*! Watson! Watson!" and the rest of the team roaring.

Things went black.

When I woke, I found myself blinking up into fluorescent lights. Holmes's tear-streaked face was hovering over mine. She seemed genuinely upset, and for a second, I thought there'd been another murder. I struggled to sit up on my elbows.

"Oh, baby," she sniffed, shoving me back down on the bed with a touch more force than was necessary. "I thought you'd never wake up!"

I completely failed to catch on, at first. But then again, I *had* hit my head. "Where am I?" I tried to ask, but it came out more like a woof.

Holmes burst into tears, putting a hand to her mouth. Her nails were painted a bright red, and she smelled like Forever Ever Cotton Candy. Then I noticed she was in a polka-dot sweater. With a *bow* in her hair.

Apparently, she'd been working on her caring-girlfriend routine.

I thought I was going to be sick, but then, it might've been the concussion; I was fairly sure I had one. Everything was out of focus, in a doubled sort of way, and the only solution I could think of was to sleep. I shut my eyes, satisfied that I'd fulfilled my end of our makeshift plan. I had an injury that was bound to keep me in the infirmary for at least a day. Enough time for Holmes to poke around.

Somewhere across the room, a voice said, "Oh, you two are too much," and I snapped my eyes open again. From the little supply station, Nurse Bryony beamed at us. "Do you know she hasn't left your side for the past three hours? You blacked out for a bit, and then you were drifting between asleep and awake, and the whole time she just sat and held your hand, fretting. Poor thing."

The accent was American, but the cadences were faintly, unmistakably English. I don't know how I hadn't noticed it before. Or was it in my head? This time, if I ignored the halos I saw around all the lights and the soft little hum in my head, I could almost pay attention.

"How long will he be here?" Holmes asked, laying her hand against my cheek. "We have dinner reservations for tomorrow in town. It's our two-month anniversary."

Her fingers were cool and soft against my face, and I found myself leaning into her touch. Then I froze. "Sorry," I whispered to her, mortified.

"What are you apologizing for?" she asked, her voice surprisingly rough-edged. With her other hand, she brushed my hair back from my face.

The nurse cleared her throat, cutting into my confusion. "I'll keep a close eye on him. It's not bad enough to send him to the hospital, but I still don't want to take chances. You might have to reschedule your plans, just to be safe."

Holmes smiled down at me. She wasn't Hailey. She was something much more insidious. Charlotte Holmes without the edges, all combed and clean, well loved and loving in return. I knew it would be gone tomorrow, all of it—the gentle way she touched me, the glitter of her undivided attention, the bows and the perfume. It would all go back into her costume box, and she would be the real Holmes again.

Because this wasn't real, even if she spoke to me in what sounded like her real voice. "Do you hear that? You should be fine," she said.

I shouldn't have wanted it the way I did.

I was beginning to go, I could tell, and I knew I would wake up back into our old life. The lights winked at me; they liked the secrets I told them. But silently, I reminded myself, secrets are best when kept to oneself. They began blowing out, one by one, like candles. "Good night," I told Holmes, pulling her hand to my chest, and then I was awash in sleep.

"WATSON," SHE HISSED. "WATSON, WAKE UP, I'VE GOT TO GO. Night check's in ten minutes."

The room was dark, but I could see light coming in from under the door, where the nurse's desk was. Thankfully, it seemed my head had cleared enough to form coherent sentences. "Did you find anything?" I asked. Or tried to ask. It came out cotton-mouthed.

Holmes handed me a glass of water with an impatient look. I was right; she was herself again, and I suppressed a flare of disappointed guilt.

After a gulp, I repeated my question.

"She went out for a smoke, and I picked the lock on the medicine cabinet. There's a store of protein powder in with the other prescriptions, for Gabriel Tinker, according to the tag, but the canisters were all empty. I tasted a bit of powder I found in the cabinet, and it seemed innocent enough."

Tinker was the rugby team's fly-half, the one who'd been

sleeping on the field. "You *tasted* it? Why couldn't you take it back to your lab and examine it there?"

She looked affronted that I should even ask. "Efficiency."

"Right, okay, you nut." I pulled myself, slowly, into a sitting position. Holmes tucked a pillow behind my back. "So let's break it down: she's from England. That's why we flagged her file originally, right?"

"She was born there, but she moved here when she was a teenager. Or so she said when I pressed her, after I shed a few homesick tears. My face is still swollen. I forgot how uncomfortable this whole crying business is."

"No powder, no England. Two near misses, then," I said. "Unless you somehow wronged her back when you were a toddler, if I've got her age right. Twenty-two?"

"Twenty-three." Holmes got to her feet. "If she is, in fact, our culprit, she wouldn't be telling the truth to us anyway, so it hardly matters. As it stands, I can tell she's hiding something, but that could just be the sort of reserve you have around students. I'll try to track down an actual sample of that powder tomorrow, because what I tried tasted more like dust than protein."

"Shouldn't we focus on someone who we have a clear lead on? Like, I don't know . . . August Moriarty?"

"No, I don't think so," she said matter-of-factly. "I'm off to write my *Macbeth* paper. Be careful tonight. And maybe shower. You smell awful."

When she left, I realized I was starving. I wolfed down a roll of crackers I found next to the bed and took the small cup of what looked like Tylenol, washing it down with the rest of the water. As I set the glass carefully back down on the table—depth perception was a bit of an issue, post-concussion—I realized what I'd done. The woman taking care of me might be a poisoner. With a fixation on me and Holmes. And I'd put myself into her overnight care, tossing back the pills she gave me without a second thought.

The light in the next room flicked off. I stared at the door, willing it to stay shut, willing the nurse to pack up her things and leave. I willed this feeling to be just paranoia from my head injury, to remember the cluster of Moriartys sharing space on our wall. I willed Bryony to just be an ordinary woman who took a job at Sherringford because of the pay and the beautiful campus and because she didn't mind taking care of teenagers with the flu, not because she'd tracked Holmes and me across an ocean to frame us on Moriarty's orders.

The knob turned. The door swung open.

"I'm headed out," Nurse Bryony said softly. "Can I get you anything?"

"No, thanks." *Leave*, I thought. *Go home.*

But I heard her set down her bag. She padded into the room, smelling faintly of flowers. An ordinary, pretty-girl smell. I swallowed hard. The room was beginning to sway, like a ship, and I wished badly that Holmes was still there.

"You're nearly out of water." Nurse Bryony refilled my glass at the sink and took another roll of crackers from the cabinet above, setting them both by my bed. "There. Go easy on these. I'm surprised you're not more nauseous."

I wondered if Dobson was nauseous, before he died. I'd never had a concussion before. Was nausea a symptom? Was it a symptom of arsenic poisoning?

That's it, I thought. *Holmes can come up with the next plan.*

In the half-light, Bryony was a dark silhouette, all except the shining hair that fell across her face as she leaned down over me. She had a strange, hot electricity to her. I thought, in my confusion, that she might kiss me, or slap me across the face, that she would pick up the pillow and smother me with it.

But she put a cool hand to my forehead instead. "Get some rest, Jamie, so you can see that girl of yours again tomorrow," she whispered, her breath hot on my face. "The other nurse will be in first thing." She gathered her things and left.

I didn't even try to sleep. Instead, I stayed up listening to the quiet clock of my heart, wondering every moment if I was about to stop breathing. I'd been careless with my life, I knew I was, but if I died tonight, I was going to be furious. I debated texting Holmes a thousand times. If I was wrong, I'd look like an idiot.

Around dawn, I threw the water glass to the floor, needing to hear something shatter. It was plastic. It bounced. When the morning nurse came in—an older woman with round Midwestern vowels—I was shivering with the effort to stay awake.

But she washed and filled the same cup, gave me pills that matched the ones I'd taken earlier. She made some crack about how I looked as if I'd been chased through hell, and I was overcome with the sensation that I was missing something, something huge.

WHEN I FINALLY GOT SIGNED OUT OF THE INFIRMARY, IT WAS dinnertime. Mrs. Dunham insisted on escorting me back to my room.

"Now get into bed," she said, waiting with crossed arms until I did. "I've already talked to Tom, and he's going to bring you something back from the dining hall. I want you to call me if you need anything, or if you start feeling terrible, and we'll get you right to the hospital."

"Yes, Mrs. Dunham," I said unhappily. I was horribly ripe—I hadn't showered since before rugby practice—and starving, and ragged at the edges from my all-night vigil, and I just wanted to be left alone.

She bustled around, gathering extra blankets for my bed and picking Tom's clothes up from the floor. "I got special permission for an after-hours visit, if you'd like to see Charlotte."

"Thanks. I don't really need anything else," I said, because she was genuinely sweet, and she wasn't showing any signs of leaving.

"I love that you two are friends," she said. "Those stories were my favorite when I was younger."

I smiled tightly at her. It was terrible, the way my stomach contracted at that sentence. I'd used to love hearing people talk about the Sherlock Holmes stories, and now I couldn't help making anyone who mentioned them to me into a suspect. "They were mine too."

When Tom returned, he was juggling a sandwich, a pair of apples, and a cup of hot cocoa. "There you are," he said, arranging it all on my desk with a flourish. "I heard you ate it pretty hard at practice. Incredible catch, though, according to Randall."

I tore into the sandwich. "How are you? How are things with Lena?"

"She's good. What's Charlotte paying her off for? Lena's, like, rolling right now."

"That's from poker," I said, mouth full. I wanted to leave the investigation behind at least long enough to get through dinner.

"Well, are you and Charlotte still prime suspects?" he asked, pulling over a chair.

I shrugged. It hurt to. "Can we talk about something else? What did I miss in my history class? I got all my other assignments."

His face fell. "Nothing really," he said, and waited, as if he expected me to cave and tell him all about my adventures. I wished he knew how stressful and humiliating those adventures actually were. It wasn't my job to educate him on that, though, so I let the conversation die, crunching into one of the apples he'd brought. Eventually, Tom gave up on me.

Holmes swung by an hour later. Thankfully, I'd had a chance to shower. "How's the patient?" she asked as she perched on the edge of my bed.

I was always suspicious of Holmes in a good mood. "Has someone else been killed?" I asked, only half-joking.

She smiled at me. "Better. Try again."

Without turning around, Tom tugged out one of his earbuds, then the other. I don't know why it annoyed me so much, his clumsy attempt at spying. Maybe I was done being grist for the gossip mill. I lifted an eyebrow in his direction to tip Holmes off, but she'd already noticed. She whipped out her phone.

"I've got a date," she announced, texting furiously. My phone lit up silently on the bed between us, and I craned my neck to see. *Apparently Wheatley's brother keeps snakes in NJ.*

"Where'd you find the guy? Craigslist? The sewers?" *Any missing?* I texted back.

Shepard's running it down. "Funny. You're funny. Look, I thought tomorrow you could help me write a poem for him. Maybe show it to Mr. Wheatley tomorrow after class, get his opinion?" *Interrogate him.*

Why don't you? "Love poems? It sounds serious."

"Oh, quite. He's dreamy." *Because you're his student. He doesn't know me.* She swung her legs off the bed. Furtively, she fished a chocolate bar out of her coat pocket and slid it onto the desk. It was a Cadbury Flake; she must've ordered it online. I don't know how she knew it was my favorite. "Feel better," she said, smiling crookedly at me, and then slipped out of the room.

Tom stuck his earphones back in with a sigh.

So you didn't find anything on Nurse Bryony? I texted her.

No. Sciences 442 at lunch. I heard her footsteps retreating down the hall. *We'll make a plan for Wheatley then.*

I LINGERED BY MR. WHEATLEY'S DESK AFTER CLASS, WAVING
an inquisitive-looking Tom on to his next class. I had a free
period at the end of the day, so I wasn't in a rush.

Wheatley was talking to one of our class's better poets, a
shy, small girl who wrote exclusively about communing with
nature in her native Michigan. As I waited, he gave her a series
of book recommendations in his meandering, sleepy voice, and
she scribbled them down. Our journals were identical. I tucked
mine discreetly back in my bag, feeling a little cliché, and tried
to focus on remembering the strategy that Holmes and I had
hammered out at lunchtime.

Finally, he turned to me. "Ah, Mr. Watson," he said to me.
"What can I do for you?"

I shuffled my feet. "I wanted to talk to you about my
poems," I told him. "I'm having some trouble putting them
together. They're a lot harder than stories. I was wondering
if you had any books I could borrow to do some outside
reading."

He nodded thoughtfully. "I have something in my office I
could lend you. Follow me."

Wheatley's office was the kind of book-lined cave that, in
other circumstances, I would've let myself get lost in. There
was a hooded copper lamp on his desk that spotlit a stack of
our manuscripts, and I recognized my most recent short story
on the top. In the corner, a stand-up globe was turned so that
a dusty Europe faced out. I sat gingerly in a chair and took a
harder look around.

I didn't have the facility for observation that Holmes had, I knew that. But I'd always liked cataloging the details of a place and its people, using it as grist for my stories. Maybe that interest was more about romanticizing my surroundings than deducing from them, but it still spurred me to look closely at the authors of the books on his shelves (Kafka, Rumi, some Scandinavian mystery writers), the kind of rug on his floor (it had a folksy, hand-woven feel), the kind of coffee he was drinking (he'd brought it from home, in a stainless steel mug). I'd been too muddled and, frankly, scared to look that closely at Nurse Bryony when I was in the infirmary, and I was determined to have more to show for my efforts this time.

Wheatley hummed to himself as he ran his finger along a bookshelf. Though he was a nervous teacher—a pacer, a hand-wringer who started each sentence two or three times—he seemed at ease now, in his office, and I wondered if it was the confidence of a man who knew he had me in his power. Or maybe he just liked me, and was more comfortable speaking one-on-one. It was impossible for me to tell. I wished that Holmes were there.

"Found them," he said, pulling a few books from the shelf to hand to me. "There's a book of poetry prompts, in case you'd like to practice, and a collection of essays by contemporary poets that you might find useful in thinking about the impetus for writing a poem."

"Thanks." I tucked them in my bag.

"Your fiction is good, as I told you at homecoming," he said. "Clean and sharp, and very readable. Some of your plots are a bit far-fetched, but I don't mind the wish-fulfillment aspect of it. I think it runs in your blood, maybe. I read all your great-great-whatever-grandfather's stories when I was a boy. Wonderful. The movie adaptations from the thirties were very good, too."

I'd always hated those films—they'd portrayed Dr. Watson as a bumbling idiot, and Sherlock Holmes as an automaton. But I saw my opening, and took it. "They're great, aren't they? My favorite is the one about the snake. 'The Speckled Band.'"

"I know that story." Mr. Wheatley shuddered. "I hate snakes. My brother keeps them on his farm, and I—well, I make him visit *me*. Can't do it. After I heard what happened to that Dobson boy, I couldn't sleep for days."

His distress seemed genuine, but I couldn't be sure. "He was attacked by a snake?" I asked innocently.

"After he died," Mr. Wheatley said. "I'm surprised you don't know. Didn't the police talk to you about it?"

"They talked to *you* about it?"

He squirmed a little in his chair. It was strange to see an adult act so squirrelly. "I keep a close tab on the news. I have a friend on the force. You know."

I could tell he was lying. But it didn't mean I knew what the truth was.

"That reminds me," I said, trying a different tack. "I wanted to know about how to write from our lives, especially when things get weird and . . . unbelievable. Can you still do it? Write about them? You talk a lot about how we need to write from our own experiences, but when awful things happen—"

"You can talk to me about it, if you need to," he cut in. "It might help you organize your thoughts. You could even write me a story about it. For extra credit. After all, you've skipped almost a week's worth of classes."

I looked at my hands, wondering what he'd try to get out of me. It might be useful to play along.

Also, I could use the extra credit.

"Sure, I could try that," I said.

He pulled a legal pad out from under the stack of papers on his desk and balanced it on his knee. "So," he said, lifting a page or two and sliding a piece of cardboard beneath it. "What are you finding so unbelievable?"

"Well," I said, "it's a little weird that my best friend is a Holmes. I never really expected that to happen."

"Hm," he said, making a note. "Tell me more about your relationship with Charlotte Holmes?"

Even though I'd led him to the topic, I still found his tone obnoxious. I gritted my teeth. "Like I said, she's my best friend."

"And yet you went to the dance together. She could have more complicated feelings. It's important to consider these kinds of things," he said, slipping into teacher mode. "For character development."

If anyone had complicated feelings, it was me. And those were none of his fucking business. "We're talking about Charlotte Holmes here. I think she has complicated relationships even with the skeletons in her lab. Nothing is straightforward to her."

I thought I'd dodged the question, but his eyes lit up.

"She keeps skeletons in her office," he said, scribbling it down. "Interesting."

"Her lab," I corrected him. Too late, I remembered what Holmes had taught me, about how easy it is to get people to correct you.

"Where's her lab?" he asked, not looking at me.

"I can't remember," I lied. "She doesn't let anyone in there."

"Very private," he said. "Good. She has kind of a goth look to her, doesn't she? Is it cultivated, do you think?"

"Holmes wears what she wants to wear. Like I do." I frowned. "She's not some agent of death. Or a cartoon. I always thought she looked very London, that's all. I don't understand how this would help me write this story."

"Character development," he repeated. "Tell me, when she investigates, does she behave much like her famous forebear?"

"Sherlock?" I asked. "I don't know, I haven't exactly met him in the flesh."

Mr. Wheatley laughed, then abruptly stopped. "No. Really. Does she?"

It went on for a long time. I let him draw me out bit by bit, noting carefully to hear where he directed the conversation. I told him that I'd been struggling to write down the story of Dobson's death and the police's investigation into my life, but Mr. Wheatley didn't want to talk about Dobson at all. I took it as a sign that he already knew all there was to know about "that poor boy" and his murder. And though everyone on campus knew now that Holmes and I had found Elizabeth unconscious in the quad, he didn't even ask about her either.

But Holmes? Mr. Wheatley wanted to know everything: about her childhood, about her older brother (whose name he readily knew), about the circumstances of her coming to Sherringford. Thankfully, my own knowledge of her was patchwork enough that I could plead ignorance. But it was all incredibly damning, watching him write down her whole dossier. Why could he possibly want that information except to use it against us?

That is, until he ripped the sheet he'd been writing on from his legal pad and handed it over to me. I stared at it for a minute, not understanding. "There. Sometimes it helps to say it all aloud before you start shaping your piece. But it all sounds very hard to deal with, Jamie, like I'd said before." He leaned over to scribble something at the top of the paper. "If you'd prefer to talk to someone else, here's the name of the school therapist. She's very kind, and you shouldn't be ashamed about making an appointment. Most people eventually do."

I folded the sheet and put it in my pocket, feeling distinctly ashamed. He'd just been trying to help after all, if a little ham-handedly. Mr. Wheatley was a good man, and he was concerned about me, and still I had been imagining him to be out for my blood. Wondering if he had lowered that rattlesnake onto Dobson's convulsing form.

Was this what it was always like, doing detective work? How could you ever let yourself get close to anyone? No wonder Holmes was so determined to keep herself apart.

When I left Wheatley's office, I went straight to Sciences 442. It had only taken an hour alone for Holmes to trash her lab. The carpet was an explosion of open file folders, their

pages spread out like snow. Something bright green was frothing over on a Bunsen burner, and the entire room smelled of cilantro. In the midst of all this chaos, Holmes was slumped on the floor in her uniform like a black-and-white bird, smoking a cigarette and reading *The History of Dirt*. It was so gigantic that she had to brace it against her knees. Above her, the vulture skeletons swung lazily on their strings. During one of our marathon research sessions, I'd decided to name them Julian and George, and today, Julian's skull sported a small knife that looked as if it'd been stabbed there. I shuddered.

"Your book looks great," I said, picking a path across the room. "What's the sequel? *Worms and You?*"

"Don't tease, I know nothing about American soils. And the idea of tracing a murder victim by the contents of their shoe soles is hardly far-fetched." She turned a page, and I could see that she was incredibly tense. "You sound disappointed. You don't suspect Wheatley, then."

"I don't," I said. "Or Nurse Bryony. Or maybe I suspect both of them because we have a disappeared dealer, and I want someone concrete to suspect. I'm in some muddled state where I can't tell what I think."

"It's because you care," she said. "About nearly everyone. It's remarkable, really, but in this instance, it clouds your judgment. It's why I try to avoid sentiment."

"That's heartless," I said, stung. All this time, had I been nothing more to her than someone to carry her bag?

"I said, I *try* to avoid it, do keep up." She shut her book and fixed her lantern eyes on me. "Trust me, if Milo were involved

in a murder plot, I'd find it very difficult to assist him. It's not *heartlessness* if it saves lives."

She was spoiling for a fight, but I made myself back down. I thought of the Cadbury Flake on my desk, the time she leaned over to straighten my glasses in the middle of a conversation. She was either much better or much worse at this whole caring business than she thought. "Wheatley's getting information about the two of us somewhere, and he's definitely watching you closely."

"That surprises you?" she asked.

I bit back a remark about her being the center of the universe.

"Well, yes. No. I don't know. He also seems genuinely afraid of snakes," I said, wanting to defend him. "And genuinely concerned with what's happening to me."

"I'd suspect him less if he seemed indifferent," Holmes pointed out. "Did he try to dig into your oh-so-compelling trauma?"

"No." I paused. "Well, a little. He referred me to a therapist."

"Psychology." She snorted. "All the same."

I threw up my hands. "What about the other names on the suspects list? You know, the ones who aren't Romanian royalty or pop stars. The Moriartys. What about August? Is he really dead?"

"Nothing to report." Holmes drew on her cigarette, her eyes narrowing. "Honestly, sod all this, none of this is *correct*. We have the data and the access but we've made no progress, and I've smoked at least twenty of these horrible things today and I am developing a wretched dependency, just you watch, we'll be out in the middle of some sodding field watching a perfectly captivating murder take place firsthand, and I'll have to run off in the middle because I need to have a Lucky Strike right then or *I'll* be the one doing the killing." She stabbed out her cigarette against the love seat's arm, and in the same gesture, lit another. I'd heard her run off on tangents before, but none this frustrated or angry.

"Then stop. Smoking."

"Do you really want me to revert to the alternative?" she snapped.

"Maybe we should take the night off," I said. "Go get pancakes, plan for tomorrow."

I could have blamed myself for having wound her up in the first place, but Holmes had been itching for a confrontation from the moment I walked through the door. The look she gave me then was the one you saved for cockroaches, shoe in hand. "This is what I *do*. You want me to stop? You think you can talk about it like it's a *game*?"

The acid in her tone ate away the last of my patience. "I'm saying that you should take a night off, not that you should abandon it completely."

"You can't handle the pace, then."

"No! God, if we're so stuck, why won't we just call in your parents—"

"I refuse to have them involved—"

"Don't you think that getting your head on straight can

take priority, for once, to proving yourself to your family?"

She pulled herself up, as proud and straight as an ancient queen. Her face was a perfect blank. The only glimmer of Holmes I could see was in the anger darkening her eyes.

"Yes," she said in a flat voice. "I hadn't thought of that. I, of course, have no personal stake in this matter. Since this is all an exercise to please my *parents*."

"Holmes—"

"So yes, take the night off. In the meantime, I'll be tracking down the person who murdered my rapist and tried to murder *your* little girlfriend and then almost had us arrested for it. It might even move faster without you, as you've proven yourself so extraordinarily useless."

It was the first time she'd ever said anything that cruel to me. The word *useless* hung between us, like a millstone on a piece of thread.

"How can I help you," I snarled, "when you keep so much information to yourself? There's a Moriarty plastered all over that wall that you refuse to talk about. You've told me nothing about your relationship with him."

"With him? Don't you mean *to* him?" she asked. "Is this about the case, or your jealousy?"

Her hand flew up to her mouth as if to stop the words from coming out. But it was too late.

"Okay, then." There was nothing else to say. I put my coat on, not sure where I was headed but knowing that it was some-where the hell away from here.

"Watson." Holmes got to her feet.

"I'm fine."

"I know I can be perfectly beastly—"

"You can," I said. "And why don't you just call me Jamie, like everyone else, since I'm too *useless* to be your Watson."

Holmes's mouth opened and snapped shut. I slammed the door hard enough that, behind me, I heard the satisfying crash of a beaker shattering on the floor.

eight

I PACED OUTSIDE OF MICHENER HALL, BLOWING ON MY hands to keep them warm. By the time I banged through the front door, I was mostly in control of myself again. Mrs. Dunham was manning the front desk—did she ever go home?—but I walked straight past her without a word, not wanting to test my hard-won composure.

Usually, my room was empty the hour before dinner, but that day Tom was watching a video on his computer, eating a chocolate bar. On the screen, a girl performed a burlesque routine to a song sung in French. I recognized a few of the words: *leave it, leave it all*. Biting her lip, she lowered one strap, the other.

"Are you okay?" Tom asked, hitting Pause. The girl in the video froze obediently.

"Fine," I said. "Bad day."

"You don't seem to have a lot of good ones," he observed. There was a smear of chocolate on his argyle sweater-vest, and I realized the wrapper on his desk was from the Flake bar Holmes had given me. It shouldn't have been a big deal— Tom and I had standing permission to raid each other's food stashes, within reason—but I took it like a blow to the gut.

"I don't see why that's shocking, considering," I said, and willed him to go away.

Ever since I'd come to Sherringford, I'd existed in a state of constant loneliness without ever actually being alone. Privacy was an illusion at boarding school. There was always another body in the room, and if there wasn't, one could enter at any moment. Being Holmes's friend might have taken the edge off that loneliness, but it didn't dissipate entirely. At best, our friendship made me feel as though I was a part of something larger, something grander; that, with her, I'd been given access to a world whose unseen currents ran parallel to ours. But at our friendship's worst, I wasn't sure I was her friend at all. Maybe some human echo chamber or a conductor for her brilliant light.

I hadn't realized I was thinking out loud until Tom cleared his throat.

"I had a friend like that once," he said.

"Oh?" I said, uninterested. But Tom had a thoughtful expression on, and I didn't want to be cruel.

"Andrew," he said. "He was the only person I really kept in touch with after I left for Sherringford, and last summer, we hung out all the time. He's this all-state football star, and he always gets perfect grades, and I swear he could get away with murder because of it. Because ninety percent of the time, he was so good, he could stay out all night downtown, partying, and he'd come in at dawn and his parents would just buy that he was out late studying. I felt . . . invincible when I was around him."

"What happened?" I asked.

"Cops caught us drinking down by the lake, and he pinned the whole thing on me." Tom flashed a self-deprecating smile. "His family is like a big deal—they have all this money, and we don't, not anymore—so they got the charges dropped. But I was in the doghouse for months. The worst part of it was that he stopped talking to me. If anything, I should've been the one who got to tell him to eat shit."

"I'm sorry." It was hard to imagine Tom being on anyone's bad side. He was the guy who could wear a baby-blue suit to homecoming and still have one of the hottest girls in school as his date.

"It's not worth it being the sidekick," he said. "I bet she just uses you to do her dirty work. Andrew used to do that to me."

"Sometimes," I said, hiding how close to the bone that cut.

He gave me a knowing look. "So she doesn't even let you do that."

"No," I snapped. "She trusted me to sniff out Mr. Wheatley. And I went out and got a fucking concussion because no one would investigate the school nurse. I don't call that doing nothing."

Tom looked like I'd hit him. "You *what?*"

"All right, it was stupid, and I couldn't have planned it exactly—maybe I would've broken my arm, or twisted my ankle—but I couldn't exactly fake having to stay in the infirmary all day, could I? How else could Holmes have snuck in there without breaking in? The door's alarmed, they keep everyone's medicine in there."

"No—I—"

He was casting around for words, but none were coming. Did he really think that I was so useless I couldn't help her out at all?

"I didn't know you were that stupid," he said finally.

"Thanks, you twat."

"Don't mention it," he said. "Look, I'm meeting Lena for dinner, so I gotta go. I'm doing some work at the library after that, but we can talk more about your life choices tonight, if you want to."

Tom and Lena. Mine and Holmes's shadow-selves. Or maybe we were the shadows, and they the happy, well-adjusted versions. "Don't worry about it," I said. "I'm fine."

After throwing some books in his bag, he took off. He must've bumped the keyboard as he went, though, because the video he'd been playing unpaused. The girl on the screen began shimmying out of her clothes again. I plunked down in Tom's chair and closed the window, then sat there for a minute, staring at the notes Tom had pinned above his desk, the tiny mirror he'd put there.

That's when I noticed it.

His desk and mine were across from each other, meaning that most nights we did our homework back to back. The only mirror in our room had been clumsily hung to the right of where I sat, its bottom half obscured by my desk. If I sat up in the middle of the night, I'd catch a glimpse of my reflection and panic that we had an intruder. That was, more or less, all that mirror was good for.

I didn't mind that much. I cared a bit about what I wore on the weekend, but our school uniform was exactly that, a uniform, and so the way I looked in it didn't change. Tom, on the other hand, wore all kinds of product in his hair, and rather than lean awkwardly over my desk to apply it, or do it in the bathroom (which he claimed was "embarrassing," as if he'd be dispelling some notion that his boy-band mop grew in that way), he'd tacked up a locker-sized mirror above his desk.

All this is to say that, when I looked up into Tom's mirror, I was at the precise angle to see that there was a gap between my own mirror and the wall. A small gap. A centimeter.

In that centimeter's worth of dark, I could see the glimmer of a reflection.

Something was back there.

I walked over, got down on my knees, made blinkers with my hands to block the overhead light. Still I couldn't make out what was behind it. After straightening a wire hanger from my closet, I rattled it in the gap in an attempt to dislodge whatever was back there. I hit on nothing, even when I ran it from top to bottom. When I looked again, I could still see the glimmer of light reflecting off something.

Was it a lens?

I took a deep breath and tried to gather my thoughts. On the bed, my phone buzzed, and I seized it, thinking it might be Holmes. It would be a relief. We'd both been horrible to each other, we'd both been keyed up, and defeated, and lost—I couldn't imagine what being lost felt like for someone as whip-smart as Charlotte Holmes—and I refused to believe that she'd meant what she'd said. It had to be her. She'd come right over. Everything would be fine.

But the text was from my mother, asking if I'd forgotten our weekly call. She'd try again later tonight, she said, and signed it with kisses.

I looked back into the gap. The light was still shining.

Someone had been in here. Someone had put this thing in my room.

In a sudden, towering wave of rage, I jerked the desk away from the wall, scattering my textbooks in the process. Standing in the space I'd cleared, I braced both my hands against the mirror and pulled. It refused to give. I planted my feet, trying to remember what Coach Q had taught us about taking down a bigger opponent, and pulled, harder. Harder. There was a faint cracking sound—probably its bolts beginning to pull from the plaster—but it still refused to move. Panting, I stared at my reflection. My eyes were all pupil, my face sweaty and red. I looked how I did at the end of a rugby match. Like a Neanderthal.

Fine. I'd be a Neanderthal. With a grunt, I picked up my chemistry text from the desk and slammed it into the mirror.

It didn't give on the first try, or the second. Around the tenth, I stopped counting and instead watched the webbed crack grow from the middle of the mirror to its edges. Outside, in the hall, someone yelled *What the hell is going on,* but I ignored them; it wasn't hard to. The mirror may have been sturdily constructed, but like all things made of glass, it eventually gave. There was a great loud splintering *crack* as it broke, and I spun away, throwing the textbook up to shield my face. It hadn't shattered out so much as down, but some pieces had flown out and stuck into the flesh of my hands. I was in such a fury that I couldn't feel them there.

Because when I turned to look, I saw a small, circular lens, the size of my thumbnail, with a cord that ran into a wireless device. It'd been adhered to the wall with a bit of tape.

But how could the camera capture anything through the mirror? I bent and gingerly picked up one of its larger pieces—I'm not sure why I bothered; my hands were already bleeding—and turned it front to back. Both sides appeared to be glass. A two-way mirror.

What came next I can only describe as a fugue state. I'd understood what it was to lose myself in the past, when I'd been in a rage, but this time the feeling was coupled with crippling fear and violation. Someone had seen me get dressed. Someone had seen me sleep. And though I couldn't find a microphone on the camera, I was sure that this someone had also recorded every word I'd said.

So there had to be an audio recording device, as well.

I tore the books off my shelf, dumped out my desk drawers,

went through every pocket of every pair of trousers hanging in my closet. I took my Swiss Army knife and cut open my mattress, not caring about the fine I'd have to pay, and searched every inch of it with my bleeding fingers. I got on my hands and knees and pulled up the carpet in our room inch by inch, using the knife to help me along. I cut open the curtains, then looked down the hollow rod that held them up. And I adamantly ignored the noise in the hall that had now increased to a fever pitch—a fist was pounding on the door, and a voice that sounded like Mrs. Dunham's shouted *Jamie, Jamie, I know you're in there,* but I'd already shoved Tom's desk chair under the doorknob and thrown the deadbolt. It was easy to turn the volume for the outside world all the way down, what with the screaming panic in my head.

When all was said and done, I'd come up with two electronic bugs, each the size and shape of my thumbnail. One had been affixed to the wall-facing side of my headboard. The other I found on the bottom of my desk chair. I held them in my cupped hands, striping them with blood. Their data must have been sent to the transmitter wirelessly, because they weren't attached to anything with any cords that I could see. I set them down on my desk in a neat line, along with the camera, which I'd yanked the cord from. Then I threw them into a pillowcase. If they were still transmitting, the spy on the other end would be looking into a black screen.

I heard a buzzing sound. Was it from blood loss? Not unlikely. My room looked as if some howling, wounded beast had ripped it up with its claws. Everything I owned was on the floor, a good deal of it tracked red from my hands, and I hadn't even searched through Tom's things yet. I'd been able to control myself that much, to wait until he returned, but there was still the problem of the bugs. What to do with them? I thought, woozily, that I should call the detective. I should call Holmes. Come to think of it, there was still shouting in the hall. Was I imagining it?

My name: *Jamie, Jamie, Jamie.*

"Go away," I hollered, and eased myself down into the chair. I was beginning to feel the cuts on my hands, the glass that I'd pushed still further into the skin with each new thing I'd rifled through or discarded. I should go to the infirmary, I thought, but I didn't want to tip off anyone—anyone who hadn't already heard the commotion, that is—and Nurse Bryony was still sharing space with Mr. Wheatley on my no-fly list.

I hunted through my shaving kit for a pair of tweezers, put a T-shirt between my teeth, and got down to the business of pulling out the glass. It wasn't sanitary, God knows, but it also hadn't been a good day for making decisions. *You don't seem to have a lot of good ones,* Tom had said. He wasn't wrong. I nearly bit through the cloth trying not to scream, but I didn't manage to keep myself from crying. It wasn't so much from sadness or pain as acceptance of the impossible, a great well of *this is wrong* bubbling up all at once. I wondered absently if the transmitters on my desk were picking up the sound. One more shameful thing in with all the rest. I resisted the urge to smash the audio bugs like the insects they were—I'd need them as evidence, after all.

What I didn't understand was why they'd bugged my room. Who was I, anyway? I wasn't the extraordinary one. I was Jamie Watson, would-be writer, subpar rugger, keeper of the most boring journal in at least five states. I couldn't even get people to call me by my full first name. If I was important, it was only as a conduit. Holmes's only access point.

What information had I revealed, unwittingly, in this room? What had I given away?

With a growing sense of horror, I realized that I'd given away plenty, even some that day. Mr. Wheatley; the faked concussion; the search through Bryony's things: I'd said all of it out loud. I'd spent the week after the murder telling Tom about all our suspicions and our findings, what we'd found in Dobson's room. I'd even bitched about August Moriarty. God, how stupid could I have possibly been?

By now, I was sure they knew I'd found their bugs. I needed to get over to Sciences 442 and sweep our lab, see if Holmes could trace the signal. If she couldn't, I knew that Milo could, and I knew he wasn't more than a phone call away.

The shirt I'd been wearing was ruined, smeared with blood and bits of glass. I stripped it off and shook it out before I tore it into makeshift bandages for my hands. The knots I'd made would hold, but not for long. Maybe we could steal Lena's car keys again and go to the hospital. *We*, I kept thinking, *we*. I knew she'd forgive me. She had to. Without each other, we could, quite literally, die.

I put on a clean shirt and flung open the door only to trip over Mrs. Dunham. She'd slouched down against the wall outside my room, legs kicked out before her. It was clear from her face that she was crying.

"Jamie," she said hoarsely. I knelt down beside her. "What have you done to yourself? Look at your hands! And your face—are you hurt? I heard the worst noises coming from your room."

"I didn't mean to scare you," I told her. "I'm fine. Everything's fine."

That phrase was beginning to sound meaningless.

She leaned over to look inside my room and pulled back in shock. "Oh, *Jamie*. What have you done?"

"I've got to go," I said, "but I'll explain later, I promise, I've got to find Holmes."

She grabbed at my hand to keep me from leaving, and I bit back a yell of pain.

"I guess that means you haven't heard," she said, and her eyes misted over with tears. "Oh, Jamie, I didn't want to be the one to tell you. But there's been an accident. A horrible, horrible accident."

MRS. DUNHAM SAID IT'D ONLY HAPPENED TEN MINUTES before—had it only been ten minutes since I found that camera? It could have been seconds, or years, for all I could tell—and that campus was being evacuated, building by building. Michener Hall was empty except for the two of us. She'd thought I'd destroyed my room on hearing the news. Because she, unlike everyone else, knew where Holmes's main haunt was.

They were blaming it on a gas explosion, she'd said.

I'd pelted across campus at a dead run. It was beginning to snow, a powder-dusting that clung to my bare arms and the bandages on my hands. I'd forgotten my coat, my phone. My heart beat harder as I got to the quad.

From clear across campus, I could see that the sciences building was a smoking ruin.

My phone. Where was my phone? What if Holmes was trying to call me? What if she was trapped in the building somewhere? That was the worst possibility I'd allowed myself to imagine, that Julian and George's flightless bones had collapsed on top of her, but that she was fine underneath—a little sooty from the smoke, perhaps, but fine . . . but then, I wasn't giving her enough credit. Holmes was a magician. She had to be standing outside, whole and hale and intact, smoking a cigarette as she watched it all burn. Most important, she'd be alive. Still furious with me, I'd give the universe that—she could never want to speak to me again for all I cared—so long as she was alive.

All of that went straight from my mind when I saw it. It wasn't possible. The northwest corner of Sciences was blown clear through: the corner where Holmes's supply closet was. Battered pieces of granite had thudded mightily to the ground. Through the smoke, I could see the building's interior walls, tattered and stacked like the pages of an old book lit with a match. Here and there, bits of broken wall were still smoldering.

Somewhere in the distance sirens sounded. Uniformed

police officers were cordoning off the area, pushing the few bystanders back into a huddled mass of winter coats. Over a bullhorn, a voice ordered any remaining students to report to the union for further instructions. An officer had set up a standing light that sharply illuminated the building's entrance. There would be a thorough search, he was saying. The firemen would pull out any survivors.

Survivors.

I pushed past him, and the other officer waving a pair of plastic flares, and then past a yellow-suited fireman—there were fire engines behind me, now, flashing their lights—who snagged me by the arm. The look I turned on him must've been that of a feral dog because he loosened his grip for the half second it took me to shake him off. I took off in a sprint toward the front door, and was instantly tackled to the ground.

They wrestled me back toward the emergency vehicles where they assigned an officer to be my babysitter and made me sit under his watchful eye on the edge of the fire engine. They didn't want to arrest me, they said, but they would if I tried to take off again. So I sat dully while the red lights washed everything with fire. At some point, the officer, in a moment of compassion, pressed a cup of something hot into my bandaged hands. He tried to convince me to put on his jacket, but I wanted his pity even less than I wanted his attention. Possibly I insulted his mother. I couldn't remember. He kept away from me after that.

I wondered what Holmes's funeral would be like. I felt sick for a while, and then I stopped really feeling anything at all.

Someone must have taken my wallet from my pocket, or done some calling around, because suddenly my father was there at my elbow. He led me to his car, where the heater was running full blast, and said something about taking me to the hospital. My hands. I'd forgotten about my hands. They were the first words of his I'd registered.

"*No.*" I felt my body come alive with terror. "No, Dad, someone is after us, and I can't go to the hospital. I have to find Holmes. Don't you see? I can't tell you until I know it's safe but there's something very *wrong* going on and I need her. I need her here, do you understand?"

I can only imagine what I must have looked like, half-mad with terror and grief and covered in my own blood, ranting at him from the passenger seat.

But my father did an amazing thing. He put the car into park. Slowly, as if he might scare me into flight, he reached over to cup the back of my head. "I understand," he said. "For now, let's just go home."

He put it into drive and turned on the headlights. And there she was, standing in their white glow.

Holmes's skin was smoked black from the explosion, her hair flecked with snow. Her violin dangled from her fingers. She opened her mouth, and I saw her say my name.

I was out of the car in a heartbeat, and in the next, she was in my arms.

Holmes was always Holmes, even after a terrible shock. With the utmost care, she reached around me to place her Stradivarius on the sedan's purring hood. Only once it was secure did she allow herself to be held, and even then, she kept her palms on my chest as if to brace herself. She was slight, and freezing cold. Her posture, as always, was perfect.

"You're alive," I murmured, tucking my head over hers. "I'm so sorry."

For once she didn't chide me for stating the obvious. Instead, she let out a long, shuddering breath. "The only thing I saved was my Strad, and I had to go back in for it. Watson, I was in the bathroom, and if I hadn't been—the bomb was planted in our lab."

I laughed hollowly. "They're saying it's a gas explosion."

She shifted to look up into my face. "A homemade bomb, and in our lab. There was shrapnel stuck in the walls. Watson"—she kept returning to my name—"I assume you look such a mess because you've found wiretaps in your room, and not because you've taken up cage fighting."

"The cut hands," I guessed, seizing on this chance to feel normal, "and what else?"

"The fact that you're stuck all over with glass like some porcupine. Camera behind the mirror, and then, of course, you'd look for the audio. Which made you feel both personally wronged and suspicious—if you don't trust someone, your left eye twitches at the corner. Right now, it's happening every three seconds. By looking at the kinds of mud on your shoes, it'd only take moments to trace your route from Michener—"

I pulled her back up against me, and she battered my chest with ineffective fists.

"You are doing this to shut me up," she complained.

"I am," I said, and she began to cry. I backed off. "I'm sorry, I didn't mean to—"

"It's not you. This is horrifying," she said through her tears. "I'm not in the least sad. Why am I crying?"

My father bundled us together in the backseat under a moth-eaten blanket; I insisted that we wrap her Strad in another. I tucked her under my arm, and she wept quietly the whole way.

ABBIE, MY FATHER'S WIFE, HAD MADE UP THE GUEST ROOM, and after we arrived Holmes took a cursory look at the bugs from my dorm room, pronounced them dead, and put herself straight to bed. While my father went to call the school, my stepmother pulled me aside to ask where she should put the inflatable mattress.

"Are you having sex with her?" Abbie asked, and promptly looked mortified. "I'm sorry. I'm not used to teenagers, and I can't believe the first thing I've ever said to James's son is . . . I don't really know how to . . . are you two having sex?"

"We're not," I assured her. Bizarrely, this was proving the perfect way for us to meet—unscheduled, without expectations. I didn't have the energy to hate her. Honestly, I couldn't feel anything except tempered relief. Holmes was safe, if in shock. We were being looked after, if only for a night. And Abbie had an open, charming face, with a spray of freckles across her nose, and I was so tired. I decided to just get it over with and start liking her.

"Then I'm putting you in with Charlotte," she said, "so don't start tonight. Having sex, I mean. And your nose is blue—are you hypothermic? Go run yourself a hot bath."

Upstairs, I peeled off my makeshift bandages in the bathroom sink. I had to soak in the tub with my hands resting over the sides so I wouldn't bleed into the water. Afterward, I put on some of my father's old sweats and let Abbie lead me down to the kitchen table. After giving me some Advil, she cleaned out the wounds in my hands with antiseptic and, with a pair of tweezers she'd sterilized, took out the rest of the glass shards under my skin. Then she got to work on my scalp. I clamped my mouth shut to keep from yelling.

My father came in halfway through the process. He'd been on hold all that time, as Sherringford's lines were jammed with panicked parents calling in. Finally, the school had sent out a mass email. He read it off to us there at the table. There hadn't been any casualties from the "gas leak," thank God, though the physics teacher had been in his lab and suffered "minor injuries." But Sherringford was shut down for the rest of the semester.

It's about time, I thought.

My father kept reading something about rescheduled finals, and incompletes, but I didn't pay much attention because I didn't care. There was too much else to think about. The letter said that, after the explosion, students had been evacuated to a nearby Days Inn under the supervision of the RAs and house mothers until their parents could come retrieve them. Tomorrow, Sherringford was bringing in a specialist team from Boston to sweep the campus for other possible "leaks," and after they gave the all clear, students would be escorted, in roommate pairs, to get their things. They'd give us each ten minutes to pack. The schedule for each dorm had been attached.

My father put his smartphone away and looked me hard in the eye. "Charlotte is here. She's safe. And I've been very patient. But now I need you to either give me an explanation for why you've fifteen vicious cuts and an exploded science building, or I'm taking you to the hospital."

Abbie's hands stilled in my hair.

I tried my best to sketch it out for him: my fight with Holmes, the bugged room and the broken mirror, the home-made bomb, our suspicions about Mr. Wheatley and Nurse Bryony and the Moriartys, what I'd said to Tom in our room.

My father had out his ever-present notebook, and he jotted things down as I spoke. When I came to the part about August Moriarty—how the records on him just stopped, what Milo had scrubbed from the *Daily Mail*, the thing Charlotte wouldn't tell me—my father made a disgruntled sound. "Jamie. Number fifteen: if you wait for full disclosure from a Holmes, it might be years before you learn a damn thing."

I threw up my hands. "Tabloids, Dad. The *Daily Mail*. Have they ever been an accurate source of information? And anyway, I couldn't look it up even if I wanted to."

"You," my father said sadly, "still have rather a lot to learn. Don't you remember the stories I used to tell you about Charlotte?"

"Yes," I said. "I'm not stupid."

"Since you're not stupid, you have, of course, reasoned from that information that I've kept tabs on her since she was a little girl. And that I most likely have a file or two up in my study that could fill you in on some of this."

The answers had been there all this time.

All this time. In my childhood home.

I opened my mouth to ask him for the file when he looked at me and said, "You know, if you hadn't been so unfairly angry with me, you might have gotten your hands on it weeks ago."

That settled it. Because I might have had a burning need to know the truth about Charlotte Holmes, might have obsessed over it for an endless string of awful nights—but I still resented my father more.

"I don't want it."

He looked like I'd struck him. "What?"

"You heard me," I told him. "This is between the two of us, and I trust her."

"But—"

"I trust her, Dad." It was true, after all.

"Of course. Of course you do." My father sighed, pinching the bridge of his nose. "Right. Anyway, that detective of yours has been calling me all night. Do you not have your mobile? No? That explains it. I'll call him back and tell him what you told me"—he lifted his notebook—"if you'd like to go to bed."

"Yes, more than anything." I stood unsteadily. "No hospital, then?"

He gave a surprised laugh. "Are you mad? Someone's trying to kill you. No, you're staying right here." Shaking his head, he disappeared into the hallway.

Abbie was putting away her first-aid kit, smiling to herself. Did she think all of this was fun? I subtracted a few of the points I'd given her.

"What exactly is so funny?"

"It's like you're his mini-me," she said. "Oh, it's awful, all of it, but it's like a spy movie! I mean, how cool."

Well, my father had married the right woman. She was just as insensitive as he was.

"My best friend almost died today," I said to her. "It was a really close call. I don't think that's *cool*."

She patted me on the shoulder. "If you hold on a sec, I'll get a fitted sheet for that mattress."

I stomped up the stairs with an armload of linens. In the guest room, Holmes was curled under the floral coverlet, sound asleep in her clothes. She'd scrubbed some of the dirt from her face, but not all of it, and she looked like a Dickensian orphan against the white sheets. I unfolded the blanket from the end of the bed and tucked it over her, standing for a long moment to watch the moon move across her hair. She was alive. She would wake up tomorrow to scheme and argue with me, to bring me terrible sandwiches, to push against me until I made myself a better partner. Her sad eyes and her sharp tongue and the way she touched my shoulder when she thought I wasn't listening. I was always listening.

She was right there, and still I couldn't believe it. I resisted the urge to brush her hair away from her forehead. She stirred, and I pulled my hand back.

"Watson, what is it?"

"Nothing. Go back to sleep."

"I shouldn't," she said, pushing herself up. "We need to work this case. Something terrible is about to happen."

I gently pushed her back down. "Not tonight. Nothing will happen tonight. Go back to sleep." I pulled my mattress up next to the bed and lay down; it sighed out a long breath of air.

"Watson."

"What?"

"I'm sorry I picked a fight with you," Holmes said sleepily. "But you should know that I had a good reason."

"I know, I was being an idiot." I really didn't want to do this now, I didn't, but I would if I had to.

"No. It wasn't your fault." Her voice was fading into a thin whisper. "The note said you'd be killed if you stayed, so I fixed it. I was horrible until you went away."

I sat straight up into the dark, but Holmes was already asleep.

HAD IT BEEN ANY OTHER DAY IN THE HISTORY OF MY LIFE, and I'd been told something like that, I would have stopped sleeping altogether.

But that night, I was out in the space of ten minutes. It wasn't that I felt particularly brave, or that I'd resigned myself to my violent, rapidly approaching death (though that wasn't a bad plan, really). My body had just proved itself physically incapable of handling more terror. Enough, it decided, and shut the whole thing down.

I woke as the first rays of sun crept into the room. More precisely, I woke to a toddler-shaped eclipse.

"Hi," he said, placing a sticky hand square on my mouth.

I removed it carefully, sitting up. "Hello," I said. "How did you get in here?"

Holmes's bed was rumpled and empty, the door wide open.

"I like ducks." He looked disconcertingly like pictures I'd seen of myself as a child. Guileless eyes, wild dark hair. My mother used to say I could get away with murder, and looking at him, I believed it.

For the record, I'd never resented my half brothers for anything that happened between my father and me. They were little kids, and none of it was their fault.

Besides, he was pretty cute.

"I like ducks too," I said, and scooped him up to take him downstairs with me. Thankfully, I wasn't inexperienced at talking to babies—I had a whole mess of little cousins. "What's your name?"

"Malcolm," he said in a shy voice. "Your name is Jamie."

"That's right." I bounced him a little as we walked into the kitchen.

"It snowed!" he yelled, pointing out the back door at the expanse of white lawn.

I wondered what the wreckage of the sciences building looked like this morning. Our destroyed lab open to the air, all shrouded in white. With a strange pang, I wondered if Holmes's collection of teeth survived.

Abbie turned around from the stove where she was making pancakes. "Oh no, Mal attack! Sorry about that. I wanted to let you sleep in."

I shrugged, juggling Malcolm to my other arm. "It's okay, he was just saying hi. Have you seen Holmes? I need to find her, and kill her."

She gave me a dubious look. "In the family room, with your father and Robbie. He's showing her the cat."

"I didn't know you had a cat," I said, trying to make conversation. I did, in fact, know they had a cat. I was really hoping to get one of those pancakes.

Abbie frowned and didn't offer me one. "It's skittish and hates everyone. Robbie spent the last hour trying to find him for her."

"Come along," I singsonged to Malcolm, "we're going to meet Miss Charlotte, who thinks that keeping Mister Jamie in the dark is a fun, fun game."

In the family room, my father and Holmes were examining a piece of paper they'd laid out on the coffee table. The cat—a handsome tabby—was purring on her lap.

"But it hates me," the small boy at her feet was saying plaintively. "Why does he like *you*?"

She looked down at him, considering. "Because I have a bigger lap for him to sit on. Wait ten or so years, and then he might like you better."

Robbie burst into tears.

"Right," my father said. He took Malcolm from me and grabbed Robbie by the hand, leading him from the room as he sobbed. "Let's see if your mother has finished with those pancakes."

Holmes hardly noticed. She whipped out a tiny magnifying glass and leaned over the paper. "Watson, come here and tell me what you can make of this."

"Is it going to explain why you kept direct communications from our stalker a secret from me, choosing instead to inflict some serious psychic damage with the end goal of getting me to leave you to deal with a bomb all by yourself?"

"Yes." She didn't even look up. "Come here."

She'd squared the note in the middle of the table. As I approached, I saw that she'd laid a sandwich bag between it and the wood.

Holmes handed me a pair of latex gloves. "They were in your stepmother's first-aid kit," she said by way of explanation. "Go on. What do you see?"

I read it aloud.

IF YOU KEEP DRAGGING JAMES WATSON
INTO THIS HE WILL DIE TO
TONIGHT
HE DOESN'T DESERVE IT THE WAY YOU DO
THIS WON'T STOP UNTIL YOU HAVE
LEARNT YOUR LESSON

"A grammar error," I said. " 'To,' instead of 'too.' Spellcheck wouldn't catch that. And learned is spelled the English way. 'Learnt.'"

She gestured impatiently. "What else?"

"Well, it's a death threat. Though they seem to like me more than they like you." Gingerly, I lifted the note by its corner. It was square, cut from regular printer paper, thin to the touch. There was a crease down the middle, probably from where Holmes had put it in her pocket. The ink was black. I held it up to the light, but I couldn't see anything special about the rest of it.

I told her my observations, and she nodded, pleased. Maybe I wasn't so useless after all.

"What did you come up with?" I asked her.

"All the things you didn't," she said, and took the page from me. "Our letter-writer is most likely a woman, and she's writing it on her own behalf. Look, she's used one of those specialty sans-serif fonts, the kind that doesn't come standard. You'd have to download it, and you wouldn't put in that sort of effort if you were someone's lackey—you'd just use Times New Roman, whatever the default was. And that would be the smarter move, too. Either she's so up herself she feels she doesn't need to cover her tracks, or she wrote this in an absolute hurry and that was the default font."

I took it back and squinted at the font. "It doesn't look all that weird to me."

Holmes sighed. The cat on her lap turned its baleful eyes

toward me. Apparently she'd found her spirit animal.

I scrubbed at my face. I needed coffee. Or a sedative. "But how do you know it's a woman?"

She snatched the page back. "All it took was a few minutes' research for me to find the origin of this font—it's called Hot Chocolate, how twee—along with a few hundred others on one of those design sites. Well and fine, but that was the ninth hit on Google. The *first* was a website that catered to 'sorority life,' and I found our Hot Chocolate on the page about creating invitations for parties."

"So she's a sorority girl," I said.

"She's someone who looks at sorority websites," Holmes corrected me. "But that was only one search term. After working out the algorithms, I tried one hundred and thirty-nine others, beginning, of course, with the most common syntactical search strings and moving, systematically, to the least likely"—here, my eyes began to glaze—"but each time, this website came up first. I doubt that anyone who makes a typo on their death threat looks past the first Google hit. And this website was absolutely covered in glitter."

"How did the note arrive?"

"It was slipped under my door yesterday morning, like so." She folded it back in half. "Look at that crease. It wasn't just casually folded. That was done with a blunt object and a considerable amount of pressure—you can tell from the dimpling at the seam. Someone was upset when they wrote this and took it out on the paper."

Obviously. It was a death threat. The horrible weight of

what Holmes had done yesterday fell back on my shoulders. "So after you received it, you chased me out, and then . . . waited for someone to come by and kill you?"

She regarded me evenly. "It seemed a good chance to meet them, didn't it? But I expected them to come by with a gun. Bombs are a coward's weapon."

"And if you hadn't been in the bathroom on the other side of the building, you would have *died*." I bit down on a knuckle, reining in my flare of temper.

"I know. That's why I made you leave." She popped the note back into the bag. "I'll have your father give this to Detective Shepard, I'm sure he'll want it now that we're finished. You did very well. You just missed one thing."

"What?"

Leaning over, she held the unsealed bag under my nose. "What does that smell like to you?"

Forever Ever Cotton Candy. I coughed, waving a hand in front of my face. "Didn't you say you could only get that off Japanese eBay?"

"Yes."

"So where the hell did you even find out about it?"

"August Moriarty gave me my first bottle for Christmas," she said. "I'd mentioned that I liked cotton candy in passing, and he'd hunted high and low for a perfume that scent. It had only been manufactured in Japan, he told me, and discontinued in the eighties." Her eyes went faraway. "I wore it for a few weeks, even though it's heinous, because . . . well, no matter. It did prove to be useful, in the end."

I stared at her. Mom jeans and an oversized sweater—borrowed from Abbie, I could deduce that much—and her face assiduously clean. The sun dappled her hair. I had no idea what she was thinking.

"Holmes," I said slowly, "how is this not a warning from August Moriarty?"

"It's not. It's a woman's work, Watson, clearly."

"So . . ."

"Nurse Bryony," Holmes said, as if it was obvious. "Do you really think Phillipa is likely to be visiting a Delta Delta Delta website? More so than the woman who spent all of homecoming requesting old R. Kelly songs and telling me about her sorority formal? The profile is an excellent fit."

"But the perfume points right back to August."

"She most likely wears it too." Holmes shrugged. "Stranger things have happened."

"Have you smelled it on her?"

"People don't wear the same perfume every day, Watson. I'm sure I'll find a bottle in Bryony's flat. It's in Sherringford Town, and we can search through it while she's away."

"Holmes. How does this explain anything about the dealer? Or the forger's notebook? Or the guy in the morgue?"

"Do you not trust me to have this worked out?" she said. "Because I do. They employed one agent, and that agent failed. So they hired another. There. It's sorted."

"Holmes—"

"Earlier, when I spoke to Detective Shepard, I asked him to bring Bryony in for questioning tomorrow at ten a.m. We'll toss her flat then." She gave me a sympathetic look. "I know the feeling. I'm always disappointed at the end of a case. But we'll find another."

I was beginning to believe it, now, what she'd said about the dangers of caring too much. How emotions only got in the way. It sounded to me exactly as though Holmes was ignoring some obvious conclusions in favor of devising any theory that let August Moriarty off the hook. How hard would it be for him to plant a typo, or to use a special font, to write this note the way a woman would? He knew what Holmes would look for, how she'd interpret it: he could feed her exactly what she wanted to see.

The worst part? She'd kept on buying that perfume he'd given her. Even though it was expensive. Even though she hated it. It was foreign, and hard to find, and that letter was doused in it.

I knew what I had to do.

"It's a good plan," I told her. It would be one, too, if there was any chance Bryony Downs was guilty. "But look, I still feel really awful from yesterday—I didn't sleep much, thanks to your sense of timing, ha—and the pancakes smell amazing, but you know, Malcolm got me up so early—I think I need to—"

"Are you all right?" she asked. I was beginning to sweat.

"I feel terrible." The truth. "I need to go lie down." Also the truth.

"Go," she said, waving me away. "I'll wait for the detective. And maybe I'll go through the note with your father again. He can't follow my reasoning."

I ran into my father at the foot of the stairs. "Can I see that file?" I asked him in a whisper.

He looked at me sadly. "In my study, upstairs. In the second drawer." He had a kind face, my father. I'd remembered a lot of things about him when we moved to England: his dorky enthusiasms and plaid ties, the stupid nicknames he had for Shelby, the way my mother used to shout at him as he slumped at the kitchen table, head buried in his hands. But I'd forgotten how kind he was. How much he'd always trusted me.

"I'll give you some space," he said, and after I found his study, I locked the door behind me.

nine

I PUT THE FILE ON THE DESK.

My father had clipped things from newspapers, printed articles off the internet. It went chronologically: the oldest information was at the front. I resisted the urge to flip to the back.

No. I'd ease myself into it. Into betraying my best friend.

It started with the usual sorts of things. Sherlockian societies and book clubs. Fan sites for my great-great-great-grandfather's stories, but far more for the film and television adaptations. Flipping through the pages, I found printouts from some of the fan sites that tracked the movements of the Holmes clan. They were intensely secretive, Holmes's family, and so gathering kernels of information had become something of a sport for the greater world.

I folded out a taped-together family tree, one in my father's own handwriting. Watsons, always the record-keepers. At the top, he'd placed Sherlock. Then came Henry, the son he'd had so late in life, categorically refusing to name the mother. I traced through Henry's sons down to Holmes's father, Alistair, and his siblings: Leander, Araminta, and Julian. A small line connected Alistair to Emma, Holmes's mother; below that was a fork each for Milo and Charlotte Holmes.

I browsed through the articles about Holmes's first case, when she tracked down the Jameson diamonds. In a photograph with her parents at the Met's press conference, she stood pale and solemn-faced between her parents. On one side stood her father, looking at the camera with hooded eyes. Her mother had blond hair and a dark-red smile, one possessive hand on her daughter's shoulder.

Enough of what I already knew. I flipped through to the last page and worked backward. Information on Leander Holmes's charity. The page before it was a clipping from a Yard fund-raiser. And the one before that, like a lump of pyrite nestled into all that gold, was from the *Daily Mail*.

It was a single paragraph, down at the very end of a long stream of gossip, squeezed between a bit on the Royal Family and another about Shelby's favorite band:

> *Remember how the oh-so-secretive Holmeses made a big splash last year inviting boy-genius heartthrob (and DPhil student)* **August Moriarty, 20**, *to be a live-in tutor for*

*their daughter **Charlotte, 14**? The two families have had bad blood between them for more than a hundred years now, and daddy **Alistair** wanted to make a very public peace offering. Well, it looks like things at Casa Holmes took a turn this past week. **August** was escorted out by the police, and not for diddling with the children! Our source tells us that he got caught feeding **Charlotte's** dirty little drugs habit. Oxford's already expelled him, the Moriarty family's disowned him: what's next for the former future professor? As for Miss Charlotte Honoria Holmes, we hear it's boarding school or bust.*

So her middle name was Honoria.

I had to read it again. A third time. A fourth. And then I made myself read between the lines. Was I feeling *bad* for August Moriarty? Was that what this was? Anyone else would look at the age disparity there and think, *Oh, that asshole took advantage of an innocent young girl,* but Charlotte Holmes wasn't innocent. She was imperious, and demanding, with a self-destructive streak that ran as wide as the Atlantic. I thought about the way she'd run roughshod over Detective Shepard when she'd wanted in on this case. About how she'd convinced me of my own worthlessness when she'd wanted to be alone with her homemade bomb. Her blackmailing a math tutor into buying her drugs was only a hop, skip, and a jump away.

The worst part? I'd almost known. I'd made an educated guess, that night in the diner, and she'd let me believe it was the whole story—that she was sent to America because of her drug problem. Never mind the Moriarty at the center of it all.

If any of this was true, August would have a million reasons to want to bring Holmes down. I racked my brain to remember what Lena had said that night at poker. If she was right that Holmes was upset about August her freshman year, it was further proof that she did actually have a heart, and a conscience, despite her protests. (Honestly, if I were Holmes, I'd be worried he was living on a street corner somewhere.) Milo had come to visit and said . . . what? That he'd take care of things. But Lena hadn't known *how*, only that Holmes had been happier after Milo left. At the time, I'd thought, oh, drone hit. And now I just wanted to know how much it had set Milo back to pay August off. I hoped August had been given a sizable check, maybe a little house by the sea. A book-lined study where the poor bastard could continue doing his math on his own terms.

It would've been one thing for a Holmes to fall in love with a Moriarty, I thought bitterly. In fact, it'd be sweepingly, crushingly romantic—and on cue, my imagination began to color it in. Charlotte and August, our star-crossed lovers, locked in a constant battle of deductive wills. Missile codes swapped via elaborate games of footsie. Having veal cutlets in the garden while debating whether to annex France. Et cetera, ad nauseam.

The thing was, Charlotte Holmes didn't fall in love.

And even if, somehow, she had (my stomach roiled again), she'd fucked him over in the end. Jesus, Holmes had screwed a *Moriarty*. A whole family of art forgers and philosophers and blue-blooded assassins sitting in their ivory towers, connected to the lowest reaches of the underworld by the gleaming strands of their ambition. Sure, they weren't all bad, but enough of them were, and after this business with August, every last one would have reason to be out for Charlotte's blood.

I tried to yank myself back from the brink. I could be doing that same thing I did in the diner—seeing ninety percent of the story, but missing the ten percent that actually mattered. Maybe I was all wrong. For one thing, the *Daily Mail* wasn't exactly known for their journalistic integrity. And maybe August really had encouraged her habits—maybe she was the innocent one.

Then why was he trying to kill her?

Well, I thought, as long as I was being awful, I might as well go ahead and be petty with it. I opened my father's computer and, half-covering my eyes, put Moriarty's name into an image search. He was a dork, I told myself, a math nerd; he probably had gelled hair and an overbite.

The page loaded slowly. The pictures came up, one by one.

He looked like a Disney prince.

I shut the laptop hard.

FOR ANOTHER HOUR I SAT THERE, PARALYZED IN MY DELIB-erations. When I finally reached a decision, I didn't feel any better. I spent an hour on Google, trying to dig up what I needed—but as I suspected, it was nowhere to be found.

All right, then. This had to get even more personal.

As silently as I could, I unlocked the study door and crept into the hall. All was still. Downstairs, I heard the lonely, spectral sound of Holmes's violin; she was safely occupied. In the guest room, her dirty clothes were gone from the edge of the bed, but her phone was sitting out in plain view.

A few weeks back, she'd decided to give me the passcode—for emergencies, she'd said. Her eyes had glittered as she rattled it off.

"I thought it was supposed to be a random string of numbers," I'd protested. It was a weak protest: I'd been thrilled. Birthday, snow day, Christmas Day thrilled.

Holmes had graced me with her half-second smile. "If someone can get their hands on my mobile, I'm either dead, or close to it. In any case, you're the only other person I'd want to use it. So I thought I should choose a key code you can remember. Surely you can remember this."

I typed it in quickly, hoping it was still the same, hoping it wasn't.

0707. July 7.

My birthday.

With a heavy sigh, I scrolled through her contacts. There were only four of us on the list: home, Lena, me. And Milo.

"One of the most powerful men in the world," she'd told me. And the only person she'd listen to, if she wouldn't listen to me.

I stabbed out the text one letter at a time. *Milo, this is James Watson.*

"I've been solving crimes ever since I was a child. I do it well," she'd said to me. "I take pride in how well I do it. Do you understand?"

Your sister is making a massive mistake, one that might cost her life. I need your family's help.

"They don't believe I can do it anymore."

Come if it's convenient. Even if it's not . . . just get here.

I sent it. Then I deleted any evidence that I'd sent it. It was a futile gesture: God knew it would be a moment's work for Holmes to sniff out my betrayal. I debated trying to make good on my original lie, to get some sleep. But I didn't see how I could. We weren't simply being framed anymore. We were being hunted. If we weren't going to be thrown in jail, August and his accomplice would make sure we'd die instead.

And who was to say he wouldn't make an attempt on our lives while we were here? I froze. How hadn't I thought of that before?

Malcolm and Robbie, I panicked, and dashed down the stairs to find my father.

He was at the front entrance, waving to Abbie and his boys as the minivan backed down the driveway.

"Oh," I said.

"They're going back to her mother's for a few days," he told me, shutting the door. "Charlotte made quite the compelling case for it, and now I feel remiss in not already having sent them away myself." He sighed. "Detective Shepard's in the kitchen, if you'd like to speak to him. Did you find what you needed?"

"Is that Jamie?" Shepard called. "Ask him what the hell Forever Ever Laffy Taffy is."

But Holmes's violin was still crooning. I followed the

sound as if in a dream. There, in the family room. Dressed again in her usual clothes, all the way down to her trim black boots. Against the bright window, she was like a shadow gone abstract, the instrument tucked under her chin. She moved the bow with exquisite slowness. A high note, and then a languorous descent.

She paused, midnote, like some beautiful statue. It wrecked me, watching her.

"Watson?" she asked without turning.

I plodded forward as if I'd been summoned to the judge for sentencing.

"I just spent a good hour telling the detective about the explosion. As if I knew anything he didn't. Oh, and your father said that your assigned time to get your things from the dorm is at ten thirty tomorrow. So I might toss Nurse Bryony's place alone." She held the Strad up to examine its strings and plucked one, listening. "Is that all right?"

"I'd rather go with you," I said, in as normal a tone as I could manage.

She whirled to look at me, her eyes gone dark as a storm. Rapidly, she took in my face, my posture, my bare feet on the carpet, and when she reached her conclusion, she reared back as if I'd struck her.

"You said you wouldn't," she whispered.

"I need to hear it from you," I said. There was no use now in pretending. "What happened between you and August Moriarty?"

"You don't—"

"I do, I need to know."

"Watson, please—"

"Tell me," I insisted. God, I was terrified. I hadn't known that *please* was in her vocabulary. "Just—will you tell me."

Tightly, disbelievingly, she shook her head, like I was a man on the street who'd made the mistake of demanding her wallet and PIN number and ten minutes with her in an alley. Like I hadn't seen the knife she'd been carrying in plain view. In that moment, I invented and discarded a hundred things I could have said to her—platitudes, reassurances, accusations—only to have her walk past me and straight out the front door, the tap of her boots the only sound in the silence.

In the kitchen, Shepard said to my father, "Sororities? Hot cocoa? Um. Can you walk me through it again?"

I DIDN'T TELL MY FATHER OR THE DETECTIVE SHE'D LEFT, FOR the simple reason that I didn't want them to stage a search. She had every reason to want to disappear, I thought, even with our bomber on the loose, but the last thing I wanted was for her to come face-to-face with them right now. Even if I didn't have any doubts about who would win.

It did nothing to stop the sinking feeling in my stomach. Because this wasn't a superhero film (swelling music and inevitable triumph, the enemy at her feet in a tasteful amount of his own blood). This wasn't one of my great-great-great-grandfather's stories (her with hat and cane and pocket watch, dashing out to haul the villain in, me waiting by the fire for the great reveal to be brought safely home). This wasn't even an item on my father's endless list, an anecdote to be summed up in some tasteful, mannered way. I didn't even know how that could be done. *128. When you betray Holmes's trust, _____. 129. When you realize she's cared about someone who isn't you, you selfish bastard, _____. 130. When the direct result of emotions she claims she's incapable of feeling is one dead misogynist creep, one innocent girl choked to almost-death, your every private moment filmed, and Holmes nearly blown up into bloody pieces, _____.*

She'll understand, I told myself after a good hour of stewing. She'll understand why I did it. And, for now, I'll respect her need for distance—I can do that much—and when she's back, I'll apologize, and we can get on with the business of not getting ourselves killed.

That was when I remembered rules 1 and 2.

Search often for opiates and dispose of as needed.

Begin with the hollowed-out heels of Holmes's boots.

Maybe we weren't so divorced from the past as I wanted to believe. I thought, *Oh, I am one stupid son of a bitch,* and I hardly remembered to grab my coat as I flew out the door.

Between our house and the road was a flat expanse of grass, dusted lightly with snow. When I was a child, it had been its own continent, unending. But now it seemed the size of a postage stamp. It was unforgivingly white, and open, and showed no sign of her. How had she managed to move without footprints? All I could pick out were those of rabbit and deer.

We were a half mile from the nearest house, and even farther from any sort of civilization. Still, I tromped out to the middle of the road and shadowed my eyes, looking far in both directions. I saw pavement, flat land, our nearest neighbor's weathervane. I didn't see her.

Well, before I took my father's car to go out looking, I'd rule out the rest of our land. I'd be thorough. Holmes would have been thorough, looking for me.

God knows what I'd say when I found her.

I MADE QUICK WORK OF THE TREES ALONG THE SIDES OF THE house. I spent longer in the shed my father had built to store his tools. The lawnmower was there, and his sawhorses, and though it seemed like there was nothing else, I examined the shed from both the inside and out, looking for unaccounted-for space, a hidden room. I felt every inch of wood with my bandaged hands. Nothing. Still nothing.

I stalked out into the backyard and considered the stretch of open, icy land behind the house, wondering if she'd managed to turn herself the same colors as the landscape, if she was somehow standing right next to me. If she'd erased herself altogether.

Through the back window, I glared at Detective Shepard's bent head. My father was opposite him, trying not to watch me, and failing. I glared at him too.

I'd get in the car, then. I'd scour all the countryside between here and Sherringford, and I'd find her, somehow. After I was sure she hadn't OD'd, I'd let her hate me all she wanted. But my hands, beneath their bandages, were beginning to freeze. I had no intention of getting frostbite twice in two days. *Gloves,*

I thought, climbing the porch steps, *and then the car, and then Holmes—*

Below my feet, I heard snickering.

It was an ugly laugh. A laugh you'd hear from a small boy who'd just plucked the wings from a fly. Still, it was hers, and I jumped off the side of the porch, getting to my hands and knees to peer into the foot of darkness underneath.

In the frozen mud beneath the stairs, Holmes had tucked herself into a small dark ball. Her head was tipped to one languid side, considering me. I knelt there, unmoving. She saw me, it was clear; it was also clear she wasn't processing what she saw. Her bare feet were black with dirt, her hair wild.

She'd hidden herself under the porch the way a beaten dog would.

74. *Whatever happens, remember it is* not your fault *and likely could not have been prevented, no matter your efforts.*

My father, once again, was proving himself an idiot. "Holmes?" I whispered.

"Hello, Watson," she said drowsily. I crawled up next to her, past her socks and shoes all in a pile, past her tucked-up legs. Her eyes flicked over to me, unconcerned. I noticed, with a shock, that her pupils had constricted to tiny black dots. "Hello," she said again, and laughed.

"How much have you taken?" I asked, shaking out her socks and pulling them back over her freezing feet. She didn't resist, but she didn't respond either, even when I put a hand inside one of her boots and came up with an empty plastic bag. "God, have you always kept this stuff with you?"

"Rainy days," she said, shutting her eyes. Her voice wasn't ragged, or hoarse—it wasn't hers at all. "Oh, Watson. Always so disappointed."

"No, stay awake," I said, tapping at her cold face. She batted my hand away halfheartedly. "What have you taken?" I asked.

"Oxy. Slows it all down." She smiled. "Done with coke. Hate coke. Am I disappointing you?"

"No."

"Liar," she said, with sudden venom. "You expect impossible things, and I refuse to deliver. Can't do it. Won't."

"I am not expecting anything from you," I said, "except for you not to freeze to death." Shucking off my coat, I wrapped it around her. "Come on, let's go inside."

"No."

"Holmes, it's freezing, we need to get you into a hot bath." I tugged on her arm. Immediately, she clawed at my injured palm with her nails. I flinched away.

"I said *no*," she said, staring at me with eyes that were all iris and no pupil.

I cradled my hand to my chest, trying to steady my breathing. "How much have you taken?"

"Enough," she said, looking away. She was bored again. "I won't die. Go away."

"I'm not leaving without you."

"Go away. Take your coat, it smells like guilt."

"Actually," I said, "I think I'm fine right here." I couldn't make her go inside. I probably couldn't make her go anywhere with me ever again. What else could I do? After a moment, I tucked myself in beside her, hoping my body heat, at least, would do something to warm her up.

The world slowed to a standstill, as it does when things go so wrong, the bad news closing in like a lowering ceiling. I should have been thinking up a solution. A way out. Deciding if I should grovel for her forgiveness, or if I should tell Detective Shepard that she and I should be pulled from the case. But I didn't. I curled up against her in the cold and listened for her breathing. What were you supposed to do when you were dealing with drugs like this? How long would the effects last? I wished, for the first time, that I'd done something with my years at Highcombe other than read novels and swoon over icy blond princesses who'd never touch anything harder than pot. I could have gained some practical knowledge. She might be dying, I thought, and I had no way to know; the responsible thing would be to call the police, or an ambulance, or at the very least tell my father and let him sort it out.

I didn't. They'd write that on my tombstone, I thought: *Jamie Watson. He didn't.* The snow sifted down through the porch slats, filling in the tracks her knees had made crawling through the mud. I wasn't Catholic, but this had the distinct feel of purgatory: the bitter cold, the unending wait. No idea of what would come after.

After what felt like forever, the back door slid open. I listened to the heavy footfalls over our heads.

"Jamie?" my father called. "Charlotte? Detective Shepard and I are done talking. Jamie?" I held my breath. After a long minute, he swore and trudged back inside.

"Worried," she observed, after we heard the door shut. I stared at the cloud her breath made in the cold. "Good that he worries. I don't. You're nothing to me."

"Liar," I echoed. I tried to put the force of my affection behind it.

"You did once," said Holmes. "Mean something to me. You don't now."

She began to shiver. Was that a good sign? A bad one? Either way I couldn't stand it. Carefully, I pulled her into my arms, and to my great surprise she let me, curling up against my chest as pliantly as if she were my girlfriend. As if I'd held her before. As if I held her every day.

Somehow that scared me far more than the rest of it. Lee Dobson had found her this way, I thought, and my arms tensed, instinctively. Dobson had—

"Stop thinking about him," she said. "It's not yours to think about."

"What am I allowed to think about?" I asked wearily. If I had a rope, this was its end.

"Let's talk about the things you think you know." That horrible snicker. "Let's disappoint Watson some more."

"No," I said, "you don't—"

"August was my maths tutor. Did you know that? You did. Can tell by how your hands seized."

I'd thought I wanted to hear this. But I didn't. I really, really didn't. "You don't have to—"

"It was my parents' idea. For publicity. Had some bad press, and they wanted to change the story in the media. Forgiving Holmeses. Fucking liars. I hated him at first. But after Milo moved to Germany, I got used to him. It was like having an older brother again. And then it wasn't. It was something else."

"What?" I asked, into the silence.

"I loved him. And he wouldn't have me." The words came sharp and hard, sudden in their ferocity. "He was too old, he said, and even if we waited, it would be a catastrophic mess. Our families, you know. He said that I'd grow out of it. My 'crush.' Him saying that was worse than him rejecting me."

I couldn't quite breathe, hearing her speak this way, as if reciting her sins. When she spoke again, she was horribly precise.

"I wanted to punish him. To make him feel what I was feeling. So I got him to use his family connections to buy me cocaine. I knew he'd do it. I'd been taking so much, and he was so scared that, without it, I'd go through withdrawal." She drew a breath. "I wanted to make him hurt me, and then I wanted him to pay for it. The night his brother Lucien drove up with a boot full of coke, I called the police. Lucien ran, and August stayed to take the blame, as I suspected he would. After all, he felt responsible.

"My mother fired him. Then she phoned his don at Oxford to have him expelled. And after all of that was over, she sat me down in the drawing room. She'd drawn all the curtains. And she explained to me, very patiently, that this was a lesson. It wasn't to happen again."

"The drugs?" I asked quietly.

"The drugs." She laughed. "No. I'd started with 'the drugs' at twelve. I was too soft on the inside, you see. No exoskeleton. I felt everything, and still everything bored me. I was like . . . like a radio playing five stations at once, all of them static. At first, the coke made me feel bigger. More together. Like I was one person, at last. And then it stopped working, and I began taking more, and more, and they sent me to rehab. When I came back, I spent a few months going the classical route—morphine, syringes. It made everything quiet and far away. I was wrong inside, you see. I'd always been wrong. But it was too messy, the morphine, and I was found out—more rehab. So I dropped the morphine for oxy. More rehab. Then more oxy. I've never quite managed to shake it, any of it, and my parents stopped expecting me to. It doesn't scare them anymore."

The whole time she spoke, she didn't look up at me once. She was curled up in my arms like she was my girlfriend, but she was talking to me like I was an empty shell.

"What my mother was afraid of was sentiment," she said. "Of my being sentimental. With my particular skill set, it's a liability. With what I felt for August, I became . . . a worse person. I was sent away to think on what I'd done. It was never about keeping me from the drugs. It was about keeping me away from myself."

"Jesus, Holmes, that's horrible." What kind of monster would demand that her daughter not feel?

"Is it really? I think my mother was right. I don't trust myself anymore. No one does." She lifted her head to study me. She'd gone so pale that the veins on her neck stood out like pen marks. "Not even you."

It was awful to see her like this. "Holmes—"

"You thought *I killed him*. And it's almost true. He lost his life because of me. He got a job, finally. Works for my brother in Germany doing data entry. What a waste. But he's forgiven me. He's a sentimental fool. August even demanded his family leave me alone. I was disturbed, he told them, and no good would come of it. They listened. It was their last favor to him. You see, his family disowned him for taking my fall."

"You aren't disturbed," I said, trying to mean it, to make her feel better. "You aren't disturbed at all. You just made a mistake."

"I don't make mistakes," she said, and pulled away from me. "I know exactly what I'm doing."

"Even if you did. You were still forgiven. They *forgave* you. And accepting their forgiveness isn't a sign of weakness." I was desperate to pull her back to me, back out from where she'd gone, deep inside herself. I'd never wanted this. Never. "I wouldn't have thought any different of you, if you'd told me."

"You wouldn't have?" she asked, the last vestiges of the haze gone from her voice. "How interesting."

"Unfair."

"You keep using that word like it has any real-life implications."

"It does," I insisted.

"Fairness, Watson, would see August Moriarty restored to school and family and his fiancée—he really could have told me about her when I first confessed it to him, I wasn't about to stalk and kill her—but no. He's alone, in a foreign country, and friendless. Really, the parallels are striking."

"You're being melodramatic," I said, and her eyes flashed. Good. Any reaction was better than none. "I'm sitting right here, being your *friend*, and I'm not going anywhere."

"I'd be fine if you did," she snapped.

"I don't doubt that. But I'm still not going anywhere, and because I'm not leaving, I need you to listen to me." I took a breath. "I'm sorry for what happened to you. I am. It's awful, and the fallout from it was . . . unreal. And I'm sorry I broke your trust. I never wanted to hurt you. But I only did it because I was desperate. Don't you think that your trust in him and his family might be a touch unfounded? Like, have you had Milo look into their activities? Has August been in Germany all this time, or has he made any trips to America—"

"He *isn't responsible*," she snarled. "I've told you that from the start. He may hate me—he should hate me—but he isn't a killer. And if you can't believe that—Watson, I will not work with someone who refuses to trust me."

"But you refused to trust me in the first place," I said. "Why didn't you just tell me the truth? I know you have personal stakes in the matter, but so do I!"

"What stake could you possibly have in this?" She was inches from my face now. How could she not understand?

"Your life. Your *life*, and mine. Are they really worth you being right in this?"

"I would never let you die," she said, her breath coming fast and shallow.

"But what about you? What's going to happen to you?" I could hear my voice breaking as I pictured it. Her on the concrete, the blood a halo around her dark hair. Her under a slab of granite in her lab. On a slab in the morgue. In a bath of shattered glass, or poisoned in the night. Her curled up under the goddamn porch to die, her stone-blank eyes staring up at me, Jesus . . . it could happen to either of us, but if my being there meant she had any more of a chance of staying alive, then I would be there. Full stop. I was saying it to her out loud, now, pleading. "I know you don't need me, any fool could see that, but we are in this together. I will be here, right here, until it's over. You . . . you're the most important thing to me, and I can't imagine being without you, but if the moment it's over, you want to send me away, I will, I'll go—"

"You should." It tumbled out of her in a rush. "You don't see it—that I'm not a good person. That I spend every minute of every day trying not to be the person I know I *could* be, if I let myself slip. And I'll bring you down with me. I have. Look at us. Look at where we are."

"That's impossible."

"Is it?" she asked dully. I was losing her again. "Are you blind?"

"You can't be a bad person," I told her, "because you're a robot, remember?"

It really was the lamest, most halfhearted joke I think I'd ever made. But there wasn't anything else that I could say. I'd betrayed her trust; she'd kept things from me I'd needed to know. She'd endangered our lives; I'd endangered our friendship. I had no idea what was next. All I wanted was for her to look at me the way she used to, with that wry half-twist of her mouth, and make some deduction about the sandwich I'd had for lunch.

I realized then that Holmes was laughing.

I looked at her askance, in case she was also bleeding from the head. But there it was: her low chuckle, a hand thrown up to hide it. When our eyes met, there was a kind of confused electricity there, like we'd broken up and simultaneously exchanged vows. It brought back that hallucinatory fear I'd had that night in the infirmary, that Nurse Bryony would just as soon kiss me as smother me with a pillow. I didn't understand girls at all.

Bryony.

Bryony.

"Holmes," I said urgently, "what did you say August's fiancée's name was?"

"I didn't." Her eyes went vague. "I didn't know her at all, only that they were engaged, and that he left her in the wake of . . . Jesus *Christ*, Watson," and she shoved past me in her haste to get out from under the porch.

"Where are you going?" I called.

"Milo," she replied. I snatched up her shoes and crawled out after her. The two of us together burst through the door, covered in clumps of mud, shivering from the cold—we must've looked like we'd come up from some arctic hell. In a way, I guessed we had.

My father was standing with his arms crossed in the

middle of the kitchen. "Jamie," he said, a warning in his voice, as the detective stood up from the table. We pushed past them and ran straight up the stairs. "Where the hell did you two go?" he yelled at our backs.

"Five minutes," I said, spinning around, "just give us five more minutes."

In the guest room, Holmes practically fell on her phone. "Milo," she said into it, and I froze. The text I'd sent. If he ratted me out, this could get ugly all over again. "Where are you? A tarmac? I'm only catching every other word." Her voice went dangerous. "You're coming to New York. Tell me why. No, that's a lie. That is too. Fine, tell me the last time you left your apartment. Before this. No, don't give me that, you were the one who had them *put it in your office building.* Yes—no, I'm not on drugs. No. Yes, fine, I am, don't hang up. Of course I want to see you while you're here, you ass."

He was coming. He was coming, and he wasn't going to tell her that I'd asked him to. I said a silent prayer to the saint of deranged best friends' deranged older brothers.

Holmes paced, tracking bits of frozen mud into the carpet. "No, don't hang up, I have a question." She paused. "What was August's fiancée's name? I don't care. It's important—no, it's not what you think—no I'm not—did you just call me a cow, you whale? Milo—*damn it.*"

She whipped around to face me. "He hung up. The idiot thinks I want her name so I can find her and kill her."

"There's some deep irony there," I said, smiling.

Startled, she smiled back. Just for a second. And then her

phone chirped with a message. I peered over her shoulder.

Bryony Davis. Don't eat her. See you soon.

Bryony Downs. Bryony Davis. She'd barely covered her tracks.

Holmes and I stared at each other. My heart was pounding.

Shepard opened the bedroom door. "So?" he said, his brows knit. "I've examined the note. I've spoken to your father. And I appreciate your passing along Bryony Downs to me for a more, ah, official interrogation. But what is all this"—he gestured to Holmes's muddy pants and my damp hair—"about, exactly? Something I should know?"

She threw me a glance. I caught it.

"Um, well, we're dating now," she said, a hand creeping up to touch her hair. "We just made it official, and—oh God, Jamie, this is kind of embarrassing."

I tugged her hand down into mine. "It's not embarrassing," I said. "I mean, it's been such a long time coming. But I guess I was, um, blind to my own feelings."

Holmes beamed at me, and I pulled her to me, tucking her under my arm. The detective made a small, involuntary noise, like he was choking.

"We were outside in the snow—well, okay, I ran out there because I got mad because I thought he didn't like me, but it turned out he *did* like me, he was just shy, so he ran out there to find me, and—" She smiled at him, and it was strange to see how fatigue made that fake expression real. "I mean, do you want to hear what he said? It was so romantic."

Shepard put up his hands. "I have so much to do," he said,

backing out into the hallway. "You know how it is. All back at the station. Where I should go."

"We'll talk more later," Holmes assured him, with what I could tell were the frayed ends of her composure.

He smiled tightly. "Right. Yes," he said, shutting the door, and from the hall, we heard him mutter, "God, I hate teenagers."

THE NEXT MORNING WAS FOREVER IN COMING, AND STILL, when it finally arrived, I wasn't ready. How could I have been? We didn't have a plan. Or if we did, I wasn't in on it.

To top it all off, I was exhausted. I'd spent the night before taking care of Holmes while she came down. It'd happened right after Shepard left, her falling on the bed like her strings had been cut. She'd insisted she didn't want anything—no surprise there—but I'd forced water on her, and crackers one at a time from a package my father had left outside the door. It was just the two of us, silent, in that dark little floral-sheeted island. She stared at the ceiling fan, her arm thrown over her face. She didn't say a word until I stood to go tell my father what we'd figured out about the school nurse.

"No," Holmes said, grabbing my arm without looking at me. "Stay here."

"You've solved it," I told her. "You don't need to haul her in. Let the police do that."

"I still have more work to do. I need to figure out what part she plays in this. How the Moriartys have been using her." She held on tighter. "This isn't some jewel robbery. This is the woman who's killed one person and tried to kill another. Not to mention trying to ruin our lives, if not end those too. So yes, I will bloody well haul her in."

I should have pressed my case. I should have insisted. But I was exhausted, and she was exhausted, and so I didn't try.

Jamie Watson. He didn't.

I sat back down on the floor and put my head against the mattress. The hours passed that way, day slipping into night, until I fell asleep kneeling by her bedside like a pilgrim before some entombed saint.

There wasn't the barest hint of sun coming through the window when Holmes shook me awake, hustled me into my clothes and down to my father's car. I hadn't spoken a word. "Tea," she said, pressing a mug into my hands from the passenger seat. "Now drive, before anyone realizes we've gone."

As I blearily gripped the steering wheel, reminding myself that I needed to be on the right side of the road, not the left, that this wasn't England, Holmes kept up a low unending monologue, sorting the last few months through this lens of Bryony's guilt. Well. Probable guilt. If it turned out that an entirely different English Bryony was our school nurse, I'd be the first to pack it in and just go home.

"She's only gotten more desperate as she's gone along. She's dropped the conceit of hanging us with our own history, which, personally speaking, was the only part of her campaign that I found at all *interesting*. Come on. Explosions, really"—at this point I was parking the car—"there is nothing interesting about explosions. She ruined a perfectly good lab that I had painstakingly assembled, bit by bit, from things I'd taken from Mr. Lamarr's biology room—oh, don't look at me like that, I've seen you toast marshmallows on those burners, you're just as guilty as I am—and really the only thing I'll miss were my copies of your great-great-great-grandfather's stories. Categorically worthless." She led me down Sherringford's main drag to the side street that held Bryony's flat. "Honestly, I think they're being given away for free on Kindle, but I did love them. And she has footage of you *naked*, most likely, which I can't even begin to unravel the child pornography laws on that one—"

I was having trouble understanding Holmes's relentlessly chipper mood. We'd spent the day before in hell. And, okay, we were about to engage in a little breaking and entering (which, honestly, I was pretty excited for too), but we hadn't even acknowledged anything that had happened the day before. No apologies, on either side. No real conclusion to the fight. No acknowledgment of whatever it was that had passed between us under the porch. And here she was, arm tucked in my elbow like the day—it felt like years ago—I first introduced her to my father.

I turned to say something, I don't know what, and I saw her face. Relief. She was relieved. Somewhere, deep, deep down, she had suspected August Moriarty; she'd been too well trained to ignore it. And now she had good reason to pull her focus away from him and put his fiancée in her crosshairs instead.

I quickly debated with myself how I should react to this realization—jealousy? disapproval?—and decided I was tired of feeling like shit. I might as well cheer up too. Maybe she'd let me pick the lock.

"Holmes," I said. We were standing on the corner of Market and Greene, peering down the block at Bryony's flat above the flower store. It was all very picturesque, with its painted window boxes and iron scrollwork. It didn't look like the flat of someone who had killed a boy in cold blood. "Were you going to tell me why we're here so early? Her interview at the station isn't until ten, and it's just eight now."

"Bryony will be out the door by eight thirty, hair all done, looking like a starlet. She'll stop by the Starbucks outside town. She'll maybe go shopping. She thinks this is a routine set of questions, not an all-day event. Anyone who uses a vanity font on a death threat is far too confident to think they're under suspicion." She was almost bouncing on her heels. "I got into the police database this morning and got the make and model of her car. Registered to Bryony Downs, one black 2009 Toyota RAV4, license 223 APK. Or, that car right there." It was parked on the street outside her flat. "In the meantime, we are going to sit very inconspicuously in the café here until she leaves, and if all goes well, we'll have you to your ten-thirty appointment to collect your things, because those jeans are beginning to smell a bit ripe."

I wasn't sure I could survive cheerful Holmes any more than I could her junkie alter ego. All the same, I let her drag me by the arm into the café, where she set us up with two teas by the window.

It all happened as she'd predicted. Bryony emerged, in

red lipstick and sunglasses like an old movie star. Holmes told me not to be so obvious, but I couldn't help but stare at her as she drove past—that shining blond hair, the way she was singing along to the radio. I almost could have believed she wasn't guilty, then, because it was clear the consequences of her actions hadn't made the slightest impression. She'd put an innocent girl in the hospital. She'd taken Dobson's life. Even someone as disgusting as Dobson deserved the chance to grow up and become a better person. Bryony Downs should be lying on her bathroom floor, racked with guilt, and instead she'd decided she was the star of her own romantic comedy.

Holmes held us back another ten minutes. "Patience is a virtue, Watson," she said. "Besides, she might have forgotten something."

When the coast remained clear, it only took us moments to get to the front door, leading up to both Bryony's flat and the one above it. It was unlocked. As we crept up the steps, I said a quiet *thank you* for not having to pick her locked door right there on the street. When we reached it (#2, like the mailbox by her door, printed BRYONY DOWNS) I went down on one knee to inspect the lock. "It's a Yale," I said casually, "like the ones I practiced on with you. Do you think I could—"

With a disgusted sound, Holmes turned the knob.

"I see that you're still scratching your locks," she said to the man sitting there.

ten

I DIDN'T UNDERSTAND WHAT I WAS LOOKING AT.

The room in front of us was almost empty. As in, no tables, no sofas, no rugs, nails where pictures used to hang—empty. From where I stood, I had the clear view through a doorway to where two dark-suited men with Bluetooth earpieces were methodically sorting through boxes of breakfast cereal. One at a time, they opened them, dumped their contents in a bowl, and then tossed it all into a garbage bag. One of them actually whistled while he worked.

It was distinctly possible that I had dreamed myself into a surrealist film, or that Holmes was pulling some elaborate prank. I might have even believed it, too, if it wasn't for the man sitting in front of us.

He, or one of his minions, had dragged a velvet tufted chair into the center of the bare room. But he wasn't sitting on it the way you'd have expected. He didn't cross his legs, or lean lazily into the wing of the chair, stretching out one arm to check the time on his admittedly very nice watch. Those poses wouldn't have worked on him, anyway: the man was too much of a nerd. A handsome nerd, a very sleek, well-dressed nerd, but a nerd nonetheless. Instead, he sat at the edge of his ridiculous chair, tidily smoking a cigarette.

I sized him up: that was what he clearly wanted, presenting himself in the empty room like an art exhibit. Buddy Holly glasses, a sixties ad-man haircut—a hard side part, tapered at the sides—and from what I could tell, his suit was straight off Savile Row, where James Bond would get fitted for a bespoke jacket, if he were real. Holmes had said he was pudgy, but what I saw instead was a sort of softness from hours spent in front of a computer screen.

None of this would have been all that remarkable on its own. But written invisibly all over him, like white ink on white paper, was power. Electric power. The kind that snapped its fingers and brought a government to its knees. What had Holmes said? MI5? Google? Private security? How much of that was true? Drones, I thought uneasily. He controlled drones.

And I was the genius that had brought him here.

"Where are Nurse Bryony's things?" I asked, trying to sound like I knew the answer already and was just asking to confirm.

Milo Holmes ignored me. "I don't scratch locks," he said in

a sonorous voice, smooth where his sister's was rough. "That was my man Peterson. Wanted to have a go, and I thought there wasn't any harm. We weren't in a rush."

He'd had all of ten minutes to clean out the living room. I hadn't even seen him go in the door. No rush. Right.

"You're very kind, sir," one of the men said from the back, and resumed whistling. They were cracking open Bryony's eggs now.

Holmes crossed her arms. "You do scratch. Every time. I do a very pretty one, as you well know. You should've waited for us."

He drew on his cigarette. "You look better than I was expecting. My sources led me to believe that it was very bad, this time."

I swallowed.

"Yes, well, it's much less razor blades and three a.m. phone calls now, isn't it, and much more saving my own neck from the noose." It was easy for me to imagine them as children: Milo, inexorable as a tank, and Holmes, the dervish circling him. She was so restrained, most of the time, but when she wasn't . . . well. Then, she said things like, "Tell me right now what you have done with my evidence or I will tell Mother about you spying on our fencing instructor in the shower."

"You won't. And you know very well what I've done with your evidence."

Holmes cast one hateful look around the room. "New York? Honestly? And you've missed all the important parts. I was handling this. It was handled."

"Handle August Moriarty's ex-fiancée? Lottie, really." (*Lottie*, I thought gleefully, despite myself. *Lottie*.) "You're emotional. You really should have left this to the adults. Now that this idea of Mother's has run its course, let's bring you home. Boarding school? All wrong. We'll put you in the London flat. I'm sure I could convince Professor Demarchelier to tutor you—"

"Milo, he *hates* me, and—"

"No, you aren't thinking. What if they try to throw you in jail? Americans, with their prisons. My men would get you out before that, of course, but such a hassle. You always did like the skiing in Utah. I would want you to be able to come back. I'd want that, for you."

It was becoming abundantly clear why Holmes didn't want her family involved. Emotional? Leaving things to the adults? Sending her away? *Skiing*?

I was an idiot for calling him in. He could go straight to hell.

"I'd like to know what you've done with the evidence," I said. It came out as a growl. "And how you knew to be here, at this flat."

Milo arched an eyebrow. "Is this your bulldog?" he asked Holmes. There wasn't any venom in it, but that didn't make it better.

"This," Holmes said, "is James Watson, my friend and colleague, and you will give him an answer."

I stood up a bit straighter.

"My sister asked me a question yesterday," Milo said. "Do you know the last time that happened? November 2009. Lottie doesn't ask questions. She deduces and decides for herself. That alone would be enough to get me on a plane, particularly when that question has to do with a Moriarty. Thankfully, I was headed to New York already. And as for her things? This—this nurse?" He said *nurse* the way you'd say *gelatinous slug*. "This bank of flats has a very nice little alley behind it, and we sent away her possessions by armored car right as you walked in. My men at Greystone HQ in the city will sort through them, determine the appropriate angle, and return them to your Detective Ben Shepard."

"By the city, he means New York," Holmes said, not taking her eyes off her brother. "And by Greystone, he means the mercenary company currently razing the Middle East. Which he owns—Greystone, that is—and which apparently works as his personal honor guard, if the breakfast knights back there are any indication."

"Glad to be of service," Peterson called. The other one grunted.

"You know, none of this explains the Moriarty agent practicing your handwriting," Milo said conversationally.

"No," Holmes said. "But my ruining August's life does. His fiancée's decided to play avenging angel on his behalf."

"Two separate people out to get you," he mused. "You really are popular. I'm just not sure why you won't come to the obvious conclusion—that the two of them are working together. That this Bryony Downs creature is in August Moriarty's employ."

Holmes set her chin.

"Fine, Lottie," Milo sighed. "We'll focus on the nurse, at least for now."

"How is any of this efficient?" I asked him, changing the subject. "What is this woman going to do when she returns and finds out her things are gone?"

Milo coughed politely to hide his laugh. "We'll have proof enough before her interview with Detective Shepard is over to have him charge her with murder."

"And you know the facts of the case," I said. "You know what you're looking for, in her things."

"Obviously," he said.

"Will you come up with real proof?" I asked. "Or manufacture it?"

Milo spread his hands wordlessly.

"Do you have to ask?" Holmes said to me.

"Well, now that that's settled. Take this," Milo said, handing me his cigarette. "I want to text Uncle Leander the adorable thing you just said about James."

"*Watson*," she and I said together.

"Of course," he said. "Friend and colleague. I love it."

Holmes snatched the phone away.

"So that's it?" I asked, grinding his cigarette out on the floor. "Is this the end? Detective Shepard gets a confession out of Bryony Davis-Downs, and you take her stuff off to be freelance policed, and . . . what, roll credits?"

"It appears so," Holmes said. Already she was beginning to slump into herself, something I identified now with back porches and mud and pain-pill misery.

I put a hand on her shoulder. I couldn't think of anything else to do.

She looked at it, and then up at me. Slowly, the color returned to her face. The corners of her mouth pulled up into a smile, one that stayed.

"Peterson," she called, "won't you tell your colleague there—yes, you, with the Persian cat and the basement flat in Berlin—to call the armored truck and have them turn around. I want everything back in this room just as it was. I suppose you took photographs of the original, or you're a bigger fool than I'd imagined, disrupting the crime scene as you have. Really, why on earth would you have moved it to your head-quarters except to allow this would-be Orson Welles—sorry, Milo, you're not handsome enough to be Olivier—to pose in an empty room? How dull."

I bit my lip against my smile.

"What I could have told you from the dust trails alone would have solved this case," she continued. "As you've utterly ruined that possibility, I want any powders or creams you find brought straight to me. Cosmetics, of course, but do look for jars marked as protein powder. Any wires or tools, anything to suggest a bomb. And I want the receiver for whatever tracker you've affixed to Bryony's car. Give it to me. No. Bring it here." She held out an impatient hand. "I want to make sure that she's actually arriving at her appointment and not, oh, dashing to the airport and then on to Fiji and thereafter, gone. Have I missed anything, Watson?"

As she examined the tracker she'd been handed, I made

a show of surveying the room. "Were you going to tell him about the molted snakeskin under the chair cushion he's sitting on, or should I?"

With an undignified yelp, Milo leapt to his feet.

"Oh, yes," Holmes said blandly. "That. Peterson, do check the walls for a rattlesnake."

THE TWO GREYSTONE GRUNTS BUSILY REARRANGED THE FURniture to Holmes's specifications. Milo watched the proceedings, arms crossed, with a faint air of distaste.

That is, he appeared to, if you didn't look closely. I did. I'd learned to do that much. Whenever Milo's hard gaze fell on his sister, it softened the slightest bit. He could've stopped Peterson and Michaels at any point, ordered Bryony's place stripped bare again, frog-marched Holmes onto the nearest London-bound plane.

He didn't. He stood and watched his sister work.

It seemed safe enough for me to take the few minutes to gather my things from the dorm. Holmes had put me in charge of watching the GPS tracker on Bryony's car, and other than two quick stops for coffee and for gas, she'd driven a straight course to the police station. There wasn't really much else I could do, and honestly, I was looking forward to getting a clean set of my own clothes.

"I'll be back," I told her. She nodded and kept on directing traffic.

The day had turned out to be mild, so I left my father's car parked on the street and walked the half mile up to campus. I was suffused with a sense of well-being, the kind I associated with waking up late on a lazy Sunday, no plans, no obligations. I had no doubts that Holmes would find the necessary evidence to implicate Bryony Downs for every terrible thing that had happened. It was over. Over. And Charlotte Holmes and I were still here.

I let myself daydream about spending Christmas break with her in London. Hopefully Holmes would be at her family's flat there for the month, but if not, I'd jailbreak her from Sussex myself. We'd go get a proper curry, first thing, and then I'd take her to my favorite secondhand bookshop, the one where the owner had asked me to sign my great-great-great-grandfather's books. Maybe she'd want to see a violin program at Royal Albert Hall. And after that, I'd ask her to show me her personal London, the one she'd memorized as a child. We'd see how it had changed and grown in our absence, the way cities do. We'd both have to get to know it again as *our* London.

As I crossed the quad to Michener Hall, I couldn't help but notice how bare Sherringford was. The sciences building was in ruins, still smoking faintly, under the black tarp they'd thrown over the roof. That woman had wanted Holmes dead, I thought with a shiver. It hadn't really hit me until then. Bryony Downs had wanted to end Holmes's life. Thank God we were done with it.

I was a few minutes early, but Tom was already waiting on the steps of our dorm, shivering in his thin jacket. We both looked a little threadbare, I thought: me in my father's coat,

Tom in his raggedy sweater-vest. It was surprisingly good to see him, argyle and all.

"Hey," he said brightly. "Where have you guys been? At your dad's house? And Charlotte's okay? I've been trying to call you but it kept going straight to voicemail."

I told him about the cell phone I'd abandoned on my desk. He'd been evacuated straight from the library, he said, and put on a bus to that Days Inn without anyone telling them what had happened. "We'd heard the explosion," he said. "People were crying. It was awful. But we got filled in eventually. For the first day it was like a church in there. And now it's a total shit show, people climbing the walls. Lots of rumors. Like, what really happened in the science building? Do you have any insider info? No, tell me inside, I want—"

I said a silent *thank you* as the front doors opened, cutting him off. A bored-looking policeman consulted a clipboard. "Thomas Bradford? James Watson? Come with me. The building's secure, but they're having us stay with you as a precaution."

In my haste the other night, I'd forgotten to lock our door or even fully close it. The policeman frowned at me when a slight push threw it open. When he saw what was inside it, his hand went for his gun.

It really did look like a crime scene. The slit mattress and the torn-up curtains and the hollowed-out books. The glint of broken glass over everything. "It's fine, Officer," I said. "I had an accident with the mirror right before we were evacuated."

"Doesn't look fine," he grumbled, but stayed outside.

I turned to Tom to apologize, to explain. He'd be shocked,

I thought. Maybe he'd want to make a statement to Detective Shepard; after all, he'd been recorded too.

All the blood had drained from his face except for two bright spots of color, one on each cheek. His eyes had gone all pupil. He blinked rapidly, staring at the floor.

"Tom?" I said, as gently as I could. I hadn't meant to scare him this badly.

He jerked his head up to look at me. "When did this happen?"

The phrasing caught me off guard. Not *what*, but *when*. "The night we were evacuated," I said cautiously.

"Was it Nurse Bryony?"

I startled, then remembered that I'd told him about my concussion and the infirmary. "I don't know." It seemed the safest answer.

He went a shade paler and nodded to himself, as senselessly fast as a bobblehead doll.

"Five minutes," the policeman called.

"Hey," I said to Tom, "I promise I'll explain later, but can we—"

"Where are they?" he asked in a snarl, shoving me into the door of my closet. His cheerful, bright American face looked like an ugly mask. "Where the fuck are they, Jamie?"

It was like the floor fell open below us.

I shoved him off me and kept him there, an arm's length away. Tears welled up in his eyes as he struggled against my grip.

"What the hell are you talking about?" But I knew exactly what he was talking about. I just wanted to hear him say it.

Admit that he'd bugged our room. Confess that all this time, his friendly gossip mongering was a cover for collecting information for Bryony Downs.

"Oh my God, he's going to *kill* me." Tom stopped fighting me off. He fell back, gasping, throwing his hands up over his face, and I felt a flare of satisfaction.

That faded as quickly as it came. *He?*

The dealer. The Moriarty dealer.

"Two minutes," the policeman said. "Cut the dramatics and finish packing."

"Talk fast," I said, pulling my suitcase out from under the bed and yanking armfuls of clothes from the dresser.

"I never even got anything good," Tom said, as if to himself. "Nothing conclusive. Charlotte even stopped coming to the room. You two were always hunkered down in her fucked-up little dungeon."

"I just— I can't deal with this right now." I grabbed the novels from above my bed and dropped them on top of my clothes, one, two, three, like grenades. Textbooks, soap. I had to get in my closet but Tom was still slouched in front of it.

"Move," I said to him, but he stared up at me stupidly, and the bovine look on him eroded the last of my temper. "I swear to God I will break your neck if you don't move. I might break your neck anyway. You were spying on me, Tom? On top of all the other awful shit happening—you had to make it worse? I never did anything to you."

"He offered to split his advance with me," he said. "He already sold it, you know, he's in the middle of writing it now.

274

It's going to be *huge*, and he's going to have all this money, he'll be famous, he'll finally be able to teach somewhere better than this shithole—his friend Penelope is going to get him a job at Yale—"

I stared at him, at his horrible lying mouth. "Wheatley? You're full of shit. The dealer told you to say that."

Tom went to his desk and, opening the bottom drawer, pulled out a battered legal pad. The top page didn't have any writing on it. Not actual writing, no—someone had painstakingly colored in the indentations made by the words written on the page above. *Skeletons in her office he says starrily as if he's in love with death as much as her.* Lines and lines of florid prose. *He wears the glasses of a Beat philosopher from the 1950s but his face is all Cornwall smooth. When they dance they do not touch.*

They were Mr. Wheatley's notes from our meeting, when he'd so impressed me by interrogating me and then handing over what he'd written down. I remembered the piece of cardboard he'd stuck below the top page. The top *two* pages. I'd thought at the time that he was worried his ink would bleed through, but he had just been making himself a copy.

"He was sure you were guilty," Tom said, almost like he was pleading with me. "Back in October, I was waiting for an appointment with him to talk about my story, and I heard him say it to another teacher inside his office. You. Guilty. And I told him, no, you weren't, and it was actually this great story, you and Charlotte Holmes solving crimes, that you two were totally boning like Bonnie and Clyde, the good-guy version.

He had this idea for a book. True crime. With famous kids as the heroes. The public would eat it up. I'm a good writer, he told me that, better than you, anyway, even if my family's not famous, and I'd do a good job helping, and you'd be happy about it in the end, when you saw how much attention it got you—" He cut himself off.

"So you bugged our room."

"He had me do it. Ordered all the stuff online. The mirror was the worst, replacing it. But yeah, I'd get you to talk and then I'd review the files when you were gone, write everything down, pass it along to him. But—look at this. He's never going to pay me now."

"Why?" I asked him again. I'd thought Tom was my friend. He was one of the only constants in my life, his irrepressible grin and his motor mouth and his ridiculous sweater-vest. We watched stupid videos on his computer at night. We ate each other's candy, borrowed each other's shampoo. He was the first person who was nice to me when I came back to America, miserable and alone.

"I was doing you a favor," he repeated, like he was trying to make himself believe it.

"Time, boys," the officer boomed from the doorway. I slammed the door in his face and bolted it. I was going to get an explanation even if it got me arrested.

"Tell me why."

"Lena's family goes to Paris every summer," Tom said quietly, as the policeman hammered on the door. "She invited me. And she . . . she expects things from me. Dinners out. Presents.

You know her dad's a big oil tycoon out in India. They have a housekeeper. She has her own *plane*. And I'm here, from the Midwest, on scholarship. Do you know what that feels like? He was going to give me ten grand!"

I couldn't wring out an ounce of sympathy for him. "Seriously, what do you think Lena will say when she finds out how you got that money? Jesus Christ, everyone at this fucking school acts like they're so rich and half of them aren't, not even close. When are you going to realize that? What do you think all those people are doing at Holmes's poker game every week, wagering all their money? Here's a solution. Get the hell over yourself. Tell Lena the truth. God, she's actually a decent person, do you think she'd really care?"

"I didn't expect you to understand it. You're a show dog with a pedigree. I'm just someone that escaped from the pound." He shook his head. "It's not like I hurt you or anything. You're my friend. I was doing you a *favor*. It was going to make you famous—"

"Open up the door! Open it up!"

I was disgusted with him, disgusted with Sherringford, with the bullshit and the jealousy and the backstabbing. Furious, I grabbed the handles of my closet doors, ready to throw the rest of the stuff in my suitcase and get the fuck out of Dodge.

Something bit into my skin.

I looked down, stupidly. My hands were so cut up and bandaged that I could hardly tell what had happened. There. A pinprick of blood near the knuckle of my index finger.

I didn't think anything of it. Not until I gripped the handle with the bandaged part of my hand and flung open the door.

Clothes and shoes and the rest of my life's detritus all in a jumble on the closet floor. On the back wall were three giant, jagged lines in marker.

YOU HAVE TWENTY-FOUR HOURS TO LIVE
UNLESS SHE GIVES ME WHAT I WANT
XOXO CULVERTON SMITH

Culverton Smith. The man behind Sherlock Holmes's poisoned ivory box.

I stared back down at my bleeding knuckle. Behind me, Tom raised his iPhone with one shaking hand, and took a picture.

I RIPPED THE INFECTED SPRING FROM THE DOOR HANDLE. Took my phone from the desk (dead), and its charger. Picked up my suitcase. The whole time Tom was loudly pleading his ignorance—*this wasn't me, I wouldn't do something like that*—like the swine he was until I grabbed him by the shirt with one hand.

"This is what you can do for me," I snarled at him. "Deal with the cop."

His eyes were focused on the pinprick of infected blood on his shirt. "But what should I say?"

"Make something up. You're good at that."

As I stalked down the hall, I heard Tom's half-assed babbling. "It's my fault," he was saying to the policeman, "it's my
fault, let him go."

I made it to the front doors before my legs began to give
out under me.

Bryony Downs had won. She'd taken "The Adventure of
the Dying Detective" and turned it back on us with deadly ear-
nest, not knowing that Charlotte Holmes had used that same
story to clear our names. I had no idea what she'd dabbed
that spring with, but my brain was supplying a cavalcade of
answers. Spinal meningitis, I thought, or malaria. I used to
want to be a doctor; I'd wanted to treat the scariest diseases,
and now I couldn't stop running them through my head. Milo
was right. She had to be working with the Moriartys; how else
could she have access to this sort of thing? She was a puppet,
and this was a message directed at the Holmes family.

And the message was going to be my dead body.

I staggered out the front door and down the steps. The
next two students were waiting for the officer to fetch them,
and one of them stepped forward to help me.

"Don't touch me," I said, holding up a hand. "I might be
contagious."

Because that was the worst of it. Nurse Bryony could have
made me into some kind of bomb. A patient zero that could
take out the whole eastern seaboard. I needed to get inside,
away from everyone, and I had to start making a plan. My
parents couldn't know. There was nothing they could do. I
wondered if my father would still find all this crime-solving

fun after he identified my corpse at the morgue.

No. I wasn't going to die. I was sixteen years old. I was going to be a writer; I was going to go to college, get a flat in London, or Edinburgh, or Paris. I'd get to know my stepbrothers. Oh, God, I didn't want my little sister to be an only child. I didn't want to leave Charlotte Holmes with a controlling family and a brilliant mind and a dead best friend. I didn't want to imagine her life without me. Maybe it was selfish to think that way, but I couldn't imagine mine without her.

The sky was open and blue, guileless in its beauty. And the snow everywhere, blinding. The light was beginning to prick at my eyes, and I rubbed at them with the back of my hand. This had to be psychosomatic, I told myself; it had to be in my head. The denial working its hand around me. *I can't possibly be dying,* I thought, and tried to believe it.

One foot, then the other. Where was I going? I'd walked, I remembered, up the hill from town. The distance was impossibly far. I'd sit for a minute, catch my breath. If I could just arrange my suitcase—there.

Holmes told me that, when they found me, I'd passed out in a snowbank.

They bundled me into the back of Milo's town car, her and her brother and his Greystone mercenaries. Blankets. Something hot to drink. Holmes rubbing my chilled hands between hers, strangely smooth and firm. "No," I'd managed to say, "the blood, it's contagious," and then I saw that she was wearing latex gloves.

She knew.

I was racked with chills, and still cold sweat beaded on my forehead before trickling down my face. My mouth burned, my teeth tender to the touch. I couldn't swallow. My throat didn't work. Holmes held a bottle of water to my lips and tipped it, gently, into my mouth. I tried to pull off my shirt, thinking, in my delirium, that it was a straightjacket, and she stilled my hands. All the while Milo watched me from behind his glasses, taking copious notes on his phone. On what, I didn't know. I was a specimen, I thought wildly. I would be experimented on until I died.

When we got to our destination, Peterson had to carry me up the stairs over his shoulder, like he'd rescued me from a burning building. And then there was a bed, with sheets still warm from the dryer, a table beside it. Peterson returned to that table again and again with pill bottles, clean rags. Some-one brought in an IV drip and put it into my arm.

What was real? I didn't know. Milo came in, in a suit and watch chain; he lit a pipe by the window, staring broodingly out over the rooftops. My dog Maggie was there, too, though she'd died when I was six. But she put her shaggy head on my mattress and looked up at me with big wet eyes, telling me in silent words what my sister Shelby was reading that week (*A Wrinkle in Time*), how much my mother missed me. My hands were made of lead; I couldn't ruffle her ears the way I wanted. *Good dog,* I wanted to say. *Where have you been?*

Bryony came in through an invisible door and put her arm around Milo's waist. They talked as if I wasn't there.

"Lead him up to the mountain and put the dagger to his

throat," Milo said in his sonorous voice.

"I thought we were done with goats. I thought we only made offerings of sheep." Still, Bryony smiled into his face. He kissed her like they were in a movie, dipping her back in his arms.

Stop, I yelled, *stop*, but she was at my bedside, with a pillow pressed down over my face to keep the words inside my mouth. And then she was gone, and Milo was, too, and I was alone.

I didn't trust anything that was happening to me—Where was Holmes? For that matter, where was I?—but I was so overwhelmed by a wave of exhaustion that I let myself be carried away by it, all the way to sea.

When I woke—when I fully woke—night had fallen. As my eyes adjusted to the dark, I noticed things I hadn't before. There was a dim lamp by my bed, its mouth turned away to throw a white circle on the wall. Beside me, a machine counted out my pulse, reading it from a plastic clip attached to my index finger. My hands had been re-bandaged, expertly this time. I felt present in my body, in a way I hadn't since I opened that closet door.

There was a bright blanket at the end of my bed, a door across from me. In the shadowed corner was a chair. Empty, I thought, and as I squinted to make sure, I saw the velvet fabric, the tufted buttons.

I was in Bryony Downs's flat.

Frantically, I pulled myself up in bed, yanking the heart monitor off my finger and going to work on the medical tape over the needles on my arm. She'd taken me—she'd taken me somewhere. Had Holmes and her brother been hallucinations, too? The heart monitor screamed a warning, and the door across from me flew open.

By the time she came in, I was on my feet, panting, the desk lamp ripped out of the wall and brandished like a weapon before me.

"Watson," Holmes cried from the doorway. "*Watson*. God, I thought you were dead."

It took some doing, but I let her coax me back into bed. She called a name I didn't recognize, and a man in scrubs came in and put my IV back in. He took my vitals while Holmes hovered behind him, biting her lip. She'd pulled her hair back roughly from her face; her nose was red, her face white. She looked ascetic and harsh. She looked, in fact, like she'd been crying. I started to reach out to touch her but then drew back my hand.

"Right now, we're managing your symptoms," the doctor murmured. "We've given you medication to control the pain, and to bring your fever down. Don't try to get up. If you need to use the bathroom, let us know."

I nodded. Now that the adrenaline rush was over, my legs were trembling from my attempt at self-defense.

"You shouldn't be here, Charlotte," the doctor said. "He could be contagious, and I don't want you touching him—"

Stepping forward, she took my hand in hers.

"So be it," the doctor said, and left.

"Holmes," I asked her, "what did she give me? How did you know?"

She hoisted herself up on my bedside. I remembered the night I'd woken her this way, when she'd fallen asleep as Hailey and woken up, again, as my best friend. We'd had pancakes. She'd asked me to trust her.

"It's a created virus," she said hoarsely. "Brewed in a lab. That doctor—Dr. Warner—is a specialist on this particular strain." She rattled off a series of Latin words I didn't know. "That's what it's called."

"Can you give me something easier to call it?" I asked, half-joking. "The Watson flu?"

She shrugged. "As you'd like. It was created, originally, as a bioweapon, for the rapidity with which it kills its victims. Dr. Warner works for the German government. Luckily for us, he was presenting at a conference in Washington. Milo more or less had him clubbed over the head and brought up here."

"Oh," I said. "So it can be cured?"

Holmes bit her lip again. I'd never seen her so ragged. "We think so," she said carefully. "He has some theories. Right now, he's in the other room, researching."

"The other room. Here, in Bryony's flat."

"It was my idea," she admitted. "God knows she won't be returning here after pulling a stunt like this. And I didn't want to bring you to your house, not contagious like this. So we took this place over, changed the locks; Milo called in some favors, as you can see. We'll bring in a professional cleaning crew, of course, after this is all over. The next tenant doesn't deserve to get the Watson flu in the bargain."

After this is all over. One way or another, it would be over soon. She caught my gaze, and with that magician's trick of hers, I watched her read my mind.

She shook her head quickly, hugging her arms around herself.

"You can't do that," I said quietly. "You can't fall apart yet."

She nodded, her face turned from me.

"Come here," I said, moving over in the bed. "If you really don't mind my being patient zero."

She swallowed her tears. I pulled back the sheet, and she crawled in beside me, putting her head on my chest. I pressed my lips against the dark crown of her hair. It was like those hours under the porch, the stillness, the waiting; and it was nothing like it at all. My muscles ached. My limbs were heavy. My lungs were raw in my chest. I had to brace myself against the bed as another round of shivers ground their way through me.

"How did you know?" I asked, gritting my teeth. "About the virus? About what happened to me?"

"Bryony sent me a list of her demands," she said, her voice muffled in my shirt. "Via text, of course. She had it timed to your appointment at Michener Hall. Must've gotten the schedule from the all-campus email."

"Via text? Holmes, that can be used as evidence against her."

"That's not what we're going to do."

"But—"

"Don't, Watson."

I didn't have the strength to argue with her. "What were her demands? What does she want?"

"A pony," she said.

I smiled against the pain. "The very prettiest pony in the land, on a golden lead. Only then will the favorite sidekick be cured."

"You're not my sidekick," Holmes said softly. "That's her first mistake."

"What am I, then?"

But I didn't know if I wanted to hear the answer. Not now.

She must have heard the reticence in my voice. "A pony," she said, "and three million dollars, and safe passage to Russia, a country which, given my father's history as well as the current state of US-Russo relations, won't extradite her to either Britain or America to stand trial for what she's done. Which would be moot, anyway, because she wants me to claim full responsibility for Dobson's murder and Elizabeth's attack."

"Jesus Christ." I struggled against the idea.

"She's done the thing very completely," Holmes said. There was a touch of admiration in her voice. "I should have known."

"This is not your fault," I told her, before she could go on. "You claiming it's your fault makes it sound like I'm just a piece of cargo getting hauled next to you. No will of my own. So stop it."

"But—"

"I'm dying," I told her, with a grim sort of glee. "You have to listen to me."

She laughed hollowly. "Milo has the money, and he's arranging the airfare as we speak. I've written out my confession. It's done. The exchange will be made at nine o'clock in the morning. She has the antidote. I don't know how—Dr. Warner doesn't know how it's possible—but she does, and even if she's lying, it's still a chance we have to take. We're meeting her twenty-two hours after your infection, so you should still be—ah. It should be fine."

"Where?"

"She'll text us the location when it's time."

"You're not going to jail for this," I said. "Detective Shepard won't let you. Wait, isn't she in his custody? What the hell happened there?"

"Remember when we thought she stopped for gas? She switched cars at the police station. Left her Toyota in the lot and picked up another car that she'd left there." Again, that note of admiration. "We saw her as a stupid sorority girl, and she ran circles around us."

"And where is he now? Detective Shepard?"

"Her terms were no police involvement, no sending you to the hospital. So I don't know. I've been focused on you." I felt her shrug. "That's the other part. You'll die. One way or another, you'll die if I don't take this fall. I think it's a good idea to listen to her, as she's proven herself handy with a suitcase bomb."

The door cracked open, and Milo stuck his glossy head in. If he was surprised to see his sister tucked in my arms, he didn't show it.

"You're awake. How are you feeling?" he asked.

Like I'd been run down by a truck. "Fine," I said.

"Do you want us to contact your parents?"

"Oh God. My father thought—"

"—thinks you are discussing strategy with myself and Lottie until late tonight. This afternoon, Peterson and Michaels returned his car and gave him my reassurances. As we've decided to broker with Nurse Bryony for your cure, you don't have a real reason to worry him. Though I understand how one's parents could be a comfort, in a time like this." He said the last part academically, like it was a theory he'd never personally tested.

"Right," I said, trying to keep my voice even. "No, that's fine, don't contact them."

"Get some sleep," he advised. "We'll handle this."

If I wasn't included in that *we*—and how could I be; I couldn't handle even standing up—at least his sister was. I nodded at him, and he nodded back, and shut the door.

"You're not going to jail," I said again. My mouth felt dry. "There has to be another way."

"I need to be arrested, and convicted. Or she'll find another way to end you. She was very specific on those terms."

"Holmes."

"Watson," she said roughly, "I remember a very recent conversation where you detailed all the horrible possibilities of my death. Do you remember that? Would you like to, for just a moment, imagine what it would be like to watch one come true? Think about what this is like for me."

"The trade-off shouldn't be spending the rest of your life in a cell for a crime you didn't commit!"

"No." She curled my shirt into her fist. "No, but perhaps I

should serve time for the crime I did."

"I can't talk about your martyr complex right now," I said, swallowing against the sand in my throat. "I can't." I reached blindly for the glass of water by the bed and drank it down.

She drew back to look at me. "You're flushed," she said, scrambling to her feet, "I think your fever's returning—I'll fetch Dr. Warner—"

"Wait," I said.

She was rumpled, undone, her hair coming out of its elastic to curl in tendrils around her face. There was something I had to say to her, I thought, something necessary, something right at the tip of my tongue.

I guess she knew it before I did.

Leaning over, she smoothed my hair back from my forehead. I closed my eyes at her touch. And so it was a surprise when she kissed me on the lips.

She smelled, unexpectedly, like roses.

"That's all I can do," she whispered, resting her forehead to mine.

"That's a lot," I said, and she laughed.

"No. I mean, that's all—it's nearly too much for me to touch anyone, after Dobson, and I—for you, I'm trying."

I could feel her breath on my lips. "I don't know how long I'll be like this," she said, slowly, "or if I've maybe been this way all along. I don't know if it'll ever be enough."

It was confusing, what she said, but I thought I understood it.

"You don't have to try," I said to her. "Whatever this is, already—it's already enough."

"I know," she said, straightening. "It has to be."

We looked at each other for a minute.

"If you get yourself thrown in jail over this," I told her, "I will never, never forgive you. You need to find another way, or I swear to God I will die on you just out of spite."

Her flickering smile. "Okay."

"Okay? It's that simple?"

"Okay," she said again. I had no choice but to believe her. "Your pulse is racing, and you're far too warm. I'm going for Dr. Warner." She smirked. "Don't want you to die before you can use it as a bargaining chip."

"Thanks," I said, pleased, at least, that she chalked my hammering heart up to my fever.

eleven

I WAS MUCH, MUCH WORSE IN THE MORNING.

It shouldn't have come as a surprise. Logic dictates that a deteriorating illness deteriorates. But then, logic is hard to come by when you're dying.

Whatever brief reprieve Dr. Warner's drugs had granted me ended around midnight, when I maxed out on the highest morphine dosage he'd allow me. The hours after that were . . . well, I've been assured it's best that I can't remember them.

As morning broke, I moved in and out of fitful dreams, dark, sodden landscapes that were at once cruelly hot and cut through by the bitterest winds. At the same time, I was conscious of something happening in the room around me. A hand on my forehead. A pair of voices, shouting. It all added to my unrest, since, for the life of me, I couldn't make myself understand what was happening. Burma, I thought, I was in Burma. I was in Afghanistan. No, my mother was baking cinnamon rolls in the kitchen, and if I was very good, if I made my bed and put all my toys away, she'd bring them in to me. Holmes was there too, dressed in all black. Someone had died. We were headed to the funeral.

I woke to the barest hint of sunlight through the curtains.

My room was silent. I could tell that much without opening my eyes. The effort I had to put into even that simple task left me dizzy and sweating. When I managed it, I realized that I was alone. Was this another hallucination? It didn't feel like one. There was the bedside table, there the tufted chair.

And I wasn't in any pain.

I turned my head to look at the morphine drip (that took another eternity), but I didn't understand how to read the dosage on the bag. Whatever I was being given, it was working. In place of the pain, there was a sort of bodily rebellion. I asked my legs to swing off the bed. They didn't. I asked my arm to reach out for my water glass. It wouldn't. I panted with the effort, and the panting took effort. I was about as weak as a newborn child.

"No," a woman insisted in the other room. It was a voice I recognized, but from where?

"No," she said again, angrier this time, and then fell silent.

It was Bryony Downs.

The meeting was taking place in the next room.

It was brazen of her to do it here, to walk into the enemy's stronghold and cut a deal in the place where they had every advantage. She really did think herself invincible.

The antidote could be out there, nestled in her pocket.

No. She wouldn't have brought it with her, not where it could be taken from her by force. She'd have hidden it somewhere nearby, only giving its location over when she'd gotten what she wanted. If Holmes gave her what she wanted.

Which meant, of course, that I would die, and in the next two hours.

I struggled, again, to get my legs to obey me. *Move*, I told them, as laughter pealed in the next room. *Move*. The shirt and soft pants I'd been dressed in were already drenched through with sweat. Sweat. Was that a good thing, sweating? Did that mean the nerves and veins inside me—I imagined them now, crackled black and breaking—were still healthy? Was I somehow beating this?

If I was beating this, I'd probably have working legs, I reminded myself. Grinding my teeth, I focused on my knees. *Move*.

And I did. I rolled right off the bed and onto the carpeted floor, bringing the bedside table down with me.

The crash was tremendous, and I lay in the middle of it, in the spilled pills and scattered tissues and the shards of my drinking glass, helpless.

I'd been in denial until that point, I think. But that was when it really hit me. That I was going to die. That they were going to put me in the ground, not years from now, not surrounded by books I'd written in the little flat on the Rue du

Rivoli at age seventy-three, but today. In a matter of hours. I'd kissed Charlotte Holmes once, and I would die before I'd see a second time.

The door flung open with a bang.

"Watson," Holmes said, going down to her knees beside me.

"Bring the boy in here." The voice rang out like a sweet bell. "I'd like to see him."

"Can you move?" Holmes asked, unnaturally loud. She put her hands under my arms. "If I get you to your feet, can you lean on me?"

"Yes," I managed to say, though I had no idea if it was true.

She heaved me up to my knees. "Listen to me," she said in my ear. Her black hair brushed against my cheek. "When I blink twice, you play your last card."

"Okay," I said, because *I don't know what the hell you're talking about* was seven more words than I could force out.

"Milo," she called, "I could use a hand."

Together, the two of them manhandled me out of the bedroom and into the sitting room that, when I'd last seen it, had been empty. Under Holmes's direction, Milo's mercenaries had reassembled it into what it had been, which was something like a preppy brothel. A pink shag rug. Lucite chairs around a Lucite table. A sofa that looked like it'd been stuffed with marshmallows, and a pair of men's trousers hung over its arm. An iPod dock and speakers, a haphazard setup of slides and beakers and a microscope (those must've been Dr. Warner's).

A gilt mirror spanned the whole length of one wall, gathering the entire room in its reflection—Charlotte Holmes, in her trim black clothes, sitting on a fuzzy ottoman that looked like it escaped from *Fraggle Rock*; Milo, so close to his sister that their knees were touching; and me, slumped like a beached whale on one of those clear plastic chairs. If the beached whale had lost fifteen pounds overnight, coated his face in Vaseline and blacked his eyes, and then crawled up onto a beach to end it all.

Looking at me, Bryony Downs curled her lip in disgust.

She'd come in no further than the front door. Her purple puffer coat was unzipped, but she still wore her pom-pomed hat and gloves. With her porcelain doll face, flushed from the cold, she could have been taking a breather from the slopes. Really, everything about her belonged in a catalog for Fair Isle sweaters, or an advertisement for a ski lodge in Aspen. Everything except the fanatical gleam in her eyes.

"Hi, Jamie," she said brightly. "It's good to see you."

If I hadn't been an hour from death, I would've walked right up to her and snapped her neck.

But I was. That was the point.

"Okay, where was I? Before this one's attempt to prematurely kick the bucket?" She rested against her doorframe, hands in her pockets.

"You were gloating," Milo offered.

"Yes," Holmes said, leaning forward. "Do go on, it's fascinating." She had that cataloging look to her, with her fingertips pressed together and that line at the bridge of her nose. I noticed, then, that there was a briefcase at Holmes's feet, a pair of plane tickets resting on it. Bryony's terms, fulfilled.

Her eyes flicked to the two of them, and then back to me. "I don't want to bore you," she said, clearly thinking about her getaway.

"Tell me," I coughed, in an attempt to stall her. "Dobson. How?"

"Poor thing," she said. "I'd come over to check your vitals, but I think little Charlotte here might react poorly to my hands on you. A shame. You know, this *orthomyxoviridae surrexit nigrum* virus doesn't have a precise countdown clock. It isn't a bomb. Really, you could croak at any time. So I'll honor your last wish." She put a hand to her heart in apparent sincerity. "I'll do that. Isn't that how all those stories always end? The hero explaining everything to his hapless confidant? You are a Watson, after all, so let's stick with tradition."

Holmes wasn't listening, it was clear. Her eyes were fixed on Bryony's boots. Slowly, her hand stole over to her brother's, and she took it. For comfort, or for another reason, I wasn't sure. So I clamped my eyes on Bryony, giving her the captivated audience she obviously wanted.

"Lee Dobson. Nasty thing, wasn't he? One of my first patients back in September, with a mean case of thrush. He had to come in for a follow-up, and I think he thought . . . well, you know. Attractive older woman, lusty young man. He was trying to impress me. Asking all these 'oblique' questions about narcotics, opiates. For a friend. They always say it's for a friend. How does someone react to heroin? As opposed to morphine? To oxycodone? Did they go nonresponsive? At what dosage? How pliable were they? Were they still able to have sex?"

Holmes's shoulders went stiff, her jaw set. Part of her was listening, after all. Beside her, Milo's expression was set in a determined blank.

"Oh, I was happy to oblige him and answer his questions. I had no qualms about it. Because how many other students at this school could be depraved enough to do drugs of that caliber? I knew I wasn't pointing him toward the innocent. Why, yes, I told him, your friend will be euphoric. So happy, so lazy, so unwilling to move. They should be careful, I said. Terrible things can happen to girls when they're that high. He thanked me profusely. Nearly wrung my hand off. And I had the satisfaction of knowing that I was sending our little whore here exactly the man she'd been asking for.

"And after that he kept coming back. It was clear he was infatuated with me. You can see why, of course." A smile crept over her face like a poisonous fog. "I can see you are, too, Jamie, from the way you look at me. I knew it the day that you got into that tussle with my Lee, the starry-eyed look on your face. Don't be ashamed. I did pageants, you know. Won quite a few prizes. But no. No, I was talking about Lee Dobson and that protein powder.

"Because the two of you had more or less marked him for dead. Charlotte had made her disgust for that poor boy so loudly clear, and, you, Jamie, had made an attempt to kill him. No, don't look at me like that—you would've beaten him stupid, and all for him saying things about your Charlotte that were *true*. I got all of it from Dobson in the infirmary. How he'd tried to warn you about what a slut she was. He was doing you a favor! And look at how he repaid it. Poor thing marked himself for death at that point. From my own experience"— here she huffed, like a disappointed grandmother—"I know that Charlotte is utterly ruthless. She would've taken him out eventually, especially with such a besotted baby mastiff like you by her side. I was doing him a favor, really. At least I got rid of him in a humane way.

"It wasn't hard to start dosing him with arsenic in his protein powder. A little bit at a time, building the dosage each day—I made him come to me to take it, of course. And then I had a blank page to write my story on, once he was dead. You know, I loved Dr. Watson's tales when I was young. It was so much fun to get to do a reenactment. I nicked a brand-new copy of *The Adventures of Sherlock Holmes* out of the library and made a dorm visit that night—came up through the back stairs. I'd asked Lee to prop them open for me. Had a surprise for him, I said. He probably thought he was going to get laid. I knew his roommate was on that rugby tour; he'd told me, so eager to get his hands on me. Well. By the time I arrived, he was dead. They called me to help comfort the students, after."

She studied a nail. In a flash, I remembered seeing her there outside Dobson's door, patting my sobbing hallmate on the shoulder. I swallowed the bile that had risen in my throat.

"Of course, I had help with the snake."

Holmes started. "What help?"

Bryony clucked her tongue. "Speaking out of turn," she said, and for the first time, I heard a trace of anger in her voice.

"But I'll play along. Still haven't thought through the consequences of your actions, have you? Well, birds can't change their feathers. Here's a quick education: when you orchestrated my fiancé's downfall—all for the crime of loving *me*—you ruined my life. You ruined. My *life*." She took a step closer to the two of them, almost inadvertently. When she moved, I saw the gun she'd holstered underneath her puffer coat.

"You whore. I'd been with Augie since we were kids. He'd gone to Eton, and then early to Oxford, while I went to the village school, but all the while he'd always loved me. *Me*, do you understand? I went over to the Moriartys' for every Sunday dinner. They came to my flute recitals, when my own mother was too drunk to scrape herself off the sofa. And when I was seventeen and my mother died, and my father couldn't be fucked to take me in, do you know who did? Oh, that's right. Professor Moriarty and his wife. I don't care what they did on the side—they were saints, do you understand? If they asked me to slit my own throat, I would have, for them."

"I thought you came to the States when you were sixteen," Holmes whispered.

Bryony smiled. "Do you think my name was the only part of my employment records I had falsified? No, *I* was never sent away across an ocean. No one wanted to be rid of me that badly. You see, I was to marry Augie as soon as I finished at uni. His parents paid for me to attend the University of London, and his family had already bought a flat for us to live in as husband and wife. I was to be a doctor. I'm very smart, you know. Though you Holmeses all think that there's no one as bloody brilliant as you, Augie could run circles around you with his eyes shut, and I was going to be a *doctor.*

"And then Augie took that horrible job." She ground her teeth so hard that I could hear it, the enamel and bone. "At *your house.*

"His parents warned him against it. His brother Lucien did too. They thought he was mad, going into a den of vipers like that. Your bitch of a mother and your homicidal brother and you, the enfant terrible, as his student? God, the games the Moriartys play are small compared to yours. But Augie believed the best of people. He believed the best from you, baby Charlotte. That was his downfall."

That was when I realized that she was talking about him as if he were dead. Holmes noticed, too—her eyes finally drifted up from Bryony's boots to her cruelly smiling face. But Holmes kept her immaculate poker face. Either this wasn't a surprise, or her composure was even better than I'd thought.

"The last time I saw Augie alive," Bryony said, "was the day before the drugs bust. He'd come up to London for a few days, to visit me. It was beautiful. He took me to this gorgeous restaurant. White tablecloths. We talked about our wedding. It was going to be small, intimate. In his family's backyard, wildflowers, his mother's wedding dress. We were so happy. We didn't need anything but each other." She lost her dreamy look, then. "He went back to your house the next day. I reckon you could smell me all over him. Made you crazy with jealousy. Just a little girl, but with such big-girl appetites. He told me all about your crush, you know. He thought it was *adorable.*"

So much for composure. Holmes flinched, as if she'd been hit across the face.

"The day after, you called the law down on him. After the police left, after they found Lucien and dragged him away to jail—oh, you look so *surprised*, what the hell did you think happened to him?—I drove all over creation, looking for him. The police couldn't find him; he'd made his confession and run. Oxford had expelled him. No other school would have him, not with that record. He'd panicked. Gone home. And he'd taken his father's pistol into his childhood bedroom, and he shot himself in the face."

I didn't understand. I didn't understand at all—I'd thought August had been hauled away to jail, and when he'd been paroled, had gotten a job at Greystone working for Milo. I racked my memory as best as I could. What had Holmes said, exactly, when she was telling me the story?

August stayed to take the blame, as I suspected he would . . . he got a job, finally. Works for my brother in Germany.

There wasn't anything about what happened in between.

Even in my feverish haze, I began filling in the blanks.

August Moriarty had faked his death, most likely with his parents' help. I don't know how I hadn't seen it before: he'd confessed to selling hard drugs to a minor, and the sentence for that would have been much longer than the timeline Holmes had laid out for me between his crime and his new life. His parents had given him up, Holmes had said. They would have had to cut off all public contact to maintain the fiction of his death. But they'd buried the news of it, too. I hadn't found any obituaries when I was researching him, any mention of a funeral. It was as if August Moriarty had simply stopped existing. Frozen in time as a wonder boy, working on the intricate mathematical patterns in the Arctic Circle, his thick blond Disney hair blowing in the frigid wind.

And Bryony Downs didn't know.

It would have been difficult for her to accompany him in his new life, but had he really loved her, he would have found a way, I thought. He was a brilliant man. Too brilliant, maybe, not to see the hint of fanatical darkness in his fiancée. The obsession, the wild selfishness. The willingness to do anything to achieve her own ends.

Maybe August Moriarty saw this as his opportunity to escape her. An understandable decision. Despite it leading to where Holmes and I found ourselves now.

"You," Bryony said, edging still closer to Holmes, who regarded her coolly. "You have his death on your hands. So you'll do time for a death. I'm just the middleman."

And Lee Dobson and Elizabeth Hartwell the sacrificial lambs.

Though she hadn't mentioned Elizabeth at all.

"Who were you working with?" Holmes asked.

Bryony flicked her hair. "Who said I was working with anyone?"

Holmes stared her down until, shifting uncomfortably, Bryony spoke.

"The man who convinced the judge that he'd no idea of the contents of his car's boot and served a minimum sentence.

You didn't forget who drove the car to your house to get you your fix, did you? Lucien Moriarty, you stupid child. God, the best part of all of this has been feeding you from my hand. I offered you warnings. Touched them with ungloved hands, in case you'd manage to lift my fingerprints. Printed them in the font that I write all my medical reports in. Made the spellings English, instead of American. It was a paint-by-numbers murder, and you were too dumb to learn to pick up the paintbrush. I did everything but hand myself over to you. Knowing, of course, that the moment you found me out, Lucien would close the bear trap. You do know what Lucien does for a living, yes?"

"He's a fixer," Milo murmured.

"Precisely," Bryony said. "Gold star, you. Except for the part where he's a Moriarty first. They have connections you can only *dream* of. Tell Lucien you want a rattlesnake as window dressing for your little scene, and he'll make an untraceable one appear. Tell him you want a beautiful little suitcase bomb, and he'll hire a professional to make you one. Tell him you want a plastic jewel shoved down a girl's throat, and she'll choke on it. Tell him you want a new identity, a passport, a job at Charlotte Holmes's boarding school, and he'll give it to you wrapped in a bow. God, the very *lack* of evidence should have been a clue. I gave up my dreams of being a doctor for this. Do you hear that? *I gave up my dreams to make you serve the sentence you deserved.* I'd nearly all the credits necessary for a nursing degree, and if that could get me here and to you faster—well. For once, sweetie, you were the hottest ticket in town."

She knelt down before the ottoman, put her hands on

Holmes's knees, leaned right into her face. "This is why I'm a better person than you. Are you ready? I could kill you right now. No"—she held a finger up to Holmes's lips—"that suitcase bomb was never intended to kill you, don't be stupid. I was just *disgusted* by the thought of you and the Watson boy playing house in there. Acting out your roles. Do you want to know why I set up Dobson's murder as a remake of 'The Speckled Band'? It's a reminder. They're stories. They're stories, and this is real life. *You are not Sherlock Holmes*, and you won't ever be."

Holmes stared straight down her nose at Bryony's sneering face. And then she turned her head to me and, slowly, unmistakably, blinked her eyes twice.

Play your last card, she'd said. What card could I possibly play? Only sheer force of will kept my eyes open now. I could barely speak, much less get to my feet and make a stand. If I was supposed to be the muscle in this operation, I was totally out of commission.

But she knew that. So what could she mean?

Last night—a hand on my forehead, a deliberate, closed-mouth kiss. Roses. And her smile as she walked out the door, telling me not to die before I could use it as a bargaining chip.

Oh.

I let my eyes fall closed. I willed my breathing to slow. And I fell, heavily, out of the chair onto the thick pink carpet.

"Watson!" Holmes cried, a perfect parody of the last time she'd thought I was dead.

Stumbling. Footsteps. Bryony saying, "Oh, *damn*," as she

crouched above me. I could smell the Forever Ever Cotton Candy. A man's cold fingers on my cheek, then moving to my neck to take a pulse.

"He's alive," Milo announced. "He's alive, but barely."

"Don't move him," Holmes said. "I'll get the blanket from the bed."

I opened my eyes to slits. Bryony was still crouched over me, an unexpected look of concern on her face. "Jamie," she said. "It'll be okay. This will be over soon, as soon as your girlfriend agrees to let me go."

I was actually beginning to think that wasn't the worst idea.

More footsteps. Milo saying, "Couldn't you take a look at him, Bryony? For his sake?" Bryony's bit lip as she took her eyes off the bedroom door and fixed them on me.

The sound of a handgun being cocked.

"Get up," Holmes snarled. "With your hands behind your head."

Nurse Bryony got to her feet, stiffly.

"You're wearing a wire," Holmes said. "It's wrapped around your handgun holster, which is in and of itself very clever, as most of us would notice the gun and then instantly avert our eyes. I am not most people, as you well know. So yes, hello Lucien, I'm happy to know that you're well and having your crony deal drugs to the Sherringford milieu, and as I've said in the many letters I sent you in prison, I am very sorry for my part in your two months' incarceration, though I'd wager that one of the dozens of other children you sold coke to would've ratted you out eventually. I hope that you've enjoyed being an accessory to murder."

She walked forward, the gun steady in her hands. "I'd suggest that you don't attempt to blow the suitcase bomb that I found in the linen closet, as I've already defused it. I didn't even need to take to Google for that one. But then, thanks to my father, I imagine I've forgotten more about designing explosives than you've ever learned."

She was close enough now that she and Bryony were eye to eye. With wild eyes, Bryony opened her mouth, and Holmes lifted one black boot and stomped the heel of it onto the nurse's foot.

"Now, now. Speaking out of turn. I'm afraid that I'm not as tolerant of that as you. I really should be taking lessons."

Bryony whimpered against the pain, her hands still tucked behind her head. Swiftly, Holmes pulled the pistol from under Bryony's coat and tossed it to Milo, who caught it neatly.

"Bryony Downs," Holmes mused. "What can I say? If I could apologize to August, I would."

I noticed that she was still maintaining the fiction that August Moriarty was dead, even now, when throwing the truth into Nurse Bryony's face would be the ultimate punishment.

But Holmes was still speaking. "I've been through three separate rehabilitation programs. I may, in fact, simply be a terrible person at heart, but the difference between you and me is that I *fight* it. With every single atom of my being I fight against it. I might be an amateur detective but you are a bloody psychopath, and I would rather put this gun in my mouth than let you skip away to St. Petersburg where you can prey on teen-age boys on my brother's blood money. You orchestrated my *rape*, and you call me a whore? No. This is the absolute end of the line."

"And you're just going to leave your friend to die," Nurse Bryony said in a harsh whisper.

It was what I'd asked her to do, after all. To keep herself out of jail at any cost. I tried to breathe through the panic clench-ing my lungs.

Holmes sighed. "No, of course I'm not," she said, and I almost died right there from relief. "My brother's men are retrieving the antidote from Watson's dorm room as we speak. It's a clever place to hide it, isn't it? The same place where you infected him? Wanted us to really be *kicking* ourselves when we found it. But it was easy enough to deduce from the uni-versity keys sticking out of your pocket, and not your handbag, and the glass shards embedded in your boot soles. Those, I confirmed when Watson here so obligingly fainted and you got to your knees to examine him. Shards of one-way glass, specifically. Any second now, Peterson will text me that he's found the antidote."

As if on cue, her phone chirped.

"How could you know that," Bryony said. "How could you know that for sure," and I was surprised to hear an element of jealousy in her voice.

"Because, right now, you look furious," Holmes said. "So thanks for the confirmation."

Nurse Bryony spat on the floor.

Holmes rolled her eyes. "It was a bloody stupid place to hide it anyway, far too close to your flat—which is perfectly awful, by the by. So close, in fact, that we'd have fetched it and injected Watson before you had proper time to make your getaway. Why, really, would we let you abscond with three million dollars' worth of my brother's money when you had no further cards to play?

"Though I suppose you had Lucien as a last resort. Hello again, Lucien."

Milo's phone rang.

He startled. It was like seeing the Sphinx jump. "No one is supposed to have this number," he muttered, picking it up, and then, into the phone, "Yes. Fine. I'll put you on speaker."

Lucien Moriarty's voice crackled into the room.

"Hello again, Charlotte," he drawled.

Bryony's eyes flickered back and forth. "This wasn't part of the plan," she hissed.

"No, no, darling," he said. "Your part in this is done. Hush, now. Dear Charlotte. You had a question? I'll give you one answer. As your consolation prize."

"Consolation prize?" Holmes laughed. "I won. Lucien, I am quite literally standing here, holding the gun."

"So there's nothing you want me to clear up. Nothing at all. No questions about the drug dealer"—and here, his voice changed to a dark snarl—"who stuffed a plastic gem into that little prize turkey? Who was so obliging as to hang himself to break any remaining links between him and his employer? No questions about that employer who is, even now, calling you from Russia?" A laugh. "That's me, by the way. In case you're as slow as you seem."

I tried to swear, but I couldn't force out any words. Holmes's hand shook. It was almost imperceptible, but I saw it. She'd taught me to notice things, after all.

"Fine," she said. "You win. So tell me. Why did you make it so easy for us to catch Bryony?"

"I never wanted you in *jail*," Lucien purred. "That was never the plan. The plan was to torment you, and how can I do that from within a jail cell? Oh, you could lose yourself within weeks in a juvenile penitentiary, but you could also start a riot. Or break yourself out. No, this was a practice round. I wanted to see what was important to you. I wanted to see how much this foolish boy trusted you. I threaten him, and you kiss him. Cue strings. Cue the applause."

Milo whipped around to stare at his sister, but her eyes were fixed on the phone.

"It's good to know what matters to you, Charlotte. So very little does. My brother didn't. Your own family doesn't. But this boy . . ." I could almost hear him licking his lips. "No, I don't want you in jail. I don't want you to have the satisfaction of this being over."

No one in the room was looking directly at anyone else. I wondered, briefly, if anyone remembered that I was quite literally dying on the floor.

"Well. Go on. Take out the trash," he said. "I see that your antidote is waiting at the door."

A click, and he was gone.

"I knew about his plan," Nurse Bryony said into the silence. "I knew this whole time."

"No," Holmes said, pressing the gun to Bryony's temple. "You're a terrible liar. How sad, you've made me resort to *guns*. How incredibly cheap. Milo, tie her hands. I hope you're ready to take her . . . wherever you're going to take her. I don't want to know."

"I promise not to tell you," Milo said, in a tone that suggested he'd said this many times. He bound her hands neatly in a zip-tie, put her own pistol to the base of her neck, and led her out the door.

I'd missed something. But then, I'd missed a lot of things.

"Holmes," I managed, but Peterson chose that minute to charge in. With brutal precision, he pulled a syringe out of his pocket, flipped my arm, found a vein, and stabbed it in.

"Sir," he said respectfully, and left the two of us alone.

"Hi," Holmes said, getting down beside me. "You look terrible. I'm sorry I didn't tell you everything. I just needed—"

"—my reaction to be genuine," I said, coughing through my smile.

"Precisely."

"Holmes," I said again.

"Yes?"

"Hospital?"

She nodded seriously, as if the idea had only now occurred to her too. "I think that would be wise."

twelve

Five days later

"WHEN'S YOUR FLIGHT?" HOLMES ASKED, PLAYING WITH THE ends of my scarf. "You could always fly back with Milo and me tonight. The offer's still open." Her brother had set aside a seat for me in his company jet.

"I'd like to," I said, "but I think I owe a few more days to my father after all this. I'll be back in London next weekend."

He was, understandably, still upset with me for not having told him I was dying. Ever since I'd been brought home to recover, I'd watched him struggle to understand how he should feel. One minute, he was begging me for a description of Nurse Bryony's face that day in her flat—"Was it more like a snake's, or an assassin's?"—his hands clasped in schoolboy glee, and the next minute he was forbidding me to bring in the mail because it was too dangerous with Lucien Moriarty still at large. My father liked reading about adventures, liked talking them through over a glass of whisky. He even liked the thought of his son having them, up to a certain point.

I had, in this past week, plunged off that point and into a very troubling ocean.

"Well," he'd said, cleaning his glasses, "I suppose you're looking forward to getting back to your mother and sister."

"I am," I'd told him honestly.

"And I imagine you won't be wanting to return here in the spring when school reopens." He hadn't looked at me as he spoke.

"Actually, I've heard that someone got me a full scholarship for the year." I'd hidden my smile. "And though the creative writing teacher left something to be desired, I did make one or two good friends. And I found out my stepmom makes really amazing mac and cheese."

His eyes had shone. "Ah."

"Dad," I'd said. "If your methods were a little obnoxious . . . well. I'm still happy to be here."

He'd patted me on the arm. "You're a good man, Jamie Watson."

It might have even been true. At least, I was trying.

We both were.

"Well, if you stay, you can take over my duties as Robbie's *Mario Kart* opponent," Holmes said now with a wry smile.

"That little bugger is very good. I'm used to playing by myself, though, so maybe I'm just easy to beat. Milo was never one for games."

"You had a Wii," I said, disbelieving.

"Of course." She raised her eyebrows. "Why wouldn't I?"

I shook my head at her.

We'd been spending our days in my father's house after my brief stint in the hospital. After I'd been released, Dr. Warner had stayed on in a nearby hotel, coming by each morning to examine me. But other than a lingering veil of fatigue (I was sleeping fourteen hours a night), a sickly sheen to my skin, and a tremor in my hands, I was well and truly cured.

Despite my clean bill of health, Holmes had appointed herself my nursemaid. This meant I was served endless bowls of tasteless soup (rule #39 finally rearing its ugly head) and gallon after gallon of water while confined to the living room couch. She kept the room dark, the boys from pestering me (when they'd actually have been a welcome distraction), and the television firmly off. I couldn't so much as stand without her appearing at my elbow, ready to bully me back into lying down. When I asked, plaintively, for something to do, she'd brought me a biography of Louis Pasteur. I promptly used it as a coaster. ("But he invented vaccinations!" she'd cried, seeing the water marks on its cover.)

That isn't to say that I didn't have visitors. Mrs. Dunham came by, with a present of Galway Kinnell's first book of poems. She took one look at my face—I did look kind of like a ghoul—and burst into tears. Which was strangely okay. It sounds stupid to say, but after several months of being unparented (my father clearly didn't count), it was almost nice to have someone make a fuss.

Detective Shepard came by, too, in a bluster of frayed nerves and exhaustion. After railing at Holmes for her unprofessional behavior—"You confronted a murderer! In her own apartment! Without telling the police, and with your best friend dying at your feet! And now we have *nothing* to show for it!"—for a good half hour, he paused for breath. And Holmes produced a flash drive from her inner pocket.

"You recorded her confession," the detective had said, weakly.

Holmes smiled. "My brother did, but yes, I thought you'd like this. Though I gather you'll have some difficulty finding Bryony Downs, née Davis. Milo has—what's the term? Oh, that's right—disappeared her."

"Holmes," I'd hissed. Wasn't that supposed to be a state secret?

"What?" She was clearly enjoying herself.

The detective was not.

"Oh," I'd said then, remembering. "I guess there's something I should probably tell you about my creative writing teacher."

"Is there anything else?" Shepard had snapped, when I finished speaking. "Missile codes, maybe, that you happened to pick up? No? Good." He'd left in a huff, slamming the door behind him.

"I rather doubt we'll be invited to assist with solving future murders in the sunny state of Connecticut," Holmes had sighed. "More's the shame."

Lena came by, too. In her bright coat, she perched at the end of my father's armchair and caught us up on all the gossip I'd missed. (Tom had come with her, but Holmes had barred him at the door.) She and Tom were still together, she told us. Holmes forced her mouth into a smile that morphed into a real one when Lena asked if she could come visit over the holiday. "For a few days in January," Lena had said carelessly. "I'll be coming through on my way back to school and I thought it'd be fun to tell my pilot I needed a long layover. We could hang out!"

We both agreed. I always did like Lena, after all.

On the quieter afternoons, when no one came by the house, I found myself sorting through my journal from the last few months, looking at the notes I'd made, the crackpot theories I'd had as to Dobson's murderer, the list of possible suspects that seemed so laughable now. To these, I added sketches of scenes. The jar of teeth on Holmes's laboratory shelf. How her eyes dropped closed as she danced. My leather jacket around her shoulders. The way my father stood so nervously as I walked toward him for the first time in years. It all began to form a story, one I wanted to continue, one thread at a time, onward without a visible end.

Maybe Charlotte Holmes was still learning how to pick apart a case; maybe I was still learning how to write. We weren't Sherlock Holmes and John Watson. I was okay with that, I thought. We had things they didn't, too. Like electricity, and refrigerators. And *Mario Kart*.

"Watson," she said, "you don't need to pretend that you've forgiven me."

This came out of nowhere. "For what?"

"For—for what I did to August. For me not telling you the whole truth, again. You know, in the future, stop me when I think I'm being clever. Because I'm shooting myself in the foot. If we'd both had all the facts at the beginning of this mess—"

"If," I said. "That's a big if. Look. I've forgiven you. You have my implicit forgiveness, you know, even when you're driving me crazy."

"You got dragged into this because of me," she said. "Nurse Bryony was making me do my penance. She used you to get to me."

"So the next crime will have nothing to do with either of us. It'll be a very benign car theft. In another country. A warm one. We'll solve it very lazily, lie on the beach between interrogations. Drink margaritas."

"Thank you," she said, very seriously.

"Don't thank me, you're buying the plane tickets." I stretched out on the couch with my head in her lap. "Fiji is expensive."

"I don't want Fiji. I want home." She put her hands in my hair. "Jamie."

"Charlotte."

"Do come home soon. It won't be London without you."

"You never knew me in London," I said, smiling.

"I know." Holmes looked down at me with gleaming eyes. "I intend to fix that."

Epilogue

AFTER READING WATSON'S ACCOUNT OF THE BRYONY DOWNS affair, I feel the need to make a few corrections.

Perhaps more than a few.

First off, his narrative is so utterly romanticized, especially as regards to me, that the most efficient way of breaking down its more metaphorical misconceptions would be in a list.

To wit:

1. When I speak, I don't sound like Winston Churchill.
    I sound like Charlotte Holmes.
2. Why on earth would he name my vulture skeletons? They aren't deserving of names. They're *artifacts*. And one of them tried to kill Mouse (Californian vacation, very lazy

cat, vultures have no sense of smell), which made me rather upset, and which is why the two idiot things were hanging in my lab until they exploded. Which, for the record, I am fine with.

3. I took Watson to the homecoming dance because Lena's friend Mariella would have certainly asked him if I didn't, and she eats boys like him for breakfast before flossing with their bones. (See entry two, re: California condors.) I told Lena I'd take him and then forgot to tell Watson until very late not because I'm shy about my enjoyment of dancing and/or pop music, but because I was busy. To be precise, I was busy studying how quickly blood congeals within an iPhone. I had to draw rather a lot of my own for my test sample, and then I was forced to sleep due to its loss, and then I had to pay Lena back for her bloody mobile. (She didn't mind. She even let me draw some of her blood, too. Mine is O negative and hers is O positive, which made for a pleasing symmetry.) It was all very interesting, and homecoming is not, and I only went to find him when my test beaker exploded. The blood never quite came out of the ceiling.

4. Tom looked frightful in his powder-blue tuxedo. In this, as in many things, Watson is far too kind. I never corrected him on the subject because at least one of us should be. Kind, that is.

I suppose the rest of his account is more or less bearable, if I ignore the proliferation of adjectives. But it appears that I am willing to put up with many things for the sake of Jamie Watson. He is fond of watching old episodes of *The X-Files*, which is, to the best of my understanding, a show about a rather appallingly dumb man who is nevertheless very attractive, and aliens. It's tolerable if I pretend there isn't any sound. We began when he was still in hospital, and now we're three seasons in and he shows no sign of giving it up. He was the same way about curry shops in London during our first few days home. I heard quite a bit of rot from him about the curative powers of chicken jalfrezi. He is incapable of eating Indian food without getting red sauce on his clothing; I've taken to carrying a bleach pen.

I am doing all kinds of chemical researches on snake venom. I aim to know everything about it by the end of the month. While Watson was ill I learned all there was to know about oysters, because Watson's father gave them to us at a dinner at his house, and they were delicious. At that dinner, Abbie Watson asked me to watch her two young sons while she did the shopping the next day, most likely because I happen to be a girl and she assumes that this is what girls do for spending money. I agreed, and taught them how to make bombs from dung, and where best to hide them. She didn't ask me again. Watson's father thought it very funny, and Watson did too, though he refuses to admit it. I can tell he's hiding a laugh when he curls his mouth in like he's eating a lemon. Sometimes I say terrible things just to see him do it.

There haven't been any more murders, which makes things a bit dull, though I suppose it's only been a week since we wrapped up our last case. There was an official inquiry into Mr. Wheatley's actions that resulted in his termination; for his part, Tom was merely suspended. Watson has insisted on forgiving his old roommate, which I consider rather foolish. He and Tom had an obscenely long and emotional phone call that I heard every word of from the next room. That said, I don't like to see Watson upset, and so I have withheld my opinion on the matter. As the Americans say, we have bigger fish to fry.

I am fairly sure that Bryony Downs is dead, though I allow Watson to go on believing that she is in Milo's custody. I do think that my theory may be the kinder one. For his part, August Moriarty sent me a card on my birthday. *Verbum sap.*

Lucien Moriarty has been spotted in Thailand. I asked my brother to fit him with a microchip, like the kind they have for dogs, and he categorically refused. Ergo, we are relying on Milo's operatives to trace his movements.

We will be back at Sherringford in the spring. Watson's scholarship meant he was paid up through this year, so we have decided to stay. His family hasn't any money and I don't much care where I study, as my most important work is independently accomplished. Milo agreed that it was best to remain here, for now, though naturally my parents were displeased.

I'm rather beginning to enjoy displeasing them.

I am one week clean and don't wish to say any more on the subject.

A final note on Watson. He flagellates himself rather a lot, as this narrative shows. He shouldn't. He is lovely and warm and quite brave and a bit heedless of his own safety and by any measure the best man I've ever known. I've discovered that I am very clever when it comes to caring about him, and so I will continue to do so.

Later today I will ask him to spend the rest of winter break at my family's home in Sussex. (I must remember to tell my parents, though I'm sure they've already deduced my intentions.) My always-amusing uncle Leander is due in for a visit. We will look for a good murder or, at the very least, an interesting heist to solve. Watson will say yes, I'm sure of it. He always says yes to me.

ACKNOWLEDGMENTS

First of all, so many thanks to my wonderful editor, Anica Rissi, for her keen eyes and edits and her belief in this book. I am so indebted to you. Thanks too to Alexandra Arnold and everyone else at Katherine Tegen Books and HarperCollins. I feel so incredibly lucky to be a Katherine Tegen author.

To Lana Popovic, my amazing agent, editor, and friend— you have encouraged me every single step of the way. I know for sure this wouldn't be a book without you. Thank you, from the bottom of my heart, for taking a chance on me.

Many thanks to Terra Chalberg for championing this book abroad and to everyone else at Chalberg and Sussman, wonder agency.

Thank you to my friends Chloe Benjamin, Rebecca Dunham, Rebecca Hazelton, Emily Temple, and Kit Williamson for being amazing, encouraging readers, and to my professors Liam Callanan and Judy Mitchell, who told me I could. And to Ted Martin, for his endless patience for discussing Sherlockiana with me.

I'm deeply indebted to William S. Baring-Gould for his

Sherlock Holmes scholarship—his *Sherlock Holmes of Baker Street* was invaluable, and I've littered this novel with loving reference to his work. Endless thanks to Leslie Klinger; his *New Annotated Sherlock Holmes* has sat dog-eared on my desk for the last two years. I'm greatly indebted, too, to all the other scholars and writers who have played the Game before me.

Thanks to my parents, for being my biggest champions from day one. To my grandfather, for giving us the Holmes stories in the first place. Thanks and love to Chase, for his love and patience while I've filled my hours and covered our walls with this book. I never thought I'd find somebody like you. I am so lucky I did.

And finally, and most importantly, thanks to Sir Arthur Conan Doyle for giving us all Holmes and Watson in the first place. This is, more than anything, a work written for love of them.

JOIN THE

Epic Reads
COMMUNITY